HEART LIKE A HOLE

A Novel by

Paula C. Deckard

This book is a work of fiction. Names, characters, places, and incidents are the product of the author's imagination or are used fictitiously. Any resemblance to actual persons, living or dead, events, or locales is entirely coincidental.

Library and Archives Canada

Heart Like A Hole / Paula C. Deckard

ISBN (paperback) 978-0-9959574-2-8
ISBN (eBook) 978-0-9959574-1-1

Author's Pages: https://paulacdeckard.com, www.terrible-lies.com

Cover art by Egemen Oezyay

DEDICATION

For my family

"How old were you when you first let a man make love to you?"

- *Dr. Caligari*
The Cabinet of Caligari (1962)

This room has the flair of an operating theater. I think I will stay. I have nowhere else to go. The halogen bulbs are nice and dim, throwing light on the examination table. However, the light does not reach me. There is a pool of blood forming in front of me, but I feel no pain. Perhaps it's not me bleeding after all, but her. I believe that you can make your own God out of your very own blood. I close my eyes and see this beautiful child floating on the surface of the red sea. I have been there. It's where I fell in love. She is staring at the sky, mapping out her future. I see how in the future, she will grow up to be a successful woman like me. Her father loves her very much, and yet he doesn't know how she really feels. Unfortunately, I will never meet her, and I can't tell her that I am sorry.

According to the building map, there are four laboratories on this wing, and they're all connected, but I haven't got the energy to visit them all. At least I've made it into one of them. My heart rate is going down. There is not much blood left in the left ventricle to pump into the aorta.

My body is still fighting as I watch internally. I feel how it is compensating. It's trying to maintain blood pressure by pumping whatever is left to my brain, heart, and lungs. It's drawing away all the blood from my skin and my limbs. I have a conscience, after all, and it's paying attention to what keeps me alive.

CHAPTER ONE

He is looking at me while my uterus and vagina contract and grip his penis tightly. It should feel as though you need to pee. That's the moment you let your body release all the tension in the form of pleasurable waves.

I read all about it. Blood floods the pelvic area, and a high amount of muscle and nerve tension builds up in your lower body. But most of the time, I don't even get to the needing-to-pee point, and if I do, I can't do it. I'm still learning to control my teenage body.

At least I am aroused because my breasts are swollen. I am wet enough down there too, which is easy to control. If I stop the moisture from producing itself, the penis will rub against a dry wall, and often my sensitive cervix will start to bleed.

That's when they get scared. But I am not playing innocent today.

I look down at him, and he looks back at me since I have slowed down the movements. I don't know whether to make him come now with one big thrust or focus more on what's going on inside me and what I want to achieve.

He begins to rub my clitoris with his hairy fingers. But I feel absolutely nothing. I do not need to pee, either. What if I trick my body into it?

He moans as soon as I contract my vagina and continue the movements. It's starting to feel good again. Maybe focus on that, and I will eventually come? How many people do I have to sleep with before I feel that sensation again? I should feel relief in my brain and tingles down my spine. Perhaps I need to pretend I'm in love with him or open up his body.

But he has already cum.

"Sorry, I got to go," I say, "I have school tomorrow."

"You what? How old are you?" he says.

"Not much older than Alicia."

"How do you know my daughter?"

After dressing myself, I say, "She and I had detention together last week."

I leave the motel room almost instantly and head down to the bus station. My Nokia screen displays a message from Dad, "Where are you?"

My heart aches. I did say I'd be home by nine to do more reading for my upcoming biology test, and I promised not to disappoint him. It's a promise kept because I know Mendel by heart. The vagina-and-brain connection is what I'm studying – with a stopover at the heart. Only surgeons have permission to access human anatomy. And I have a long way to go.

*

Accident patients are open wounds and broken bones; they expose blood to the world. But instead of feeling most alive, they feel vulnerable and frightened. Sick patients, on the other hand, are the victims of inner attacks. Their bodies are going through disruption of cell activity. Either way, I like both types of patients. Their bodies speak the language of pain, which flows through flesh and blood. This particular language defines the real struggle of survival. As a surgeon, I aim to remove or alleviate a patient's pain and preserve his life.

Sickness and accidents affect a person differently, but both come by surprise. A surgeon doesn't like tackling surprises, especially in operating theaters. Patients expect that when a doctor puts them to sleep, everything will be all right again when they wake up. And usually, everything is – on my table anyway. You come by patients who don't even notice if you take a tiny blood sample.

Here is an example: Todd Wilson is a machinist whose hand got sheared off by the rotating blades of a sprocket. His blood was all over my table when he arrived. The hand was too mangled to reattach. Nevertheless, Todd's angry mother insisted on keeping what was left of the hand, saying it made up for Todd never helping her with the shopping. He told me that his mother had kept it forever frozen. I'm not sure if my mother would have done the same. She didn't keep my pigtails when a girl had cut them off in the classroom.

There was no second date with Todd because he failed the climax test. I seem to have lost the ability to feel my sexual climax. Usually, during intercourse, a woman's arousal increases, and a great amount of blood rushes toward the pelvic area. By the time she reaches her climax, her labia flatten, and open, vehement muscle contractions occur along with a continuous rise of heart rate and blood pressure. If physical stimuli are linked with the process in one's brain, then why are descriptions such as "the tingling in the spine" or "on the verge of losing consciousness" foreign to me? Women don't always come, but they know when they do, as they can feel it. The glands secrete a sweet-smelling fluid through the urethra, which brings a sense of relief to the brain. I'm very familiar and in touch with my own body; however, there is a lack of sexual compatibility with a partner, as that particular relief is not reaching my brain. I vaguely remember the climax phenomenon from when I was a child. Back then, I still had feelings.

Todd, however, was an interesting accident patient

on my table. Of all men, he seemed to have the most fascinating tongue. The tongue is one of the strongest muscles in our body in terms of dynamic strength. Its four intrinsic muscles make it a playful and agile organ. On the other hand, some would say the strongest is either the masseter or the gluteus muscles. Yes, there are many ways to measure strength, but I don't go by the muscle group's size.

I go by the hardest working muscle—the heart.

A year ago, I accepted the unconditional offer of a post at Mount Sinai Hospital in New York. Even though I was a graduate from Yale, I'd have expected the hospital to send me over to the School of Medicine first, but I'd underestimated myself. If you instantaneously get hired at Mount Sinai, you don't complain. Ever since the recession hit its peak, the hospital has avoided hiring more surgeons than necessary. But if you have sub-specialisms, you're more likely to get hired.

Having first gained my Doctor of Medicine and Doctor of Surgery degree in New Haven, I became an ophthalmologist's temporary assistant with only a minimum of involvement in operations, such as holding the retractor. Still undecided in my mid-twenties about which area of expertise to pursue, I returned to New Haven Hospital to immerse myself in further surgical training to become a general surgeon.

Eventually, New Haven accredited me with the status of fellow.

My consultant Dr. Phillip Dick used to praise my precision and reserved nature in the operating theater. He became my mentor.

One day when philosophizing about heartbreak, he got me interested in cardiology. I was assisting him in a severe cardiothoracic surgery. The anatomy of the thorax has always been my favorite. He said that each heart could be fixed, but I didn't believe him. He said that life needed a purpose and that mine would be to heal hearts, as only this way could I mend my own. All emotions that I've ever known felt crushed under the weight of a huge pain, leaving a sense of numbness like a paralyzed patient with damage to the spinal cord. Dr. Dick's subsequent retirement propelled me into a new life project, so I applied to Mount Sinai as a general surgeon and junior cardiac surgeon.

In cardiac or cardiothoracic surgery, we aim to maintain a working distribution system for the blood flow, which we call oxygenation. That way, we allow the heart and lung to rest while blood and air are still distributed to the body. So far, at Mount Sinai, I've only watched and assisted as a junior, but soon the destiny of a heart will be in my hands. Meanwhile, I'm keeping busy with abdomens, kidneys, and thyroids, or I submit to the hectic routine in the Emergency Unit.

Mount Sinai has always attracted me. It was built as one of the first Jewish hospitals in America in the 1850s. What initially drew my attention to this hospital was that Abraham Jacobi, the Father of American Pediatrics, had been a visiting physician.

He is the reason why I think all pediatricians should be men and men only.

People still talk about the American dream. I have hope. I believe in my strengths, and I will take risks to give my life a purpose.

Some former work colleagues at New Haven hospital say I'm going to New York to get lost. They are small-town people who believe that the big city is a labyrinth. Apparently, people who have high hopes either go to New York or California to throw the dice. It's all or nothing. But that's not why I came to New York City.

I've always wanted to work and live in a big city full of activities, individuals, and action. I wanted to dive under, find hiding places and observe without being noticed. These opportunities were difficult to find in Connecticut. Living in New York, your face in the crowd just comes and goes. People forget about you. People have important appointments to attend. In the end, you are nothing but a ghost, with a never-ending line of patients.

Fifth Avenue is the road of life, starting at Washington Square Park, which is beautiful for leisurely autumn walks. Whenever you think Death is holding his scythe tightly behind you in the operating theater, you'll find balance under the Hangman's Elm in the park, thinking about all the hanged citizens in the eighteen hundreds – all those wasted lives. The death of patients, on the contrary, isn't as upsetting. At least you know you've tried.

If you are in a different mood and want to lead yourself astray, you turn northwards through the center of Midtown, where no one will look you in the face. In Midtown Manhattan, everyone has someplace to go. If you don't, then breathe the city air, follow the smell that leads you toward the hot dog vendor or please your nostrils with the sweet scent of caramelized peanuts. Or keep on walking eastwards till you arrive at Central Park, where Mount Sinai is situated on the eastern border at 100th Street and Fifth Avenue. This is where I am standing – outside the building, staring at it.

***

Although it is my day off, I drop by work to pick up the documents on tomorrow's minimally invasive heart surgery. I feel foreign here when I'm not veiled underneath a lab coat. Busy work colleagues throw me a brief smile as they walk past. Some may even think that I'm a visitor. My cream-colored cotton blouse, my neutral knee-length black skirt, and my Prada pumps are the dress code of busy New Yorkers. And yet, I wonder what these people really see.

William Dylan, our best neurosurgeon, approaches me with open arms as if expecting a hug, but I keep mine folded and pressed against my chest.

He has been a successful neurosurgeon for eight years with a subsequent fellowship accreditation. However, Will is a devious person who reads people like an X-ray generator. His eyes are scanning me from top to bottom. He reads and determines a body's electric signals in the same way as I read and evaluate blood counts. The last thing I need is someone claiming to know all about my brain and peripheral nerves. Though it is an interesting way to judge people.

"Here comes the lady whose shell I can't crack. You look stunning today, Elle. How are you?"

"I'm good, Will."

Suddenly I spot my supervisor Stuart McCormick – the savior coming to my rescue. He is the attending cardiothoracic surgeon and the only one who looks me in the eye.

He places his hand on Will's shoulder, signaling for him to leave. Will shoots me a wink before leaving. Stuart always runs his hand through his wavy brown hair when thinking sharply and tilts his glasses before speaking.

"Parker!" he says. "Good to see you on your day off. Tomorrow's surgery starts at seven, not at eight."

"What?" I say.

My patient Mrs. Hughes, a seventy-two-year-old lady, is in a critical condition with cardiac dysrhythmia, an irregular heartbeat. We've only met once before when I'd interrupted her conversation with Stuart. The moment he introduced me as his *partner*, she threw a fierce glare at me, presumably mistaking me for his wife.

Mrs. Hughes and her son have been arguing about her insistence on composing her Living Will document, also known as the Advance Healthcare Directive. Once signed, she will hold the right to make her own decisions on future medical treatments. She can decline analgesic or cardiopulmonary resuscitation, but it's more complicated than that.

"Did she hand in her Living Will?"

"Yes, she did. If she falls into a coma, she doesn't want to be fed through a tube. Hey, please have a word with Mrs. Hughes, will you? She doesn't seem to like you much!"

I'm not surprised. She has now made tomorrow's surgery almost absurd. Signing these forms can only mean that the patient is either religious or has a death wish, whichever it is – I find these decisions hard to approve. Even if fed through a tube, she will still be a living organism. Patients who fantasize about death have stepped into the wrong place.

"Don't worry, I'll be assisting you tomorrow morning," Stuart says.

It's upsetting that my first responsible heart-related surgery will be done on her. I'm still a junior cardiac surgeon, but Stuart is gradually giving me the upper hand for surgeries that do not involve full access to the heart chambers.

Before paying the old lady a visit, I go to the staff changing room. There, I bump into Sarah Donald, our pathologist. She is twenty-nine, two years my junior, a graduate from Stanford University with a specialization in surgical pathology. Her unbearable Hollywood smile is a movie with no plot. Ever since she set foot inside this hospital, I have noticed her sycophantic nature; she has the tendency to cling to our well-known male surgeons. She got hired instantly ten months ago because the Pathology Department had been short of staff. She proved her outstanding skills in identifying specimens' state (body tissues, fluids, cytologic material, etc.) by merely looking at them. My dad has this skill, too: he can smell whether or not you're ill, similar to the way animals perceive pheromones.

This woman seems to recognize good in almost everything. Except once, I remember performing a percutaneous liver biopsy on a patient, and when I handed the liver tissue to her, her face turned pale, and you knew the tissue was malignant. That look of hers was more genuine than that perpetual Hollywood smile.

"Hey, don't you have a day off?" she says.

"Technically, yes, but I can already see myself staying here overnight."

"Nice shoes!"

I look at my old pair of Prada pumps and then grab my white sneakers from the locker.

"You and Stuey are operating on that crazy woman, right? Have you spoken to her? She seems really grumpy! Earlier this morning, Stuey had to hold her back because she was beating her son. Has she got anger issues? Why are they on such bad terms?"

Her inquisitive nature is another characteristic that I associate with a child's curiosity.

"I don't know. I will find out in a minute."

"Oh, you're going to do a ward round? Good luck! Oh, and did you see Willy Billy? He's really flirtatious today. Sometimes you wonder whether someone performed neurosurgery on him before he came here, haha."

I quickly put my lab coat over my blouse and walk towards the door. "Well, you know what he's like."

I open the door and step outside.

"Hey, you forgot…"

I close the door.

Ward rounds are nerve-wracking. While I am already here to speak to Mrs. Hughes, I might check on all the other patients awaiting surgery in the next few days. It's late in the afternoon; hence the high number of visitors arriving after their work has finished. I greet Julia, the head nurse, at reception, and then I head down to Room 308. I'm attempting to peer through the window in the door when a man comes out of that room.

"Oh, I'm sorry, Nurse!" he says and rushes down the hallway. I watch how he bumps into another woman.

"Brad! How's mom?" she says to him.

"It's not a good time to speak to her, Tess. Let's go."

He grabs her by the arm, and both disappear in the corner. I walk into the room and find Mrs. Hughes sitting up on her bed with a stern look in her eyes. There's always something about the eyes of seniors, eyes that are unable to hide their personalities. My former ophthalmologist who used to tutor me once said that eyes don't reflect one's soul but one's past.

"Good afternoon, Mrs. Hughes. How are we today?"

She scans me from top to bottom as if I was an object at an exposition.

"As usual. Living suicide at its slowest... Don't you have a day off? What brings you here after shopping for fancy shoes?"

I suddenly notice that I haven't changed into my white sneakers.

"I could hear you miles down the hallway!"

Her patronizing smile is the first smile I've ever seen on this old woman's face, which is covered with numerous liver spots. She has a mole on her lower lip, too. The smile evolves into hoarse chuckles; she's coughing up phlegm. Her sharp shoulders indicate a kind of determination and stubbornness that you don't want to mess with. For an old lady, her posture is still excellent.

"Was that your son? He looked distressed," I say.

"Leave him be. Kids will never listen to their folks."

I sit down on the chair next to her bed; it's still warm from Mr. Hughes' behind. I look at her brittle hands, fingers still sharp with obstinacy.

"And you, my dear..."

"What about me, Mrs. Hughes?"

"You've picked the wrong job!"

"What makes you say that?"

I still can't believe that my first accountable heart-related surgery will be on her. It's not even a real heart surgery, but the implantation of an ICD. She coughs again and touches her forehead.

"Are you feeling faint?" I say.

"Don't we all feel this way? What are you going to implant into my heart again? What's it called?"

"It's a defibrillator, and the implantation does *not* occur in your heart. Has Dr. McCormick gone through the procedure again with you today? You must know exactly what we're going to do."

She is not listening. The cardioverter-defibrillator will be implanted into the ribcage area with electro wires connected to the heart's appropriate chambers. That little apparatus will automatically correct the heart's rhythm with electricity when it's at fault. This is to improve the quality of her life.

"Your husband is a looker, isn't he?" she says as though plunged into delirium, and then, "I know my heart is out of beat, out of rhythm, but isn't that the way it is when old age kicks in?"

Her sudden mental transition from clear-headed to demented is worrying, given that she also seems unaware of tomorrow's event.

"You reckon I'm old enough to die in a nursing

home?" she asks.

"I'm sorry?"

"What will my grandchildren think of me?"

"I wouldn't know…" I say.

For a second, I see sadness in her eyes. I don't want to insinuate anything. I sense a low heart rate coming from her, which makes me think that she may have a sinus node dysfunction. She suddenly strikes me as weak.

"Having a cardiologist as a husband means you won't ever have your heart broken," she says. "My Bradley was a ladies' tailor. You see, you have no reason to check on *your* man – stop wasting your time on me."

I clench both of my fists while sitting still in the chair. No one has brought the old lady any flowers. Why would anyone?

"What about you, Mrs. Hughes? Don't you think you wasted a lot of time checking on Bradley?"

She glares at me.

I move closer to her and say, "I am here to discuss the operation with you."

Her eyes begin to narrow as if I've said the meanest thing ever. "You are wasting your time, Doctor," she says.

"Apparently so."

I stand up.

"All I can think about is my living will," she says. "I made a decision to withdraw all life support systems. There is a chance of falling into a coma tomorrow, right?"

Her voice has become hoarse, and I can picture the yellow phlegm in her throat. I'd prefer a devout Christian to a lost existentialist and cynic in a situation like this.

"Well, Mrs. Hughes, since you're so on keen making your own decisions, there's always the Do Not Resuscitate document that you can sign."

I hurry toward the door. It is now that I hear the clacking of my old Prada pumps. She has finally shut her mouth.

CHAPTER TWO

I see in this morning's updated paper that Mrs. Hughes has insisted on a full anesthetic. Usually, we only inject a pain-killing local anesthetic for minimally invasive surgery, leading the patient to feel dazed. Without reading any further, I shake my head and place the paper next to the computer for the report later on.

I'm in the scrub room with a scrub nurse when I hear them wheeling Mrs. Hughes into the anesthetic room with Stuart and Howard. According to Howard, our anesthesiologist, Mrs. Hughes' request for a full anesthetic is to help her sleep. Well, as long as she and I don't have to exchange eye contact, I'm good.

There is a monitoring nurse, a scrub nurse, Howard, Stuart, and me in the operating theater. Seeing Mrs. Hughes lying calmly on the bed of the fluoroscopy machine is a soothing sight. She has transformed from a mad lady into an angel.

"Don't waste your time," I hear her say.

I wonder how healing her abominable heart will make me feel better since her unpleasant personality shows no sign of appreciation – not towards me, nor towards life. Has she lived her life to the fullest? How would Dr. Dick guide me in a situation like this?

My favorite part of the human body is the thorax – the gates to the heart. I remember once in the dissecting room, Dr. Dick caught me doing some aggressive handiwork on an old female patient's chest. Sometimes you want to cut a body in a way you would open a sealed cardboard box, starting from the sternum and then down…

"What on earth, Dr. Parker? What did this old lady *do* to you?" he'd said.

I won't forget that terrified look on his face and the reflection of my face in his dilated pupils.

"I'm…sorry. It won't happen again."

And it never happened again. That incident was before he and I became close; that was the catalyst that made him pay more attention to my developing surgical skills. I became gentle. I started to listen to the bodies.

After death, Dr. Dick will donate his body to the National Anatomical Service. We'd jokingly agreed that I could have his thorax, and it will be treated with care. Other students were bidding for his head.

However, Mrs. Hughes's private life isn't my business. I just want to be close to her heart and make my way in, but I need to control my euphoria. I make the first small incision underneath the clavicle and another one slightly below. Her skin feels like dried tofu. My hands are usually hungry for flesh and blood, and the more I am responsible for the patient's well-being, the hungrier they get. Fixing their hearts makes me visualize my own open thorax on the operating table. I see my pumping heart behind the gates, and I wonder who will ever have the power to break through them and save me. Mrs. Hughes is different compared to the other patients. She is not looking to be saved. No one can persuade her to let go of the grudge against her husband's infidelity.

Stuart passes me the ICD-device. I adjust the lead, which is attached to the top of the device. I slowly insert it through the incision and into the vein. There is no chemistry between us; her flesh feels cold. I visualize her cardiac vein and marginal arteries, ready to spit poison into my face.

My life! My decision!

But you are on my table, old lady.

With the help of the fluoroscopy machine, Stuart navigates me towards the right chamber of the heart so I can attach the lead in the right ventricle. Each chamber of the heart has a purpose, the flowing of oxygenated and deoxygenated blood. These four connected apartments accommodate all human emotions, but mine. It's a pleasure to invade one of those secret rooms. Perhaps she has some kindness in store.

The fluorescent view on the screen makes me think of a black and white silent movie in which someone pokes a mole with a stick, or it could be something I've dreamt. To my surprise, I find it is Mrs. Hughes's heart.

Lastly, I place the ICD generator under the cold skin. The installation of a bugging device has been completed.

"Good job, Parks," says Stuart after the suture.

Frankly, this wasn't much of a challenge. The surgery lasted no longer than two hours.

Stuart and I walk to the doctor's room to write the report, leaving Howard to administer oxygen to awaken Mrs. Hughes.

"By the way, what did you and the old lady talk about yesterday?"

"Why?" I ask.

"I meant to ask you earlier..."

Suddenly the monitoring nurse storms in. "We have a cardiac arrest!"

"CPR," I say. I readjust my mouth mask and rush back into the operating theater.

"Parker, wait!"

I don't understand Stuart's slow reaction to this emergency. I tell the nurse to fetch the external defibrillators while I double-check the pulse and breathing – nothing.

Don't do this to me, Mrs. Hughes.

She has long stopped talking to me on this table. All I see are images of Mr. Hughes dropping her off at a hospice where she has no one to talk to.

I don't understand why Howard shows no reaction, either. It's as if everyone in the OT is under some form of paralysis.

"The ICD is not reacting."

My words seem to fall on deaf ears.

"Stuart?"

"Parker..." he says.

I look at the monitor and see that the generator is still transmitting electrical shocks to the heart, without success.

I want to demand higher voltage, but I'm unable to utter a word.

"She signed the DNR document yesterday."

While sterilizing the equipment in the scrub room, I look at Stuart through the glass window. He is in the office next door, writing the report. I've asked the scrub nurse to go tell Mr. Hughes about the adverse outcome of that surgery. Mr. Hughes was right. I am a nurse. Right now, I am doing the job of a nurse.

Stuart and I are facing each other. I turn the microphone and speakers on so he can hear the flowing water. He looks up at me for a second and then carries on writing.

"She was becoming demented," I say.

As I dry my hands, I notice that they are trembling. I grab the instruments and rewash them in the sink.

"I think she just didn't like you," Stuart says.

I didn't read the papers properly. The Do Not Resuscitate document must have been signed straight after I'd left yesterday. Apparently, her daughter Tess was the witness. You can tell that Tess empathizes more with her mother. That was why Mr. Hughes wouldn't let her see their mother yesterday.

I will miss that spiteful heart. But after all, I hardly ever have pleasant conversations with women. My mother never gave me a chance.

"Are you OK?" he says.

It sounds like we've just had a domestic row in the kitchen. I have to picture my mother and Dad back at home in Connecticut.

Stuart often calls me *partner*, but in the most discreet manner. He reflects sincerity in a way that reminds me of Dr. Dick. But in a flick of a switch, Stuart becomes callous again. I don't like this ambivalence about him. I'd rather he were indifferent on a regular basis.

He has just turned thirty-nine and is one of the youngest cardiothoracic surgeons in New York. He is also a member of the American Heart Association. He will most likely be a consultant at Mount Sinai and at the Columbia-Presbyterian Hospital in less than five years. I can't say I trust him as much as I trust Dr. Dick, not yet.

So, this is the first chapter—my first official heart surgery. A broken heart failing to fix someone else's broken heart. I hope Dr. Dick won't ever learn about this failure.

From the corner of my eyes, I see that Stuart is still watching me.

"Did you really tell her that we were married?"

He smiles. "Yeah, why not? She was creepily flirtatious."

After drying my hands again, I leave the scrub room, walk down the sterile corridor towards the door to the wards. I see Sarah in the hall with a sympathetic look on her face. Who does she think she is anyway, wearing nail polish at work?

"I'm so sorry to hear," she mumbles.

"Don't…"

I walk past her towards the elevator.

The moment the elevator door opens, I see Mr. Hughes with two teenage boys and a little girl – all three crying. They get off.

"Hello, Mr. Hughes."

"I need to speak to the doctor," he says.

"Where is Granny, Daddy?"

The little girl looks so pure and innocent. I remember my hair looking like hers when I was ten or eleven.

"I *am* the doctor, Mr. Hughes. I operated on her. After the implantation, your mother had a cardiac arrest, but we had no right to resuscitate."

Mr. Hughes knows that Stuart was involved in the operation. I will indeed send him to Stuart if he asks, and I also have no problem reporting the entire procedure of the operation to him, such as, how I successfully attached the lead to the right ventricle. But instead of inquiring, he embraces his children. All I hear now are unbearable sobs.

"I'm sorry for your loss."

I quickly step into the elevator and watch how it shuts the world out. I feel a tightening of muscles in my shoulders.

On the ground floor, I see Tess Hughes crying with one hand pressed against her head.

CHAPTER THREE

I turn towards the cafeteria to get a black coffee. I debate whether to check my blood pressure now or maybe have a quick nap.

It's late in the afternoon, and I have two hours before treating my new patient Bruce Dwayne. According to his records, he is a thirty-five-year-old painter with corneal scarring. I imagine the Caped Crusader entering my practice room with an eye injury. He has been transferred to me for an eye examination since our actual ophthalmologist from the Eye Unit, Dr. Mellor, is on leave.

I walk to my office with a cup and a small jug of coffee. My hands are still ice-cold from sterilizing the equipment. In my office, I hold my hands up to the sun to warm up. In a moment, I am back in the woods.

At the age of eight, I took a walk with Dad at Mohawk Forest State Park. I was particularly fond of spotting wild deer, especially the little ones. I was squinting my eyes to take a leak in a sunny spot when Bambi knocked me over.

Before any appointments, I clean the treatment room with a clinical sanitizer. I sanitize the doorknob, stools and clean underneath the patient's seat and treatment table because often patients leave me their nasal mucus when I am not looking. I remember that my former school principal, in his office, had the habit of cleaning the furniture around the table after each pupil's visit. His office used to smell of disinfectant every time I visited. It wasn't until recently that I completely understood that procedure.

My practice room provides me with a broader range of medical equipment than the one in New Haven. The appearance of this fully established and highly professional practice is incredible. But it assures the patient of an efficient treatment under my roof. On my desk, I have my own 21.5 iMac with a retina 4k display. My nameplate is no longer made of plastic, but of metal with my name cut: "Dr. Ellen Parker."

As I leave my practice room to get disposable paper sheets, I bump into a reasonably good-looking man who, instead of looking me in the eye, has his eyes fixed on my décolletage. Both his eyes are opaque. Next to him is nurse Julia.

"There you go, Mr. Dwayne, here she is!"

While examining Mr. Dwayne's retina with my

ophthalmoscope, I see abnormalities in his fovea – a red region, which I call the Devil's bellybutton. The fovea is situated in the center of the yellowish macula – resembling a discolored belly. The vessels in his choroid are not supplying his fovea with enough oxygen, hence the blurry vision. There are also tiny blisters on the corneal surface.

"So, you call it a glass accident, Mr. Dwayne?"

"Yeah..." he says.

"Well, such scarring is rather unpredictable. The back of your eye is badly impaired. Your transfer papers indicate a deterioration of cone cells since you were thirty. You've been using eye drops for cornea treatment ever since?"

"Yeah," he says.

"So, what was the glass accident?"

He remains silent, swings his dark hair forward to cover up a part of his face.

"Well," I say, "I'm sure you want it to heal, so there are no excuses not to wear eye patches for now. We'll have to consider a corneal transplant to restore your vision anyway, I'm afraid."

"How will that work?"

"The procedure is easy. We'll remove the scarred cornea and replace it with a healthy one from a donor."

He stares at my décolletage again, but I'm sure he can't see a clear picture of my physique. I wonder whether the outline of my body in his blurry vision looks like an impressionist's painting. The opacity in his eyes clearly blocks the amount of light required to make out any kind of object.

"Is finding a donor just as easy?"

"We're not looking for an organ donation, Mr. Dwayne, so there's no need to worry. We'll find suitable corneal tissues for you."

I see indifference in those cloudy eyes.

"Could you give me some bandage contact lenses instead of eye patches, please, so I won't look like I've blinded myself?"

It's outrageous that when endangered by blindness but informed about possible healing measures, he takes our ability to fix his vision for granted. Other patients are similar. Bandage contact lenses are softer than standard lenses. They are often applied to patients after refractive surgeries to smoothen the ocular surface and give the patient more comfort. It's also easier for the surgeon to keep track of the eye, and the patient will still have a usable vision. However, Mr. Dwayne is already past the threat of corneal scarring, and he'll most likely have to wear those kinds of lenses more often.

"You're a picky type, Mr. Dwayne."

He ignores my comment.

"Seriously, who's going to take me home when I

have to wear eye patches?"

"Do you have a family member or relative that can fetch you?"

He tilts his head in my direction. His eyes are partially red from the eye drops, and I see a weak smile at the corner of his mouth. The dimple represents something innocent.

It is now that I see an imprint on his ring finger. He lowers his head, and his hair overshadows his face again. It's bad for the eyes to have dusty hair brushing along the face.

"I'm going to get you the contact lenses."

"Thank you," he says.

"I will see you next week for some further examination. For now, I will take a blood sample to check for infections and deficiencies.

Wednesday is my day off, allowing me to catch up with meditation and afternoon naps, which are impractical at work. I'm always on call for emergencies, but I cherish every moment of regeneration that my body gets.

The first thing Franz Kafka did in the morning was wash his hands, and so do I, as you never know where your hands have been. Next, I put on some Synthie Pop and Industrial music. This is how a day begins.

My skin is dry. I am most dehydrated when I wake up in the morning, so I drink up to a liter of warm water with lemon before jumping into my ten-minute shower. No one would believe that I've had dermatitis since my teenage years. There is no cure for it; you can only control it – control it well.

On many occasions, I have cold showers, or I switch temperature numerous times to boost my immune system.

Dermatologists have agreed that it might be stress-related, so I decided to undergo a cosmetic session followed by meditation or Yoga. It took me months to achieve the necessary focus of Concentrative Meditation. Now and again, my breathing will still be shallow and uneven, and my mind will fill with naked patients on the operating table. Ultimately meditation has initiated me into understanding the meaning of control, the concept of balancing mind and body. It's not easy making friends with your inner demons, especially if you don't have a flashlight to light up their faces. They have eyes that can see you in the dark – your every move, your every blink.

During my beauty session, I use a facial mask to help purify and moisturize my skin. My dermatologist has strongly advised me to keep a good routine of moisturizing combined with breathing exercises or meditation.

For breakfast, I have whole grain flakes with honey and fruit in hemp milk. I try to avoid caffeine drinks at home, as they make my heart rate increase by sixteen percent. Coffee, however, is difficult to avoid at work. I like how the aromatic smell calms my brain, as it reminds me of how Dad used to kiss my hair in the morning before heading to work. His lab coat always smelled of clinical sanitizer. And there was the coffee.

I spend my leisure time in the city center, mainly on Fifth Avenue – the open road to anywhere, be it the eastern part of Central Park or Prada. I'm on my way to do some shopping there, as I'm running out of decent eligible second skins. If only lab coats were appropriate in public, I wouldn't have to worry about what to wear.

I first encountered Prada during my holidays in Milan. A Prada associate approached me in the shop, asking if he could borrow my body for his prêt-a-porter collection. He wanted my short blonde curls to juxtapose with his dark designs. I realized then how Prada's unusual choice of hides and fabrics distinguished them from other designers. Their professional tanneries allow the high quality of their hides to appear smooth and natural. As an adult, Prada clothing gives me a sense of safety, which I only ever used to find underneath Dad's brown bear rug. Prada is also the first designer to make fine nylon appear like silk. I was also offered the opportunity to present the clothing on the catwalk, but I declined. I wasn't made for walking that lane. I was made for walking through the sterile corridor into the operating theater wearing plastic overshoes. Back then, I was already a general surgeon assisting Dr. Dick in cardiac surgeries, during which he had opened the door for me to a new pursuit – one that would explain why I am here and why the past belongs to the past.

But wherever you go, the past is never far. Like Eurydice, it will walk behind you like a giant shadow, except that it won't disappear when I turn around. Instead, it will urge me to look back, to look back closely at the day I stopped feeling. When you're young and in love, you imagine your first time being passionate. What if you received a semi-impalement? However, I wouldn't have been able to deal with the attention on a catwalk anyway.

As I enter Prada, a middle-aged gentleman welcomes me. I've never seen him there before; I can't tell whether he is either well built or slightly chubby. His black Armani suit is of fine cotton but shimmers like silk – a hyperreal illusion. I can see why some would mistake it for Prada. Both brands express similar darkness, except that Armani embodies more mystery. Prada is straighter to the point. Men wear Armani to conceal their secret, whereas women wear it to allure.

"Please do not hesitate to ask for any help, ma'am. I'm Joe."

His voice is deep and friendly. Despite his sincere way of welcoming me, I notice drops of sweat on his shiny, bald head.

"I'd like to see your latest spring collection in the shoe department."

"Follow me."

They have a remarkable new range of shoes in stock, which are the exact equivalent of ones I saw in my latest dream, in which I was wearing Prada in the operating theater.

Joe fetches every pair that I ask for.

The number of sweat pearls on his head has increased. I wonder if he is only unfit. His pretty blue eyes look tired, like those of a mailman at 6 a.m.

As he helps me slip into the patent pumps, he gets in contact with my big toe and flinches.

"I'm sorry if my feet aren't pleasant."

"Oh no, no! You have elegant feet, ma'am."

I can see the sweat on his upper lip.

"Are you all right?" I say.

At this point, he stands up. I see him press the lid of

the shoebox against his crotch. He's pale. I bet his body lacks magnesium and calcium. Perhaps he has a thyroid disorder? He might also need more zinc to help him maintain a normal adrenal function.

"I like your perfume, ma'am."

"Thanks," I say, checking the size of his fingers. They are short and chubby.

"Jil Sander?"

"I'm impressed!"

He has pointed out my next most admired designer. Jil Sander is a German fashion designer and an eminent perfumer. On the fashion front, her cashmere products, or anything that's black and plain grey are most suitable for whenever I feel low.

Joe has finished dressing my feet.

"Thanks."

The high heels are sharp – I am now about three inches taller than he is. He looks at me with self-conscious eyes. I know what that Prada associate saw in me years ago, and I'm also aware of the presentation that I could have given him on the runway.

"I'll take them."

Some people feel guilty after shopping, but I don't get into the reality of wasting money, for me, money is of small value. It just happens that I picked an occupation that provides me with everything that I need and covers all sorts of insurance there is. I have worked hard for it.

As I turn left into East Forty-Seventh Street towards C'est Bon Café for some lunch, I hear someone behind me, saying, "Dr. Parker!"

I turn around and see Bruce staring at the lower part of my body, and then I remember that he can only see an outline of my entire figure.

"I'm amazed you recognized me, Mr. Dwayne."

"Nah. I could *smell* you," he says.

"Oh."

It happens that when encountering patients in public that I find myself instantly back in the hospital in my lab coat. I picture Mrs. Hughes's operation last week and suddenly smell her flesh on me like expired meat.

"I have excellent smell-sensors."

He is in an incredibly good mood for some reason. But right this moment, I can't help believing that I smell like carrion and death. Has her dead body passed on some form of pheromone?

"I know our appointment isn't until Friday but would you like a coffee?" he says.

We are inside the café; I am not comfortable about the possibility of being scrutinized by the people around us. Fellow work colleagues often come here to buy their lunch.

"Have you been using the eye drops that I gave you?"

"Sure have."

"How come your eyes look so dry then?"

I carefully place my index finger on his eyebrow. His clothes reek of cigarettes.

"I don't think I need any particular smell-sensors to smell..."

"Carbon monoxide?" he interrupts me.

"...Tobacco. Carbon monoxide is odorless, Mr. Dwayne."

"Sure is. You indeed are not to be fooled with, Miss Parker."

"It's *Doctor*."

He takes a pack of cigarettes out of his coat pocket and puts it on the table. "I'm sorry, I really am."

The apology is better directed at himself. I hold the pack of Lucky Strikes up before his eyes and then slam it down on the table.

"Not so lucky, hm? Well, I appreciate your honesty, but I do hope that you care about your eyes, Mr. Dwayne."

"I suppose."

"You don't sound convincing."

"Trust me – I do, Dr. Parker."

There is something innocent about the way he clasps his hands. They look ordinary but manly. I see no dirt under his nails and hardly any wrinkles – just the imprint on his ring finger. The back of his hand is bony, and the veins visible and thick. I imagine seeing an x-ray image of his left hand, showing all twenty-seven bones – the phalanges and the carpals.

I may have lost a heart the other day, but Mrs. Hughes was only a warm-up. The next patient will appreciate life.

I smile at his hand. I feel my libido responding to a challenge.

"I hope you're ready for another blood test before the eye ultrasound on Friday."

"Another *blood* test? What for?" he says.

"Well, you've not been good to yourself, so I'll need to double-check, won't I?"

"There is no need!"

He sounds anxious, and before he can talk me out of it, I prick his index finger with a finger-stick. I only need a small sample of capillary blood. I carry a couple of finger-pricks with me everywhere I go, including a lab-on-a-chip for an immediate blood examination. I get them from the Diabetes Care section.

"Are you scared of needles?"

*

Bruce has the horn of a rhinoceros sitting on the lounge's windowsill, which doesn't correspond well with his abstract paintings on canvas.

"I know what you're looking at," Bruce says. "It's a gift from a friend."

"Nice...how much did he get for emasculating that poor thing?"

"Don't you think that if a man had emasculated an animal, he would want to keep that trophy?"

From the lounge area, I watch him prepare two cocktails on the centrally located island – a little bar designated for the preparation of drinks. His gaze is fixed on the glasses, and his hand movements as if he can see every single detail. My former ophthalmologist said that the visually impaired can see better with their hearts. I'd like to believe that, but I don't.

I move closer to the windowsill to observe the horn and wonder whether the rhinoceros was tranquilized or killed before his castration.

I remember feeding Dolly a high dose of sedatives that knocked her out instantly, allowing me to pull her rotten rabbit tooth out. Dad's toolbox was always within reach; what he hid from me were Clorox and glue.

"Forgive me for asking this..."

"I'm not a good forgiver, Bruce."

I hear no movement in the kitchen.

"Neither was my ex-wife."

I walk towards the kitchen and find him lost in his thoughts.

"My eyes have never been good. Years ago, the cells in my eyes began to deteriorate. I've been using drops for many years to stop my cornea from swelling. The day she left, I stopped using them."

"Can you imagine how painful it'd be if one of the blisters burst? You'd cry, and so would the entire apple of your eye."

"I didn't care at the time," he says.

"You'd scream and panic like someone with Mace in his eyes."

"She said I didn't know what real beauty was."

"You mean inner beauty?"

He scratches his nose.

"Physical beauty hypnotizes me and makes me do stupid things."

"Are you saying that you cheated on her?" I say. "That's not nice. She'll retaliate."

He laughs.

"What's so funny?"

"She put glass splinters in my contact lens case."

I look at him in amazement.

I walk closer to the kitchen island and hold my hand

in front of him, waving slightly with my fingers. He catches them. His hand smells of pineapple.

"Did you see that?" I say.

"I never get lost in the fog."

I gently pull my hand back. "What did you want to ask me earlier?"

"Nothing," he says.

"Please don't add too much rum to my drink; it makes me tired. I still need to go home later."

The first sip of the cocktail tastes sugary. The second sip overwhelms my tongue with rum burning down from my throat to my stomach. The aftertaste leaves a trace of chamomile flower.

"You're a good doctor, Miss Parker."

"Is that so?"

"I wasn't eavesdropping, but...I overheard a conversation about Mrs. Hughes. I also heard some of your fellow doctors – they might have been nurses, sharing some awestruck statements."

"What did they say?"

"Let's just say they admire you."

I look at the horn again and could swear that it is pumping like an organ.

CHAPTER FOUR

I'm trapped in a labyrinth made of dead people's limbs. They react like they have motion sensors inserted into them. When I walk down a path, a violent arm stretches out and grabs me, and when I'm leaning against a wall, hands pull my hair, or random feet kick me in the butt. I am half-naked, wearing my torn purple negligee. I have no clue what I am running away from or where I am headed.

All those limbs around me are passing some form of electricity to me by touching my skin. The impulses are making my heart sore. I stick my hand into my rib cage and tear out the ICD generator.

Then I hear a man calling out.

"Here you are!"

I turn around and see a masked man of about six foot seven, muscular like you would imagine a nightmarish hangman, and strong with broad shoulders like my dad.

The disembodied limbs have now grabbed hold of me tightly, forcing me down to spread my legs wide open. From behind his back, he brings forward a giant ax…

I wake up and look at each corner of the bedroom. This is not my home, and I see that Bruce is asleep next to me. My side of the bed is soaked in sweat, whereas he is sleeping peacefully. I have my panties on and can feel some vaginal discharge between my legs, which I do not wish to investigate. I see two empty cocktail glasses on the bedside table and leftover pineapple parings on the floor. I look at the horn to retrieve last night's images of an evidently drunken episode. I cannot remember.

Drunken sex is not my style.

It is 5:34 a.m., and there is a funny tickle between my thighs. Something is wrong with my estradiol levels; a sudden strength overwhelms my muscles as if testosterone has taken over my body. There is an uncontrollable tingle in my vagina, making me succumb to the lower brain.

I climb onto Bruce's body. A strange moment of déjà vu engulfs my blurry memory; I must be repeating last night's incident.

He stirs and opens his eyes slightly, gazing at my belly.

"Morning," he mumbles.

I crouch down and lean my body over him – our faces almost touching. His erection corresponds with my engorged clitoris. He moves his fingers down my flanks and takes off my underwear.

These impulses aren't me.

His mouth is trying to reach mine, but I tilt my head away. The extreme rush of hormones underneath my armpits and between my legs is overpowering and beyond my reasoning. I grab hold of his face and press his head back into the pillow.

"What did you pour into my drink?"

"What?" he says obtusely and enters me.

I fail to suppress a moan – unable to fight against his movements. I glance at the horn and then back at Bruce.

"What did you pour into my drink?"

I am out of breath. I lay my hand on his chest to fathom his heartbeat. His heart rate is higher than mine. The race of hearts has begun, but I have no intention to win this race. The faster a heart beats, the more love this person has to offer. I have no control over my moans; it doesn't even sound like me.

After a while, my muscles tighten up. And suddenly, the rush of sensations in my pelvic area has disappeared into oblivion, just like that. He stops thrusting before I do. There is slippery wetness underneath. It feels like I have just woken up from a dream without remembering its ending. At least I no longer feel detached from my own body.

I pull away from Bruce and look around the room, disoriented. Everything looks different. It's as if a dream has thrown me out like garbage. I feel alone. This is the side effect of sex. And I ask myself again: Where is this tingling in the spine and warmth around the genital area?

"I'm going to ask you one last time," I say. "What did you pour into my drink?"

"Some benzo," he says.

I hover over his body and grab his penis so tightly until he twitches. Both our cums have gone cold.

"For your information, I don't like losing control over my body. Do you understand me?"

He nods. "I'm sorry."

I let go of him, but I can see a lot more behind the fog in his eyes.

"What else was in my cocktail?"

I press my forearm against his throat.

"It wasn't in that order..."

"What?"

"There were damiana extracts in your cocktail," he says.

This explains the flowery taste in my drink but not the increase of libido. I do not believe that a plant can manipulate my mind and body.

"Why did you think I needed that?"

"I wanted you to want me. You're so hard to read."

Of course. How can he read me if he is functionally blind? My voice is loud and clear, and I don't stutter. I've been told that I talk like an intimidating teacher. I see goosebumps on his forearm, which remind me of Braille codes. Perhaps I should initiate some on my arm to inform him about my rules in bed.

"After sex, you wanted to leave, but I got you to stay for some wine."

This is the part I don't remember, and I have no desire to listen to the rest of the story as it involves too much mind game. I get out of bed and begin to dress.

"I didn't want to be alone," he says.

"We all are."

My eyes are fixed on the horn's sharp tip. It has long stopped pumping. I put my Prada pumps on and walk towards the horn to cover it with my silk scarf. I decide not to knock it over, and instead, I pull both ends of my scarf downward until the tip of the horn pierces through. Even though the sound of breaking textile hurts my ears, I also sense pleasure.

"By the way, Dr. Mellor is back this week. Don't forget your appointment tomorrow."

-

On my way back downtown, the taxicab gets stuck in the traffic in Midtown. After paying the driver ten bucks, I step out of the car and start heading down W 40th Street.

It's a cold spring morning, but at least the fresh breeze cools my head down. The smell of New York rain has revitalized my perception. It's so early, but as people say, this city is foreign to fixed routines. New York has its own dynamics.

I see two black cars, a Ford Fusion and an Audi A6 or A7 that have crashed into each other – probably drunk driving or a gangster hunt. No ambulance has arrived yet; only people watching inquisitively like old women in small suburban neighborhoods. A man standing outside the mass of people is grinning at me while I'm walking. His face looks strikingly familiar. He is wearing a black trench coat with both hands hidden in his pockets. His eyes are demonic. As soon as I hear the sirens, I begin to speed up.

I need a blood test. It's easy for Bruce to just name the substances, but whether he is telling the truth is another story.

At home, I tighten a tourniquet around my arm. My median cubital vein is always visible, which makes blood tests easy. What I like about needles and syringes are the sloping holes; they look menacing and remind me of Dad's bamboo stick sword.

He keeps it in the living room as decoration. When I was very young, I drew the sword from its sheath to survey the carbon steel blade. I remember feeling vehemently attracted to the tip of the sword, and like Briar Rose, I pricked my finger on the spindle, but unlike her, I didn't die; instead, I had an epiphany. I knew then what that sting in later years would feel like. It gave me a rough idea of what love might be like, too. I was prepared for the pain as well as for the blood.

After disinfecting the area of my arm, I anchor the vein from below the puncture site and insert the syringe fast at no more than fifteen degrees. I start to pull back on the syringe and then watch how the tube fills with my blood. I pull the syringe out and immediately apply some gauze to the wound.

A thorough blood test is essential. When checking my patients' or my blood, I always run an ordinary biomechanical analysis to I measure the sodium, glucose, cholesterol, and creatinine units, including the amount of nitrogen in the blood. But when checking some patients' blood, I pay double attention to STDs.

I apply some drops of blood to a Plexiglas before placing it on the microscope stage. It's set on low power. I lower the objective lens with the coarse knob to the lowest point. As I look through the eyepiece, I adjust the diaphragm, then when I center the specimen in my field view, I switch to high power. This always brings me back to biology lessons. You will see a lot if you pay attention to detail.

I see how my white blood cells are floating around to collect garbage. It must be an awful job. There is a lack of hydration in my blood, which doesn't surprise me. I've repeatedly been perspiring in the last six hours without having drunk anything to redress the balance. My skin is dry.

Then I see some minor sponge-shaped toxicants staggering obliviously back and forth – two different types. There is no sign of them multiplying.
I keep little tubes of drug liquids in my liquid nitrogen freezer. They are for whenever I need to identify or compare foreign particles.

The balance of my estradiol levels has been overwhelmed by a high number of estrones converted by my liver; this is due to the oral consumption of damiana. He reduced me to a slave of the lower brain, disconnected me from reason. This is my first encounter with an aphrodisiac. Mexicans use damiana leaves to make relaxation tea like every American would prepare lemon balm or regular chamomile tea. Damiana is supposed to smell and taste like cannabis, but the pineapple's sweetness must have suppressed the taste last night.

I know that many mainstream drugs originate from herbs, but my belief in medicine is founded on hard chemistry. In poorer countries, you have an autonomy that relies solely on unprocessed herbal remedies, like in Uganda, where people use banana wine as an analgesic or red stinkwood to relieve inflammation.

Well, benzodiazepine can cause cognitive impairment and amnesia.

Bruce's blood samples were perfectly fine – AB negative, lacking a bit of biotin, but no sign of any diseases. The Japanese say that AB types have split personalities, one half being shy and timid, whereas the other is confident. In other words, that's Bruce. If I hadn't wanted him, I wouldn't have screened his blood twice.

***

"She is a kid!" I hear Dad say to my Mother. "Why would she know anything about sex?"

"Someone must have shown her something! She just attempted to sexually assault her classmate, for Christ's sake!" she says.

"Why are you looking at me like I'm responsible?"

"You're the doctor in the house, having your medical books lying around everywhere!"

I don't like hearing my parents argue because I am guilty. It's always about me. I'm in the backyard looking for ladybugs and earthworms. There are always plenty of earthworms after the rain. I grab a long one by the end and place its head between my lips and begin to suck it into my mouth like a string of spaghetti. Still holding the end of its body, I start to swallow one half of its body, and then I slowly pull the entire thing back out of my throat. It feels funny. I throw it aside and watch a blackbird catch it.

I can still hear my parents fight, so I make my way toward the little shed in our backyard where Dad keeps his gardening equipment and old medical books. The shed is small, but I manage to squeeze myself in. I sit down on a pile of books and clasp my hands. One of Dad's books is on the floor. The open page shows a black and white x-ray image of someone's chest. I know that the heart is trapped behind the rib cage somewhere, and I seem to just see nine ribs on each side instead of twelve. It's nice and quiet here – no more shouting. The smell of the lawn mower's gasoline tickles my nose. My head is spinning. There is an uncomfortable tickle between my legs. As I stick my finger into my cunt, I notice how wet I am inside. I go slightly deeper, but not too deep. I'm scared, scared of this pleasant feeling that I don't understand. I don't understand the noises I'm making. It must be wrong, but I can't stop.

I'm close to something.

Very close.

My heart is beating fast. My breathing is heavy. I feel a tingle in my back.

"Princess?" says my dad, and I immediately pull my finger out. I turn around and see this bewildered expression on his fac, as if he is seeing me for the first time in his life. I think I peed on my fingers, it's slippery between them, but I do not dare to look at them. He can't look me in the eye any longer and simply gestures for me to go outside. On my way back to the house, I notice that Dad is still staring at the spot where I have been sitting.

CHAPTER FIVE

My next patient is Scott Griffith, a seventeen-year-old rock musician. I watch him kiss his girlfriend in the waiting room before he enters the treatment room with me. The girlfriend is petite and has pink hair like the skater kids in Brooklyn.

Scott's transfer papers indicate a deteriorating thyroid condition, which needs further examination. An ultrasound scan diagnosed a lump and excessive iodine production, leading to an increase in thyroid hormones. The state of the swelling doesn't look too bad.

"Ever since these goiters, I've had sore eyes. Like they're bulging," he says.

"It's a symptom that occurs under very rare circumstances. I'll give you drops."

I have seen worse toxic goiters before. I think Scott is overreacting.

He is a handsome fellow despite his tired eyes suggesting chronic lethargy. He stares deliriously at the four-panel curtain.

When I wipe his neck with an antiseptic solution, he makes no noticeable movement, not even a reaction to the cold liquid on his skin. I wonder whether numbing his skin with some anesthetic is even necessary before the biopsy.

"Is this the result of not eating well?" he says.

"Not really. According to your profile, this condition runs in your family. So it's inevitable. Perhaps you should try boosting your immune system with..."

"My immune system's a bitch, y'know."

"So is life," I say.

I look him in the face, but he's still glaring at the curtains with his adorable automaton eyes. The gaseous smell of anesthetic hits my nose like a shot of cocaine would hit an addict.

"It is very likely that your immune system has turned against your thyroid's function, Mr. Griffith, and this stimulates the antibodies in your gland to a more enhanced activity resulting in overkill."

"A shame that antibodies can't think, eh?" he says. "We studied them in biology. They just float around looking for things to do. They must be bored as hell!"

I prepare the syringe for the aspiration biopsy.

"Ironically, it is me who produces these proteins, right? I am all those hard-working cells, but the cells aren't me…"

I never encountered a smart, young patient who also believes that cells are protective patriots in our bodies, fighting against antigens – like fathers protecting daughters, keeping them from harmful intruders.

Now he glances at me in a very familiar way, as if we were related. Then he looks at the fine thin needle. He slowly curls his hand around mine, which is holding the needle firmly.

"I used to be a very hard-working cell, Dr. Parker."

"I'm sure you still are."

He slowly shakes his head; his lips are trembling as though looking for the right words.

"You don't understand. I'm not referring to this life," he says.

While shooting me a serious look, his grasp around my hand becomes firm – like an embrace between two lost lovers.

"I used to be a part of you," he says.

"You what?"

"I used to be a cell in your body when you were little."

I freeze in mid-movement. Scott slowly releases my hand, which is sweating.

"And during one particular incident," he says, "You bled me out."

I let go of the needle.

I see myself in the body of that drop of blood; I am gazing up at the grass while resting on dark plowed earth. It's freezing. Then the earth sucks me in, and my new purpose is to fertilize a daisy by offering my life.

"Are you OK, Doc?" Scott says.

The next morning, I watch how the nurses set up the operating theater while a few students gather at the back of the room. During the microscopic examination, I found that Scott's cells were no longer following their regulatory mechanism. The specimen looked like a fluid cyst on the micrograph, but the diagnosis was follicular neoplasm – possible cancer due to the tissues' continuous growth. To identify the illness, I will remove half of the affected gland for further examination.

I watch Scott's girlfriend hold his hand; she is in tears as the ward nurse wheels him towards the operating theater. It must be her first experience seeing a loved one being escorted into – what some patients refer to as – the bloody chamber. But Scott's scenario isn't about life and death.

I stop the girl from entering the room.

"You have to calm down. Everything will be all right."

"I don't like you," she says.

I don't know what to say.

"I know about you," she continues, "Scott won't stop talking about you."

"I'm just here to perform a *lobectomy*, Miss."

"Yeah, do what you have to! I read all about it. But don't you dare touch his voice box, you hear me?"

She knocks my arm with her shoulder as she heads down the hallway. I'm counting her steps until she makes a turn. I'm sure she wished our shoulders were the same height.

As I walk through the anesthetic room, I indicate to Howard that I'm ready; Scott gives me a soft smile. Other than regulating one's energy output, the thyroid is also responsible for hormonal function. Perhaps Scott's lady friend suspects me of colonizing his vocal cords.

I make a three-inch incision along the mass above where the clavicle and sternum meet and then watch the blood slowly ooze out and accumulate at the edge of the wound. When removing organs, I tend to use electrocautery to control heavy bleeding. To Scott, these bloodlines are living citizens of the body – citizens that don't easily survive outside their home.

The scrub nurse applies a self-retaining retractor to hold my fine incision open and adds another to pull back the infrahyoid muscles, allowing me unconditional admittance into Scott's mushy little kingdom. I wonder if the citizens believe in the hand of God. Will they pray to me and say, "Dr. Parker, please deliver us from evil."

As I cut through the thyroid tissue, I hear a moan. I throw a quick glance at the nurse.

"Is anything wrong, Doctor?"

I look at the bright halogen lights above my head and at all the surgical apparatuses around me.

I remember it was a very sunny day in good old Connecticut. Lines of blood were running down my leg as I stepped out to the garden. I felt like I had lost something of great value. I didn't touch the bamboo stick sword, but it touched me. The sparrows in our garden were mocking me.

"It's nothing," I tell the nurse.

After removing of half of the tissue, I see the laryngeal nerve behind the gland, and behind my mouth mask, I am grinning from ear to ear. The nerve originates as a limb of the vagus nerve, which ascends to the brain in a carotid sheath. The sheath engulfs the neck's vascular system, where vital arteries provide oxygenated blood to the brain and other organs of the head. All these nerves and veins are never-ending highways that lead you to important places and back.

The voice box reminds me of a newborn chick's open mouth. In fact, now I can hear Scott's song overlaying the tweets of the sparrows.

"Innocence's been taken during the sweet love that we are making..." he sings.

I wonder whether his pink-haired lady friend has touched his every part, including the hidden spots. Does she think a voice box resembles a music box? How poetic. But realists embrace the physical.

Generally, I like spending my lunch breaks in my office. Every now and then, I join my colleagues in the cafeteria if they invite me along. I only decline when Sarah is among them.

I get a coffee and see Julia and Howard waving at me. Having just operated with them, I'd rather go elsewhere just to escape elaborate operation talks.

"Hi guys," I say. "Long day ahead, huh?"

I take a seat.

"Hey, you want to stay away from the Psychiatry Department today. There's a complete loony on the loose," says Howard. "Isn't there, Jules?"

Our small Psychiatry Department is always interesting to enter when seeking neuro-analysis devices. It's a department of myths, a department having a hard time sustaining its reputation after the suicide of a patient who killed himself by sticking his head out of a window and slamming it shut. He broke his neck. The lack of security in patients' rooms has led the department to consider installing seclusion cells, which is a marvelous idea – cushioned walls, ground, and ceiling. The main Psychiatry Center is on the other side of Manhattan – the department there is probably a different world.

"In fact, he's harmless," Julia says, "he's just an exhibitionist!"

"You sounded a lot more terrified earlier when you told me this."

She looks at Howard with huge eyes. "Well, I *was* terrified!"

Howard shakes his head and downs the last sip of his coffee. I envy his easy body language. Readable people usually lead a very simple and pleasant life.

"So, what did he do, expose himself to you?" I ask her.

"Oh, *yes!*" she says with great fascination.

We watch Howard get up hastily and leave the table. I never knew he was so sensitive. In the operating theater, Howard is a tough character who will watch your every step. In his opinion, as an anesthesiologist, surgery – at some level – is a silent physical assault.

"Hey, Howie, where are you going?" says a voice behind me. "I was just about to join you guys!" Will pats Howard's shoulder. I wonder when the opportunity will arise to sneak back into my office.

"Well, good timing for you. These ladies are about to share some dirty fantasies about the lunatic from your unit."

Will only assists the Psychiatric Department. From what I've heard, he'll soon be an attending neurosurgeon, surpassing fellows.

"Oh, are they really?"

"Shut up, Howard," says Julia. Despite being an earnest woman in her early forties, she pouts like a High-School girl.

Both Will and I notice the expression on Julia's face as Howard leaves.

"Excuse me, guys," she says.

She gets up, about to turn right to the staff room, but then decides to walk down the hallway towards the elevator where Howard is headed.

"How long have they been dating, you reckon?" Will asks and takes a seat.

"I don't think that's any of our business."

"Readable people are so boring, don't you think? Especially if they don't communicate well. It's not going to work between those two."

"Will you please shut up?" I say, indicating that he should keep his voice down.

"Don't you agree, though?"

Will's ruthless nature is overwhelming, and I admire that. His clear-headedness, unlimited openness, and wit certainly beat anyone else's humor.

I sip my hot coffee carefully and check my diary.

"Elle, I have to tell you something."

"As long as it's not about my brain's network or dying hydrocephalic children, I'm all ears."

It must be something rather serious because his smile has faded. His gray eyes narrow, and the eyebrows are forming one straight line.

"It's about that mentally-disturbed gentleman…"

"What about him?"

"Well, I operated on him the other day. He had a bad car accident that led to a skull fracture."

"Poor man."

"Luckily, no neurological damage was visible except mild damage in the right lobe. He doesn't remember much either. But the odd thing is he remembers you."

"What?"

"His name is Norman Brooke. You operated on him just over a month ago. I checked the profile, just to make sure he wasn't some kind of stalker."

I recall that man with the demonic eyes on W 40th Street in Midtown the other morning when I was rushing back home after my stay at Bruce's place. It couldn't have been Norman Brooke, as he doesn't look half as frightening as the man I saw.

"Are you all right?"

I remember removing a gastric ulcer from Brooke's stomach about two months ago. He is in his mid-forties – a gambler and probably an underground dealer. Before the operation, a blood test indicated numerous vitamin deficiencies highlighted by drug abuse. He had tried to ask me out, but I refused. Patients with stomach diseases are prone to bad breath.

"Yeah. He was quite scary. What did he say?"

"He has vivid dreams about you," Will says.

"Care to elaborate?"

He hesitates.

I see Scott's lady friend walking into the cafeteria. She inserts a coin into the vending machine and picks a diet coke. Aspartame is a harmful and overrated chemical substance, which people prefer to real sugar.

"He sees you having sex with people."

"What? Like who?"

"He didn't go into detail, but as you can tell, he has a thing for you."

The pink head leaves the cafeteria.

"He's under supervision, right?"

He laughs. "You know what the staff in that department is like. But since Julia's little encounter this morning, he'll be under proper supervision. Don't worry, he's still in recovery mode."

A sudden image of the Obsessive Love Wheel has formed in my head. It's a hypothetical concept of how deadly the idea of love can unfold in relation to obsession.

Brooke had known about my whereabouts that morning. But he has obviously passed and survived the stage of destruction.

"You haven't encountered anything strange lately, have you?"

"No," I say.

"If you think you're being stalked, we should consult the police."

"No, I'm fine."

"I'll keep an eye on him. You'd better not step a foot in that department for a while. If you need anything, just give me a beep!"

"That's very kind of you, Will."

"You can beep me any time on the pager, you know, though, having said that, you might have to wait – I seem to have lost mine."

He rises from his seat and winks at me before heading back to work.

"Oh," he says, "and the last thing he dreamt was seeing you at Times Square. You sure he isn't stalking you?"

"I doubt it. I've not been there in a while."

-

After Sarah's good news on the benign lump later in the afternoon, I rush to see Scott before commencing my evening ward rounds. I find him on the bed, watching TV on mute while his lady friend is asleep with her head resting on his thigh. His hand is resting on her shoulder.

I smile at him. The expression on his face is full of relief, far from the delirium he was in the other day.

"How are you doing?"

"Still sore. It hurts when I swallow and when I vomit."

His voice sounds husky, like someone suffering from a bad sore throat.

"I'm happy to inform you that you can go home soon."

His smile is a swift one. He lowers his head—eyes fixed on the pink head.

"You'll get some medication to control the production of thyroid hormones. Hopefully, that will stabilize and recover the ordinary function. If not, we might have to consider radiation therapy."

He looks at me again.

"I know the term *radiation* may sound ominous, but it's not that bad."

"You should have removed the other lobe as well while you were at it," he says.

"My job was to remove only one for examination."

"You could have taken my appendix, too, for all I care."

His indifference towards his own organs is astonishing.

The pink head exhales a little moan but remains asleep.

"Is that so?" I say.

"I don't know what I can give you in return. Do you need a kidney?"

Other men only offer me drinks.

I approach him to check the bandage around his neck, and then I gently pat his cheek.

"What do you mean? I don't want anything from you," I say. "Your heart is taken, and so is your beloved voice box."

He glances at her again and then smiles at me.

"She doesn't like you."

"She has already expressed her sentiments to me."

I look at my watch; it is 9:30 p.m. I hadn't realized how I've spread myself thin with work. My shoulders are tense and my neck stiff.

I don't like ward rounds because, as a surgeon, your job is to clarify the surgical procedure to patients and defend your outlook on the surgery's necessity and maintain your professional status. Surgical healing is what we surgeons call it.

Surgery is a form of healing that you can grasp; there's a body that you can hold on to. You talk to flesh and blood, and they listen. The only difficulty when negotiating with a patient is when he raises emotional issues related to his disease. My area of specialty lies in the observation of the physical. It's challenging to provide them with psychological counseling. I can't offer to hold their hands.

The staff bedrooms are situated near the staff room. There's a door that leads you to the small residence hall.

As I enter my small bedroom, I smell stuffy air. Compared to my own bedroom in my dazzling apartment downtown, this one evokes the quality of a two-star motel room. Even the patients in the wards have more luxurious rooms than the staff. I have brought my own pillow, duvet, and anti-allergy bed linen with a dust mite-proof mattress cover. The idea of microscopic creatures feasting on the keratin layer of my epidermis is rather off-putting. Outside the bathroom door are two bottles of antiseptic liquid, a scented Clorox bottle, and disposable gloves. They didn't have any regular Clorox at the grocery store; the scented fresh meadow is only half as effective, as it contains three and a quarter percent less sodium hypochlorite.

The bathroom needs cleaning.

By the time it's 11 p.m. I finally lie down on my bed. I put the beeper within reach and grab a medical journal magazine, which is usually a good slumber-inducing read, except that I opened a page titled *Patient's Tale,* which involves the story of an autophobic man who castrated himself after the rape of a teenage girl.

It intrigues me that his self-hatred was so overwhelming that even after castration, he attempted to cut off his foot with a saw. But due to the significant amount of blood loss, he fainted halfway through. In the end, a neighbor had called the police. The confession of the rape occurred at the hospital, after which the police began to investigate, but only to discover that the victim wouldn't comply. The girl claimed to know the man but repeatedly denied the physical abuse to protect her modesty or him. Whatever reasons she may have had, I believe that she and I have something in common.

When the man was asked about his sex addiction, the ritual of denial continued. He was no sex addict. He was merely aiming for the sensation of climax. Ever since the damage to a nerve root in his spinal cord after a severe fall, he had failed to ejaculate during intercourse. Instead, it would present itself in a delayed fashion, as a nocturnal emission. After waking up, he would have no memory of the wet dream.

I've read about ejaculatory anhedonia before, but I do not have a spinal cord injury.

From the girl's side, I'm sure that a little love was evident, more than just commiseration. And the man was merely attempting to reach the peak of his sensation again. He was far from giving up on it. The attempt to amputate his foot was to help him feel alive.

It's ten past midnight. I need to be fit for tomorrow's nephrectomy followed by a three-hour conference.

The entire hospital is quiet; there has been no exhibitionist alert.

On the last page of the magazine is a short article by a New York-based veterinarian writing about little-known facts on animal science.

Male mallards tend to embark upon homosexual activities when their females are busy laying eggs. Committed female penguins sell their bodies to other males to receive pebbles to build nests for the offspring. Additionally, many male animals often assault their females sexually, even while nurturing the little ones. Male moles impregnate newborns. Lastly, sows' orgasms apparently last up to thirty minutes. I feel dizzy.

It seems that, in reality, animals aren't much different from human beings, not if sexual instinct is anything to go by. A sexual constraint is unknown to them; they do not repress anything.

Consciousness versus instinct.

If this is how we differentiate, then how much of me is an animal? Like humans, there may also be evil inside an animal, except that it cannot comprehend. It never asks itself why. It's only the array of questions that gives us humans the ability to self-reflect.

But judging by the veterinarian's comedy grin staring out of the page, I don't think he is to be taken seriously. And since when have medical magazines become so sensual and obscene anyway?

I hear footsteps in the hallway, then the turn of a key. Someone has entered the room next door. Judging by the heavy sound of the footsteps, it must be a man. For a while, I hear nothing – no noise of the extractor fan in the bathroom and no squeaking of the bed's coil springs. It is as if the person is standing in the middle of the room.

The sound of my beeper breaks the silence; it must be about my patient's kidney complaints. But to my surprise, it's Will asking me whether I could pay him a short visit to the Psychiatry Department. Since he isn't addressing me by my first name, I presume it's a matter of urgency.

I leave my room head down through the staff room towards the door to the wards. It's empty, quiet; all the lights are dim. As I place my finger on the up-button of the elevator, I feel a chill down my spine. Now I remember what Will told me this afternoon.

I suddenly hear the sound of bare feet clapping against laminate flooring. The lights have flickered for a millisecond, as though my brain has signaled danger through my eyes.

"Hello?" I say and begin to look around.

On my right, I see a dark figure standing at the end of the corridor where the several sets of lights above him are broken.

"Who's there?" I say.

He is not moving; the arms hang down, lifeless. Very slowly, the figure leaves the shadow and steps into the dim light.

I see the same demonic smile that I saw on W 40th Street the other day. It is Norman Brooke, his upper head neatly dressed in a bandage. What catches me off guard is that he is naked and glaring at me with the same facial expression and the same posture. The sight of his penis hanging limply down his pelvis initiates a sudden feeling of pain in my abdomen. I taste blood in my mouth.

"Mr. Brooke?"

"I'm so happy that you still remember me, Miss Parker," he says, "I've wanted to see you for a while."

"You should be in your room."

He takes a big step forward as if to incite me to my next move.

"I'd appreciate it if you gave me Dr. Dylan's beeper. And then I would like you to go back to your own ward," I say.

The smile around his mouth widens, and the pain in my abdomen is flaring up. Fragmented images of spears and bamboo stick swords are swirling around in my head. I carefully take a step back. He chuckles.

"Please stay. I just want to talk."

"What about?"

"I'd really like to talk to you," he says.

Now he walks towards me, stepping rhythmically to the sound of my shoes as I slowly begin to walk backward.

"About...?"

"Everything."

As this creepy dance continues, I watch how his steps accelerate. The pain in my abdomen has spread through my entire torso. An adrenaline rush would typically manifest itself as a burst of tingly sensations and an increased heart rate rather than pain.

"What do you want?"

Norman reaches out his hand as if asking me for a dance.

"Just one date..." he says.

"I already told you...!"

His hand reaches my face before I can finish my sentence. I shut my eyes tightly.

"Hey, hey!" a person shouts from down the corridor.

The moment I open my eyes, I see Stuart rushing towards us. He grabs Norman by the upper arms.

"Please!" Norman shouts.

"Back off, buddy!"

Stuart curls his arms under Norman's armpits.

The elevator door opens, and a guard hurries to take Norman off Stuart.

"You son of a...! Come back here! So I can't even take a leak without you causing trouble! Where are your clothes?"

The guard talks like Norman was a dog.

I watch him bring Norman's arms behind his back and pull him into the elevator. From behind, I feel Stuart's hands wrapping around my shoulders, and the pain begins to alleviate.

"I'm sorry, Doctor, have a good night," says the guard.

Norman's eyes are still fixed on me.

He mouths: "One date."

The mask of insanity has slipped. I've just realized that the demonic smile has never existed. Norman's face breaks into a hopeful smile before the elevator doors closed.

"God, Parker. Everything OK?"

There is this brotherly warmth in Stuart's eyes. I nod repeatedly.

"Are you sure? That dude is creepy."

"Yeah, I'm fine," I say.

"Come on; let's get you back to your room."

Stuart lays a hand on my upper back.

"Temporal lobe epilepsy," he says as we enter the staff room.

"Pardon?"

"Mr. Brooke suffered his first seizure later this afternoon. I saw it. He is very vulnerable and dazed from his medication."

His vulnerability doesn't change the fact that his naked outward appearance causes me abdominal pain.

"Well, at least he isn't dangerous then."

"I'm not sure about that," he says.

I look at Stuart and the way his thumb and index finger are touching his chin.

"Why?"

"Tell me, Parker, is he really stalking you?"

After an awkward pause, I laugh. "What makes you say that?"

"Dylan said that."

I put my hand on the door handle.

"Oh, he isn't really."

Stuart's face denotes a hint of disbelief, he tilts his glasses, but I interrupt before he has a chance to speak.

"I rejected him before. He's a rather persistent type. He thinks my feelings for him are reciprocated."

Unrequited love: it has always been a mental disease that displays itself physically in the heart and then shatters it to pieces. I know what he is going through. I know what disrepair of the heart feels like, and therefore I keep mine free from disease – it's the least that I can do.

"That's not good. It sounds like obsessive delusion," he says, "I'll tell Dylan to assign Brooke to some therapy."

I need to ask Norman questions. I don't understand why and how he watched me the other morning if he was one of the severely injured people in that accident. The more I think about it now, the more it feels like a distant dream, but I'm sure of what I saw.

Before Stuart opens the door to his room, which is next to mine, he says, "Are you OK? You've been very quiet lately."

Dr. Dick used to say that to me often whenever I did not raise my hand during group conversations.

Paula C. Deckard

"Does it have anything to do with Mrs. Hughes?" he says.

The word *No* is stuck in my throat, and before I run out of air, I choke it down.

"You did nothing wrong," Stuart says.

"I know."

I don't want to talk this way. Stuart is not Dr. Dick or a sleeping subject on my operating table. He's only there to train me.

I can hear Stuart using the tap next door – probably brushing his teeth. I take off my lab coat before hiding underneath my duvet cover. My abdomen feels calm. My beeper goes off again, another message from Will's pager: "One date :)"

CHAPTER SIX

I'm in the garden. There is blood on my hand, blood running down my legs. I have stained a daisy. Sparrows have gathered in the garden, too. The last time I had my period was two weeks ago. This doesn't feel like having a period, more like having touched the bamboo stick sword again. Is this how Princess Aurora felt after touching the spindle?

Am I dying?

Mother is back. It always takes her three or four hours to do grocery shopping. She finds me in the garden and calls me a dirty brat. A year ago, she taught me how to use sanitary towels, but I've switched to using tampons. I used to be terrified of tampons, but I am no longer scared after touching the bamboo stick sword.

She tells me to come into the house, except that this isn't our house. I walk into my therapist's office. Both of my parents enter after me and take a seat by the door. They both look worried and somewhat pale. My dad is a physician; I don't understand why he can't take care of me; he does when I have the flu. And I look after him when he has the flu.

I take a seat in front of Dr. Hymen. I don't like her. Most elderly ladies with white hair remind me of a perfect grandmother full of wisdom and warmth, but she is not one of those. Her hair is thin, frizzy and clumsily tied back. Her bemused look reminds me of a mad scientist. I think she has a wart growing on her nose.

Whatever I tell her, she won't understand. Her twin sister, my pediatrician, tried hypnotic suggestion on me when I was eight – a method applied to make the insert of a suppository practicable. Kids don't get pills for the flu or dizziness. They get suppositories instead.

Sometimes when I close my eyes, I see this infrared image in my head; I see myself lying naked on my pediatrician's table. I see how this ugly middle-aged woman scans my belly and neck with the tips of her cold fingers, triggering icy goosebumps all over my skin. When I look at her, I see a reptilian humanoid similar to the ones I see in comic books. My blood turns cold. I stare at my parents, who are as immobile as Greek God statues.

I am so alone in that room.

"Ellen, dear," Dr. Hymen says.

Is that my name? If so, it sounds so dirty coming out of her mouth.

"Ellen!" Mother hisses, "She is talking to you!"

I am numb like the penguins during winter, empty like a bear's tummy after many months of sleep.

I finally look at Dr. Hymen and see the cold Antarctic wind in her impassive eyes.

"What happened to you this morning? Your mom says you were acting strangely in the backyard."

"In her eyes, I always act strangely," I say.

Mother opens her mouth widely. Dr. Hymen gestures to her to stay quiet. I look at Dad, who is smiling at me.

"All right, I need to ask you a few things which have been worrying your parents."

She pauses as though to see if I am ready.

"Do you remember what you did when you were nine years old?"

"No."

"You played with your classmate's penis."

The word makes me chuckle.

"Do you remember?"

"No."

She looks at me, appalled. She throws a quick glance at my parents. It's a secret adult sign language, which they are not good at practicing.

" Let me ask you something else."

She takes a deep breath and exhales. Her breath smells of onions and rotten teeth.

"You haven't had sex education in school, yet, have you?"

I shake my head. "It's on the schedule for this year."

"And have your mother and your father enlightened you on this topic at all?"

Again, I shake my head. Now she throws a confused look at my parents. I believe that Dr. Hymen doesn't trust my parents; she doesn't trust me, either.

"What about your friend, Helen?"

"I have no friends," I say.

She sighs. "Tell me, Ellen, what do you want to be when you grow up?"

I look at Dad and say, "A doctor."

Again, I see a smile on Dad's face, a smile that always cheers me up when I feel low. I wish he were at home more. Maybe I could tell him about my boyfriend and Princess Aurora.

"Why?"

The abdominal pain has returned. I wrap my arms around my stomach.

"Are you all right, Ellen?"

I keep my gaze as low as possible.

"Mr. and Mrs. Parker, I'd strongly advise you to take your child to an endocrinologist."

It's such a nerve-wracking day at the clinic; my eyelids are heavy. I sense a migraine coming. My monthly blood has come a little too early. That's the only con of not using birth control – you don't always know the exact day. The IUD, however, has proven to be the best option. My natural hormones won't welcome any oral drug.

Last night's images elude me. I see images of the autophobic man's emasculation and female penguin prostitutes.

Scott's lady friend and his parents came to fetch him early in the morning when I was performing a nephrectomy. He left a CD with a song about losing one's virginity.

Julia is preparing the room for the upcoming conference. The smell of coffee, as usual, is nudging at my cerebral cortex like a sex hormone, although it is mild in comparison with the damiana cocktail of the other night.

Speaking of which, I haven't spoken to Bruce since our hazy date. Besides, our ophthalmologist Dr. Mellor has returned, meaning Bruce's further appointments have been assigned to him, who will continue looking out for potential corneal transplants.

Sometimes I do regret not having continued my ophthalmological studies, but to be frank, eyes are more deceiving than you think.

I saw Norman Brooke at Times Square the other day, and I saw his weak body last night, a weakness triggered by his obsession with me. I have a strange feeling that he might know how I can reconnect with myself and restart my heart like a computer.

Stuart and Julia are discussing the agenda of the conference. She wants to address issues concerning the safety measures taken by nurses. I take a seat at the far back.

"Elle!"

Will sits down next to me.

"Hi, Will."

"Don't be too hard on Brooke."

"I never said I was."

Sarah, Howard, and the rest of the troop settle down in the front row. There was a last-minute argument about whether some students should be attending this conference. However, the majority agrees that this would generate a dissonant atmosphere, so a separate assembly will be held later this week.

"Oh, thank goodness," Will says. "Have you ever dealt with a student? They're so sensitive."

"Remember you were a student, too."

"Never. I'm not the sensitive type, you see?"

This is the first time I find his smile endearing.

"If there was a sensitivity switch in our brains, I'd be more than happy to press the off-button," he says.

Stuart closes the door and claps his hands for attention. The projection screen displays the conference's agenda and, as usual, communication is the leading issue.

"Everybody, please take a seat," Stuart says.

There are sixteen of us in this small room.

I pretty much recognize all the surgeons in the front rows; I can tell by their hairdos, the shape of their heads, and their neck types. However, there is one woman that I do not recognize – her head is tilted to one side. She is brunette, her hair firmly tied back into a knot – or a "bobtail." Many female teachers in High School used to wear this hairdo as far as I remember; I detested those women.

"Before we proceed, I would like to introduce a colleague and friend of mine from Columbia Presbyterian Hospital. Please welcome Imogen Cunningham, our supporting perfusionist."

While everyone gives her welcoming applause, she rises from her seat and bows to us swiftly. I only catch a short glimpse of her face: bright eyes, full lips, and a big European forehead.

"It's a pleasure to welcome you," Stuart says.

Our previous part-time perfusionist Alex Campbell quit his job due to its monotony. He decided to return to medical school to immerse himself in further pulmonology studies to become a lung surgeon. Apparently, dealing with the cardiopulmonary bypass machine (or CPB) is like sitting in a Science class, building the same mechanical system over and over. I, on the contrary, have always imagined his job to be exciting. But Alex told me that all he did was build, connect and watch, whereas he wanted to be trained to repair. I cannot imagine anything more exciting than staring at a reservoir of deoxygenated blood that has been removed from the heart and lungs. That blood is then pumped through the body while the heart is not beating. The oxygenator is also interesting but more for lung enthusiasts. Later I learned that his brother had died of pneumonia not long ago. Alex had spent a while tackling the five stages of grief. Despite my unfamiliarity with these stages, I can understand why someone ambitious like Alex has chosen to alleviate his sense of guilt by pursuing an alternative path. I miss him already.

"So, you'll have a woman at the machines," Will whispers into my ear.

I picture Miss Bobtail in the operating theater; how she scrutinizes me as I open up a heart. I've often considered Howard infuriating, but this is a woman wearing a cat-provoking bobtail. Things could be worse, however. Stuart could have assigned another junior cardiac surgeon from Columbia Presbyterian to Mount Sinai.

"All right, then," Stuart begins, "We are here to discuss the lack of communication at this hospital. As surgeons and doctors, we have to establish a high level of trust... I'm not just referring to patients, but trust among *us*..."

He says this at every conference to every kind of audience, but he means it each time.

"I think it's crucial to emphasize that we are a *team*, a *big team* working in conjunction towards people's well-being..."

Will yawns into his palm. I elbow him in the ribs.

"Our work quality," Stuart continues, "is built upon responsibility. We all know that. And yet, the lives of two patients were jeopardized in the past week due to failure of communication..."

I recall one of the incidents. Last week a patient nearly died of an NSAID overdose. The intravenous fluid hadn't been set up correctly, and the patient's blood began to clot. It was all pinned on a student whose resident had failed to give thorough assistance. I thought it was a nurse's job.

I hope the other incident isn't about Mrs. Hughes. I didn't do anything wrong; it was *her life, her decision.*

Dr. Austin, our orthopedic surgeon, raises his hand. "Dr. McCormick! I believe that the worst error to commit is to leave any student unattended. They should be watched at all times, especially when working up patients."

"OK, more assistance in deductive reasoning..." Stuart says, "to determine illness."

"No, no," Dr. Austin interrupts, "this student of mine was treating a patient with a tendon rupture. In my absence, he asked the patient, who was still in recovery mode, *how loud was that popping sound?*"

The whole group of surgeons roars with laughter – it's our type of humor, and Dr. Austin knows it, except our pediatrician Dr. Liddy, the gray-haired lady sitting in the second row behind Howard. She raises her hand like a teacher's pet; she waits till Stuart gestures for her to speak.

"I had just raised the student issue a few minutes ago!" she says. "We should have the students take part in this debate. It's only fair."

This woman makes me sick.

She continues, "They make all of you laugh, but we can't treat them like teenagers!"

"They are!" I hear Will mutter, still yawning.

The debate has lasted for over an hour. The student issue has underlined the hospital's hierarchical organization, which Dr. Liddy finds problematic. But without hierarchy, there will be chaos.

A sense of cabin fever has befallen Will, whose leg won't stop shaking, and it's not a syndrome. I put my hand on his thigh to make him stop.

"Elle, please!" he whispers, "Not in here!"

Stuart throws a swift glance at us, and I remove my hand. This is a school class of clowns.

There is an overwhelming smell of people's greasy hair and the scent of stale cigarette smoke on some people's clothes. Maybe I've inherited Dad's nose after all.

The bobtail is hiding something. The way she has her head tilted sideways for so long reminds me of a hairy dog showing interest in a piece of bone. I'm waiting for her carotid artery to expose on the side of her neck.

"OK, one last thing before I pass you on to Julia…" says Stuart, "I'd like to highlight the importance of regular ward rounds. Again, patients need security. And students need experience, and this can only be achieved under strict supervision."

"Why are heart surgeons so boring?" Will mumbles.

"Well, thank you very much!" I say.

"Except you, Elle. You're an android."

"I'm a…I'm a *what*?"

"A Nexus-6."

Julia climbs the podium with a dramatic look in her eyes. Stuart takes a seat next to Miss Bobtail and whispers something to her. She giggles timidly.

"Hello, everyone."

I can tell that everyone's attention span has passed its peak. Some are rotating their heads or swinging their heads from left to right. It's hard to believe that all these surgeons and nurses are renowned specialists; they can stand for six hours doing their job, but as soon as other matters outside their solipsistic head require their attention, they lose interest. That's the only thing I have in common with these people. We like occupying ourselves with our own business. But for some reason, I believe that Stuart and Julia deserve my attention.

"Thank you, Dr. McCormick, for bringing up all these crucial points. However, I have one more to add…"

Now Howard's head is tilted sideways.

"It's the danger of contamination. The junior nurses have approached me about their fears and insecurities. As far as communication is concerned, they are afraid to speak to you surgeons. In the operating theater, they are insecure when facing body fluids; they're terrified of tattoos…"

I hear Will giggle. This time Miss Bobtail whispers something into Stuart's ear. Howard's head has not moved, and I can see his carotid artery.

"Senior staff knows the precautions," Julia says, "but the juniors and of course the students need to be thoroughly advised."

I don't like how she throws students and juniors into the same pot.

Almost three hours have passed; a four-hour surgery would have been more tolerable. Will leaves the conference room, giving me no chance to enquire about Norman Brooke.

Before I even reach the door, I hear Stuart call my name. I have two seconds to put a smile on my face.

"Parker, I'd like you to meet Dr. Cunningham. Or Immy!"

"Don't call me that!" she says.

Her nickname will forever resonate at the back of my head like the sound of kids' songs.

"Oh, this must be your trainee, the junior surgeon!" she says with a British accent.

"*General* surgeon. But yes, a junior heart specialist."

"Yes, that's what I meant," she says, "nice to meet you."

She shakes my hand firmly. Despite being two inches smaller than me, her facial features express a kind of superiority. Her icy blue eyes are targeting my green ones.

"Parker, a new patient with CHF, has been assigned to you," Stuart says, and I'm glad he says *you* instead of *us*. "Theodore Whitley, seventy-one, probably in need of a valve replacement. Either way, he'll be your first big thing. Here are the documents, go see him, talk to him."

A patient in need of cardiothoracic surgery has been assigned to me. There is probably nothing more that I could ask for.

"I will."

"All right," Stuart says, "Immy, I need you to sign some forms. And then I must dash. It's my daughter's school play today."

"Oh!" says Miss Bobtail, "Little Helen onstage! You must be so proud of her!"

Without further comment, they both walk out through the door. I know that Stuart has a child, but I never knew her gender. Helen was the name of the only female friend I ever had when I was a child. Helen is the name from which my name originally derives, meaning "bright light." She must be a true princess. I also know that Stuart is divorced, and again, I don't know the precise details, apart from speculation based on hearsay.

I ought not to antagonize Miss Bobtail; I don't want an unpleasant work dynamic in the operating room. Regardless of the general operating team, I prefer having private conversations with the sleeping subject on the table. Miss Bobtail will be the first I suspect of eavesdropping.

-

There are no more operations scheduled for today, except for some ward rounds this evening, including my new bonus patient Mr. Whitley.

To study his documents, I head towards my office to dwell in some solitary activity. Then I find a rather familiar-looking person knocking on my door. I soon recognize a former accident patient of mine, Jay Adkins.

I turn back around and pretend I'm on my way to the cafeteria.

"Ellen!" he shouts.

People are staring. I don't want any of my colleagues to recognize him as a former patient. I can't feign another smile, but I catch Jay's eye and gesture for him to follow me outside.

We are walking towards Central Park together. Having spent the morning and most of the afternoon indoors, I haven't noticed what a beautiful day it is. But New Yorkers don't really care. I see some businessmen rushing to the bus station or subway. They don't care about the sun; they are too hungry for their takeaway dinner. Nonetheless, I could be studying Mr. Whitley's profile right now.

Jay and I walk through the Woodman's Gate entrance and sit on a bench nearby. Hopefully, no one I know will walk past. The other day an ambulance stopped here to save a little boy who almost drowned in The Pool, further north of the path.

"What do you want, Jay?"

I think the migraine is kicking in. I need to at least treat myself with a ten-minute meditation before starting the ward rounds this evening.

"That's not a friendly welcome, is it?"

"When have I been friendly?" I say.

He exhales. "If that's the answer to asking you out for dinner…"

I look at the cover of the document folder. Whitley – his name makes me think of a glade with a community of wild plants. I'm staring at a bunch of pink summery flowers right now, recalling how intimate I used to be with nature when I was a child. Dad used to take my friend and me to the Sleeping Giant State Park in Connecticut for long hikes.

This little spot in Central Park smells sweet. I don't come here often during summer, as Central Park is a more beautiful place during fall.

"I'm swamped today."

He attempts to touch my face, but I move my head away.

There are five patients that I have to see this evening. Apart from Mr. Whitley, there are two men and two women awaiting surgery. One of the women is waiting to have a lump removed from under her armpit, and the other won't let me run a sigmoidoscopy to examine her bowel.

"I want you back, Ellen," Jay says.

"You never had me."

"We had a great night a while ago, and I haven't heard from you since."

For a moment, I wonder whether I should consider the life of a celibate and forget about achieving the sensation of climax. Living the life of a nun would give me the time and space to practice more meditation. When on my own, I rarely masturbate, as I find it less sensual than with a person. But in the end, the result is the same – I feel nothing.

I remember Jay being delivered to the hospital a month ago with a thick piece of broken glass stuck in his stomach. A street gang had attacked him. When treating male patients who are half-conscious, I take their blood samples inconspicuously. There is always an opportunity. Jay's blood type is B, and B holders are usually relentless hunters who don't take no for an answer. He was very healthy – high in vitamins and macrominerals, but that was a month ago.

I look at my watch. It's getting late.

"That accident was the best thing that has ever happened to me," he says.

"You can't be serious."

"I am serious."

His hands are curled around mine. Jay is expressing a sentiment that I fail to comprehend. I primarily see women conveying these emotions in movies, but it's the men who practice them, to my surprise. Women put glass splinters into their men's contact lens cases. Well, I hope Jay doesn't cry to a rejection.

"The way you held my hand in the OT..." he says.

"You were in shock."

"The way you looked after me...You have a big heart, and I never thanked you for what you did."

A big heart. I can only picture a human heart, a perfect composition of muscles. I can also see how Dr. Dick and I would remove parts of a patient's ribs to access the heart.

Mr. Whitley must be expecting me already. I need to get the job done right this time. Ensure that I am the owner of a heart like everybody else like Dr. Dick believes I am.

"You touched me deeply," Jay says.

Does he understand the art of anatomical structure, or is he throwing metaphors at me?

My beeper goes off.

A message from Will: "There will be no guard on the ward tonight."

"Listen, I have work to do," I tell Jay.

"Is that it? Is that all you have to say?"

I rise from the bench, both hands in my pockets. Wearing a lab coat in a park full of nature and tweeting birds doesn't feel right.

"I understand your sentiments. I'm sorry I don't feel the same way."

To my right, a dead gray squirrel is lying on the path. The only animal I ever dissected during my studies was a pig. I dissected its torso to access the heart. My task was to extract a bullet and sew up the hole in less than four minutes. I failed the first time, and then never again.

"Have you ever loved someone?" Jay says.

My head is spinning. I see the image of the pig's beautiful blood splashing onto my gown and glasses, tainting my gloves. Does love mean bleeding that tremendous amount of blood? Is using the bamboo stick sword the same thing as using the scalpel? I don't know. I do love both instruments. Both of them happen to trigger blood when you cut through flesh. Perhaps love is touching someone deeply in the body. And only I know this for a fact because I fell in love when I was young, and the blood that I lost was proof. The sight of blood gives me hope in my job and restores my belief in humanity and love.

I leave Jay seated on the bench as I walk away – Mr. Whitley's documents tightly pressed against my chest.

"Ellen! Please, wait up! I'm not finished yet."

I cross over the main road with my eyes fixed at the hospital as if wearing a pair of horse blinkers, seeing nothing at the side.

As I reach the hospital's entrance, I suddenly hear the screech of tires, followed by a body hitting the ground. I turn around and see a stunning BMW Cabriolet that has stopped in the middle of the road. Passers-by shockingly lift their faces to this scene. About twelve feet further up the road lies Jay, unconscious, probably dead.

Looking at Jay's bruised face and motionless body on the operating table brings a lump to my throat. Only now can I hear him clearly, talking about his love life. As a schoolboy, he was in love with a pretty black-haired girl called Susan. She would play hard to get, while he would woo her with his Mom's homemade sandwiches and Dad's French pralines, which he brought back from business trips. But the truth was that Susan was only into the gifts, not him. He didn't deserve that.

Jay has a whiplash, a broken arm, a severe ligament injury, and two displaced rib fractures. He is lucky that those fractures didn't puncture his lungs or damage any other organs in his body.

When Dr. Austin and the others aren't looking, I stroke Jay's muscles around his displaced ribs and feel how strong they are. But the BMW Cabrio was a daredevil.

At Yale, I was advised to wrap the chest carefully with a rib belt, which Dr. Austin is about to do.

"No," I tell him.

"Why?"

"He has asthma."

I indeed remember holding Jay's hand while he was in shock after the glass attack. And I also remember the wheezy sound in his chest, crying for release. The Albuterol inhaler was no help, and I had to inject him with fast-acting epinephrine to dilate his airways.

Dr. Austin makes three small incisions around Jay's knee, and I carefully pump some saline solution into one of them so that he gets a better view of the knee's interior. I've been watching Jay's breathing throughout the operation to ensure that mucus has not built up in his lungs.

If only I could say how sorry I am.

Dr. Austin is the handyman when using surgical drills, which are my least favorite instruments. Holes are drilled into Jay's upper leg bones to form tunnels through which the replacement tissue will be fixed in the knee area. That tissue is also called a graft, which Dr. Austin secures with screws and staples.

A couple of hours later, we have completed the reconstruction of his anterior cruciate ligament. His knee will require several weeks before recovery.

Does my job verify the existence of a big heart? I don't know. All I know is that I'm bad karma for Jay. If I had paid him more attention, none of this would've happened. I wonder if he still thinks I'm worth the pursuit.

Lastly, Howard injects him with some Naproxen to relieve the pain.

Soon Dr. Austin heads to the office to write the report, and Howard and the scrub nurse disappear into the scrub room. Through my surgical mask, I mark Jay's forehead with a kiss.

***

Shortly after the operation, my beeper goes off, displaying two messages: one from Dr. Mellor saying that they have found a donor for Bruce. The other message is from reception, notifying me that my father has called.

CHAPTER SEVEN

Jay is chasing after me in a Cabrio! A deadly smile exaggerates the evil intentions of this chase. His hair is now green; he has become the Joker.

My feet are dying on me, and I notice that Penguin has nailed them onto the street. He looks like Norman, but shorter. The Penguin laughs and licks between my toes.

I see Batman coming to my rescue.

It's Bruce.

"Hello, fellow little bat!" Joker says as he caresses my butt. Bruce approaches me with a pair of terrifying glass eyes on his right palm. I hardly recognize him at all. Looking through the eyeholes of his mask, I only see two black holes. On his left fingers, he's holding a pair of filthy contact lenses.

Penguin's saliva feels cold and sticky on my skin. He has worked his way up to my neck now, licking me like a wild animal.

"Our lady doctor is wet!"

"Let me go!"

Bruce doesn't move. Joker is holding a cold, sharp object against my back, slowly drawing the tip down my spine. Then he shows me a pair of pliers, as though to impress me.

"Ohh, she's getting there!"

He's drawing the tool closer and closer to my eyes. All I hear is a roar of laughter.

I rarely wake up like this, covered in sweat and vaginal discharge underneath. My sleep hyperhidrosis is the result of heavy caffeine consumption. I need to control myself. I wonder why it takes me so long to wake up from nightmares nowadays; it's as if I relish the irrationality of a falling dream. I could share this experience with a medical magazine and anonymously submit it to the *Patient's Tale* column.

It's 11 p.m. I fell asleep an hour ago. Straight after finishing the ward rounds, I was meant to practice some meditation – but I must have collapsed on the bed.

Mr. Whitley was asleep, so I didn't even have the opportunity to introduce myself. Jay's operation had required a lot of time. Judging by Mr. Whitley's dainty mouth, I could see he was sincere. In the art of Chinese face reading, a dainty mouth with fine contour lines symbolizes decency and kindness. His jaw is small and cheekbones wide, so is his forehead. In fact, he has a beautiful heart-shaped face, regardless of the sagging skin and some clumsy facial hair. He looks like the grandfather I never had. And soon, I'll be in charge of his heart.

Tomorrow morning I'm going to do some blood tests. In Mr. Whitley's transfer papers, a sonographer has indicated aortic stenosis, a valvular heart disease, which means my job will most likely be replacing his aortic valve. But persuading him to assent to the surgery's necessity will be one hell of a job since he is an old man and probably conventional. I'm sure, however, that he is more optimistic than Mrs. Hughes was.

After the rounds, I called my Dad. He's coming to New York next week for a physicians' conference. We've agreed to have lunch downtown. I haven't seen him since I moved to New York, not to mention been in touch much.

However, I forgot to call Bruce. Dr. Mellor couldn't get hold of him and asked me for advice. I grab the receiver on the bedside table and dial Bruce's number, but no one picks up. The sudden goosebumps on my arms are calling to mind those images of Braille codes. His answering machine goes off.

"Bruce. It's Dr. Parker. Dr. Mellor said you didn't show up today. Where on earth are you? Did you not hear the good news? We..."

I begin to stutter. My weird intuition tells me that he's there, ready to pick up the receiver any second.

"We have a donor," I say. "Someone's just passed away, and his family has agreed on the transplant. They're even giving away the kidneys, can you believe it!"

I pause immediately, hitting myself on the forehead.

"Listen, no hard feelings about the other night, all right? My job is your well-being."

I put the receiver down immediately. I double-check my beeper – no new messages.

There is no movement in the other room; I guess Stuart must have spent all day with his daughter after the play.

It will be a risk going up to the Psychiatry Department through tonight's guard-free zone. On the other hand, Norman could have ulterior motives. Perhaps he wants to retaliate. But his eyes, last night, dispelled all my preconceived views of him. Maybe he really just wants to talk.

I leave my room quietly, heading towards the staff room and then to the wards. As I press the up button for the elevator, I shoot a look down the dark corridor. I could be at home in bed now if it weren't for Norman.

The stuffy smell in the Psychiatry Department is worse than in the conference room. The corridor is dimly lit. It's awkwardly quiet. You would expect a patient in his room to make some kind of noise or talk to himself. On the patient noticeboard, which is depicted in chart form, Norman's name stands out as he's the patient with the fewest activities listed. But according to his schedule, he has a meeting with a clinical therapist tomorrow morning. A little note informs the therapist to go to Room 525. As I make my way to his room, I encounter a very young girl in the corridor. Half asleep, rubbing her eyes, she looks at me.

"Mommy," she mumbles, "please take me to the bathroom?"

I hear haunting echoes in my head; calling me her mother reminds me of a higher degree of womanhood that I won't ever achieve.

I escort her to her room and switch on the bathroom light. She insists I enter the bathroom with her. This girl should be in the Pediatric Department, where regular night nurses are on duty. Watching a young girl struggling to lift her patient gown somehow distorts my perception of child development, especially juxtaposed with my own maturity at a similar age. As she pulls down her underwear, a thick discharge of blood stretches between her vagina and underwear.

"Mommy, I'm bleeding," she sobs.

"Wait, wait…"

As I leave the bathroom to fetch some sanitary towels from the medical drawer, I realize that I'm in Norman's room. He's asleep, or at least he is pretending. His night lamp is on.

There is no one in the bathroom.

Watching Norman in his bed, I quietly rest on the chair next to him. He looks older than I remember; the skin reveals more wrinkles, and the straight lines running from the sides of his nose towards both corners of his mouth are sharper. I wonder how he veils his personality. Are his epithelial cells strong enough to form a second skin? These cells are known to cover things; they cover our organs with protective layers. Looking at this vulnerable man, I realize that I have been painting many people with the same brush. I haven't given them the chance to show me who they really are. Perhaps he has accepted the fact that he cannot have me. The stage of acceptance takes time. I wonder how he mends his broken heart.

I identify myself with Norman. He knows who I really am. Beneath these walls dwells this brooding compulsion that exceeds any healthy human urge to be simply content. Content is not enough – I need to be satisfied.

Norman suddenly looks more attractive to me. He had better not have given up on me.

I open up the pack of the sterile lancet and prick the tip of Norman's index finger.

He stirs.

While carefully holding his finger over the polymer cartridge, a drop of blood lands on the surface. The lab-on-a-chip is a blood test device invented for quick treatments to determine specific diseases (especially STD) within minutes. It's handy when not having the time frame for in-depth implementation. I watch how the blood drop travels through tiny passages towards a reaction site, enabling the biomarker detection to identify diseases.

"Miss Parker," he says, "it's nice to see you."

"Hi, Norman."

He looks exhausted.

"You look exhausted," he says.

I shrug my shoulders and then place the cartridge on the bedside table.

"You're contemplating sleeping with me?" he grins.

"In your dreams."

He slowly rises from the bed; I help him adjust the bed frame. Doing this brings back early memories of Dad.

On one Christmas Day, he was sick with the flu. I remember changing the wet towel on his forehead. I asked him who looked after doctors when they were ill, and he said other doctors – like me.

Norman's eyes are green, just like mine.

"How's your head?" I ask him.

"Clear."

He sucks on the tip of his finger.

"I would've expected you to come with a syringe."

I almost did, but I would need a microscope, too, if I wanted to analyze his blood here and now.

I begin to understand why Will and Stuart consider Norman vulnerable; his posture is terrible, like he has been hit by a rock. What he needs is a chiropractor. He has lost a lot of weight since his last stay at the hospital. The beer belly has vanished – the eyes no longer emanate a drug-induced look.

"Do you think I do this for fun?" I say.

"I know you can't help it. Remember you're talking to a former drug addict."

"You're confusing addiction with impulse."

I hate enunciating these terms, as they leave a bad taste in my mouth, but after all, that's the truth, and he understands.

"Impulse is not the right word," he says.

"You felt pleasure gambling and doing drugs, didn't you?"

"I suppose," he says.

"I, on the other hand, feel nothing."

His eyes express disbelief, and he doesn't blink for quite some time.

"My action," I continue, "is determined by instinct, science...logic."

"And the sex?"

"It's...to come close to feeling something."

He holds my hand and presses it.

"Compulsion," he whispers as if falling back into slumber. "You deny your fears," he says, "as well as your feelings."

Silence overshadows the room like a dark shield – an eclipse covering up the light of my day and who I am.

"I'm not asking what happened to you in your past," he continues, "but there are indeed people who wish they could wipe out their memories, deny their memories, but what's the point? The feelings will remain. The worst thing is not being able to comprehend these feelings. Suppress your feelings, and you'll start a killing spree one day."

"So, how did you overcome your addiction?"

Both his irises suddenly look like pampas grass – sharp and menacing.

"I fell in love. She gave me a good reason to cut loose, but she doesn't want to have anything to do with me."

"How come?"

"She has predetermined ideas about me." He sounds indignant.

The result should be visible on the cartridge now.

"I didn't understand why you wouldn't give me a

chance, but you would go out with your other patients. Then I figured that they were all technically healthy and bright, unlike me with the stomach ulcer and addiction on top."

Coldness engulfs the back of my head, making me face every single mistake that I have committed, chances I have wasted.

"I quit the drugs and stopped gambling. Nothing but you were left in my life like you were the best thing that's ever happened to me. I thought that accident would eventually lead me to you, but I headed for the wrong injury."

He laughs and shakes his head. Some men would do the most outrageous things for me, and never have I taken them seriously.

"But...you're here, I'm here," I say.

His smile has faded, now avoiding my eyes.

"I know," he sighs, "it's just I no longer want you."

"Why?"

"I'm sober."

I wonder if I am no better than a drug.

"But I want to help you," he says.

I'm more awake now than I was after the ward rounds. It's ten past midnight, and Mr. Whitley's appointment is scheduled for 7:30 a.m. And I should be expecting more private patients after that.

"Help me with what? I'm fine." I grab the cartridge.

The results are negative. "You know, you were a lot more interesting before this accident."

"How could you say that?"

"I saw your spirit at the crash scene. You were looking at me, seeing through me. Tell me how you did that."

He looks stupefied. "What? Were you hallucinating? I was unconscious. And I'm pretty sure my soul was with me at that time."

This is not the Norman Brooke that I had in mind. I sense that he's not telling me the truth. He must be hiding something.

A sudden beeping noise from under the bed stirs the room, making Norman groan.

"Is that a seizure monitor?"

"Yes. I'm sorry I couldn't offer you a better date, but I have to ask for you to go," he says.

"Are you kidding me? That was our date?"

"Please go."

"You know you won't see me again."

He lowers his bed and then lies down on the side with his back facing me.

"Go."

"But…"

As the convulsion begins, he reaches the edge of the bed. I roll him over so I can cushion his head, avoiding an accident or airway blockage.

After two minutes, his body is at ease again. I listen to his heavy breathing, and underneath my palm, I feel his increased heart rate. He places his hand on mine and whispers, "Go."

Mr. Whitley is a very kind and bright man. Having admired his facial features, I now diagnose unpleasant ankle edema, abdominal swelling, and besides, he has been plagued by dyspnea – shortness of breath.

I've been recording his heart sounds for an hour, checking it like a sound technician at a concert. He has been having fainting spells and looks tired. In fact, all the key symptoms of valve disease are evident.

After the tests, I tell Mr. Whitley to put his patient gown back on. As he rubs his chest, I notice how dry and reddened his hands are.

"Do you wash your hands with Clorox by any chance?" I say, smiling.

"Oh, I do," he laughs. "How did you know?"

"I used to do that at least once a day."

"I see. I thought you were going to call me mad."

I would never call you mad.

"You know," he says, "when you hear about all those viral diseases: Ebola, swine flu, EHEC—you get paranoid! If you're my age, you should double up the safety measures!"

Anyone who appreciates Semmelweis's instruction for cleanliness is one step closer to where I am.

"It's good to see that you care. Cleanliness is the first step to good health," I say.

In my office, I lay out all the phonocardiograms, echocardiograms, and other examination papers in front of him. That way, I can evaluate and bring up inevitable surgical measures. The diagnosis is clear, and I'm sure he is aware of it, too. There will be no escape from surgery, no running away from my table.

He puts his reading glasses on.

"Oh!" he cries. "Is that me? What kind of a photo session was that?"

The best of your life.

"I don't remember looking so ugly," he says.

"This is why we have to do something, Mr. Whitley."

He bites his lower lip and pretends to be still analyzing the images. In his head, I know exactly what is troubling him.

"There is a severe defect in your aortic valve. Previously this defect triggered no major problems, but now a calcification has occurred…"

I point at one of the micrographs illustrating the fibrotic valve, the three pictures resembling the opening of an alien egg. In Mr. Whitley's eyes, all the images probably look alike, but I have to make him understand the threat involved.

"That's the culprit of your current aortic stenosis."

"Stenosis?" he says.

I point at the phonocardiograph showing the result of the sounds that I just recorded.

"Here, this is an indication of what we call a systolic murmur, fourth grade. The abnormal sounds are the result of a dysfunctional valve. Before the calcification, you see…"

My finger wanders back to the previous image.

"…It was fine. And it has been fine for many years, except…"

"Now. I know," he says.

A challenging silence befalls the room; I'm trying to figure out what's on his mind, so I can continue with my persuasion.

"May I ask you something, Dr. Parker?"

"Sure."

He covers his mouth and jaw with the palm of his hand, rubbing his cheek thoughtfully with the tips of his fingers, and then places both hands on the table. Now he has lost all interest in the images and looks me in the eyes.

"Have you ever been in love?"

I take a sip of water and swallow the wrong way, leading me to cough almost uncontrollably.

"Oh, are you OK?"

I put the glass down. The accumulation of blood in my face is not an outward feature that I like people to see.

"My apologies," he says, "I shouldn't have asked you that...how impertinent of me."

"No," I gasp, "no."

Glancing at Mr. Whitley, I see how his astonished eyes correspond with his open mouth – that sweet dainty mouth.

"You're crying! What have I done?" he says.

His reddened hands are reaching out for mine. The cough has stopped.

"I'm OK, Mr. Whitley."

He presses my hands.

"Just let it out, my dear."

The seriousness in his eyes reminds me of Dr. Dick, who always knew when something was troubling me.

"This is not about me," I say, "Please, tell me about you. Tell me everything."

"Everything? Oh dear, that's going to take a while."

"I have been in love, yes. Now tell me, how does it feel for you? Who is she? What does she do?"

His eyes emit a glowing surprise.

"Oh, well," he lets out a sigh. "She's no longer with us."

"I'm sorry."

"My wife Angela was a wonderful woman, very natural and energetic. She was a vegetarian and had a strong bond with nature. You see, there was nothing artificial or superficial about her. She turned me into a better person."

He places one hand on his chest.

"This is who I am. This is my way to remain faithful to her."

I let go of his other hand to pick up his profile again and a pen to question his current marital status.

"Bridget is the name of your current partner."

"Oh yes! She brings daylight to my life."

"Does she bring daylight to your heart as well?"

He smiles. It's good to have his partner as a backup for persuasion. She surely wouldn't want him to die. Well, not until they got married, anyway. But I may be judging her too soon. After all, the document says that she owns a popular independent boutique on Madison Avenue.

"Sure she does. Bridget is a very impulsive woman, vivacious. She taught me that it's possible to love again," he says.

"So, you love her, but have you come to terms with the past?"

Having said that, my tongue now feels strange, and my lower lip is trembling. Mr. Whitley seems to be lost in thought for a moment.

"What does Bridget say about your condition?"

"She's worried," he says.

"And?"

"She says, *listen to the doctor.*"

We both laugh.

"She keeps saying that surgery is nothing to be scared of."

"So she has had one before?"

There is a little grin around his mouth. He scratches his nose as though too embarrassed to say more.

"Yes, she has."

"Nothing serious, I hope?"

"For her defense, I have to stress that she is a designer after all, and good looks play a big role."

"Elaborate?"

"She has undergone buttocks augmentation," he says.

I let go of my pen.

"And she looks stunning."

-

I am finally in my apartment, sleeping in my own bed.

Jay is recovering well. I took another blood sample after the operation, although there was no point in it. I thought you could never be sure. After all, he is still as healthy as he was a month ago. I've never noticed this innocent halo over his head until now, and I've figured that he deserves better. I saw Sarah talking to him in his room this afternoon when I wanted to check on him. I heard laughter. And I saw her body language – the way one of her legs was raised up on tiptoe, the movement of her calf was drawing half circles like a timid little girl. And she is not that type of girl.

I have accepted that the past will always creep in to say hello, and it won't go until you have said hello back.

Perhaps it's my loss when I reject a good man. Apparently, it's a common factor that we don't feel attracted to people who would do anything for us. The absence of challenge is what bores us, but some are so mentally scarred that they don't think they deserve to be happy, and they unconsciously choose misery, as that's the only thing they know.

I don't really believe in a conscience, which means that there is no right or wrong. I never concerned myself with this in greater depth, for in my case, the voice of the body has always been more dominant, particularly the adventurous travelers in my veins – human cells. Even Nietzsche put a great emphasis on the human body. It's the body that makes us who we are. It's the body that yearns for free love.

Maybe I'm getting too close to these patients, apart from Mr. Whitley, of course. He is different. I just don't know how to stop drawing blood. Where would it leave my blood list of compatible patients? There are still so many different types to encounter. It's the first step of forming an attachment to someone. I help these men to recover, but in return, they fail to help me. I believe that I have to be in love once more before I ever feel anything again.

I had a very different idea of New York before I came here. I thought people here didn't care and would leave you alone.

My skin still feels rough, even after the application of rich night cream.

Have I been using my beauty as bait? Seeking to be desired? Physical attraction? Love? Which is which? I guess it's a game that I'm unable to play. The result is always disenchantment or even alienation. It doesn't mean I'm going to stop learning the rules and strategy, though.

It is early in the morning when I knock on Bruce's door. If he doesn't attend his hospital meeting today, the corneal tissue will be distributed to another patient. According to Dr. Mellor, Bruce hasn't been to any of his appointments, not to mention returned any calls. If he is sulking in his room because of me, I will drag him to the hospital with my bare hands.

As I knock for a second time, his next-door neighbor peeks out from behind the door.

"Good morning," I say to the elderly man. "Have you seen Mr. Dwayne?"

"May I ask who you are?"

"I'm Dr. Parker, and I need him to come to the hospital with me."

"I saw him two nights ago. He seemed really distraught. His steps were heavy, and he was slamming doors so hard he woke me. I don't think he left the house yesterday."

"Bruce?"

I begin to knock harder.

"Let me in, Bruce! You hear me?"

As I grip and twist the doorknob, it opens.

Bruce's next-door neighbor and I walk into the cool apartment; the windows are open, filling the rooms with desolate air.

"Bruce?"

We walk past the kitchen and the island where he'd prepared the cocktails, then past the living room through an arched wall that leads to his bedroom. I didn't pay that much attention to the details of his apartment when I first came. Now I notice that his abstract paintings have images of red bulks tied in-line on a rope. They could be hearts or even Ben Wa balls.

In the bedroom, we find Bruce hanged. The body hanging lifeless. An angelic-like figure, floating with such effortless grace, the head tilted to one side, almost as if greeting those who enter to bear witness to the miracle. It's either the wind or the scarf that's slightly moving Bruce's weight back and forward.

My green Prada silk scarf is wrapped several times around his neck, both ends tied strongly around a wood plank on the ceiling. The high quality of Prada is too proud to let him down, despite the hole that I'd torn through it. It seems that I gave him enough rope to hang himself. Now his dark hair will overshadow his face for good.

"Oh, dear Lord. No! No! We have to call the police!" the old man says and trips lightly over the mini three-step ladder that Bruce has kicked away from beneath him. Then he storms out of the apartment with his cell phone at his ear. I hear him on the phone to the police outside the apartment.

I go towards Bruce's home telephone to check the answering machine. There are several saved voice mails from Dr. Mellor and two from me. I delete mine. Then I notice an A5 envelope next to the phone which has my first name written on top. I open the envelope and find a letter written in Braille. The warmth in my body has escaped. A freezing phenomenon has been activated, expanding through the muscles of my limbs and shoulders. I approach the dead body, and through his hair, I see a trail of dried blood running down his face.

"I told you how painful it'd be if the blisters burst," I whisper.

"The police are coming!" the old man says. "Let's get you out of here, Miss."

Even though it is my day off, there has just been an emergency call from the hospital, and I can't get there on time. An accident patient apparently, which means new blood, but I can't be there.

The police are collecting my statement on Bruce. I tell them the truth, which is that Bruce was not a happy person. I tell them about his divorce from his evil ex-wife, loneliness, fear of going blind, and his belief that he deserved it. For further inquiries about his eyes, I refer them to Dr. Mellor. I say I only came to take him to the hospital because otherwise, the tissues would go to another patient.

It's going to take me at least an hour to read that letter. I have never dealt much with blind patients, and I have never watched anyone being taught Braille. As an ophthalmologist's assistant, I had tried to learn the Braille alphabet and taught myself some basics, but I'm a slow decipherer. I liked how the series of characters (or dots) were referred to as "cells."

Dr. Austin has informed me that the patient is a female cyclist with a broken rib and arm. There is no need for me to be there, so I've messaged him saying that I'm still caught up giving a statement. In truth, I'm on the subway to Washington Square Park.

Whenever I walk to the park, I enter through the big arch; walking around the arch doesn't lead you in. People pretend they can walk through the walls of this gigantic park.

As soon as I reach the Hangman's Elm, I stop in the middle of the pathway and stare at its long-outstretched arms. Before I get dizzy, I lean against the railing. I get the letter out of my bag and begin to decipher it using a Braille spelling dictionary that I borrowed from the library.

Many mothers and kids are disrupting my concentration, but I manage to decipher the first line by keeping a constant image of a domino plate of six pips in my head. Blind people just move their fingertips across the lines of dots. In fact, I'm sure my former ophthalmologist said that blind people could see better with their hands, not with their hearts.

The first line says:

if i can't have you, i no longer want to see. i no longer wish to continue...

I take another look at the tree. They say it's only a rumor that people had been hanged here, and yet, I sense intense energy divulging its misery.

i've never been much of a fighter, but i know you are and i admire you.

I watch a young girl trip and fall. I'm expecting a sharp cry but hear nothing. Instead, she props her little body with both hands to get back on her feet.

"Come on, Penny, you're a big girl," says the mother.

Penny stands upright again and brushes off the sand from her pair of leggings. Then, she continues hopping along the path while her mother strolls behind her, smiling.

***

It has been almost a week since Bruce died. Dr. Mellor distributed the corneal tissue to a teenager in Harlem hospital. According to the kid's mother, she thanked God for the miracle.

I've been busy, or at least I've been pretending to be. Sometimes I assign myself to the Emergency Unit even if I'm not needed. It happens that other surgeons don't immediately recognize who you are behind the mouth mask, but they see that you're dressed to operate, so you're more than welcome to support. I do that every Wednesday now. I no longer grant myself any days off. I figured that I am not a hard-working surgeon. I even assisted Will during a peripheral nerve reconstruction. It was interesting to see Will's precision during surgery. He is fastidious – a perfectionist.

He cut his fingers while helping Julia pick up broken pieces of glass yesterday. Before they came to wipe off the blood, I stole two drops of blood with a pipette – one drop for the lab-on-the-chip and another for a microscope slide. Will has the same blood type as me – A. This explains our stubbornness; we both aim to have things done our way. And he is healthy like me.

I've been running many blood tests lately; it's like escaping into an alternate world of citizens that do not complain but instead make a huge working-class society function. All these citizens want is you to treat them well, and they will return the favor. It's that simple.

In my wisdom calendar, Immanuel Kant says that good doesn't exist, except for goodwill. He is wrong. Philosophers are always so preoccupied in their heads, unconscious of the fact that their cells are making the thinking possible – their own good cells.

The health of recent accident patients lacks sufficient vitamins; some of them are only middle-aged and already have a high level of uric acid in their blood.

This is a sign of possible early arthritis. A sufficient vitamin intake, if you think about it, is not that hard to maintain. And yet, people opt for vitamin pills, which only provide chemical and artificial substances, whereas five apples a day will do the job splendidly. But New Yorkers don't think that way. If they wake up with a headache, they'll take two painkillers at once without thinking any further.

Hope indeed is made physical in medicine. If only people knew that one's own contribution to health is essential, not just medicine alone. Some people don't feel the slightest guilt towards the cells' hard work. These people are takers rather than givers.

These are the things I always talk about with my dad, but he usually brings up topics about the past or asks about my current relationship status.

I hope he won't do it today.

I arrive at Fourteenth Street in Lower Manhattan, where Dad is staying at the Union Square Hotel. His conference was at Bellevue Hospital this morning. At the entrance, the receptionist guides me through the lobby into Irvington Restaurant, famous for its Mediterranean cuisine.

I see Dad at a table in the middle of the restaurant, sipping some water. He hasn't changed. Almost sixty, tall and still slender, professional-looking; in short, I'm the exact female equivalent of him and almost thirty years younger.

"Ellen!"

He greets me with a warm kiss on the cheek.

"Hi, Dad."

The environment at Irvington is casual and yet formal. The bar looks neat with its wide range of spirits lined up on four different shelves. A ten feet long wooden wall separates the bar from the restaurant part. The wall is about five feet high, with another foot of block windows built onto the top. The restaurant has about twenty tables suitable for dates or groups of four. There were no tablecloths or cushions on the wooden chairs. This is how I have my lunches with Dad.

He got me water already. We order two chicken salads.

"You work so much, I hope you're drinking enough. Think of your kidneys!"

I smile.

"I can't get hold of you these days, Ellen," he says. "Every time I call, they say you're in the OT."

"Yes, it has been busy."

He appears slightly worried about it, and I expected him to be proud. His nostrils are flaring.

"Have you changed your shampoo? You know you're not supposed to use scented ones."

"Dad!" I say, trying to stay calm.

I don't need him to remind me of my dermatitis, which is perfectly under control; in fact, I think it has disappeared.

"Your skin looks good. Just don't stress."

Twenty years ago, I would have thrown a tantrum upon that comment, but what's the point now? I simply smile and drink my water.

"So, tell me, how have you been keeping?"

"Oh, wonderfully," he says. "Don't you ever miss Connecticut?"

I look at him and see my young self in his eyes.

"Sometimes."

"We do miss you, you know?"

"I'm glad that you're still so dedicated to your work, Dad."

He lowers his eyes and starts pulling the edge of his napkin. I hope that this meeting will not end in an argument.

"Your mother is doing fine…"

I finish my water and try to avoid his eyes.

"She sends her best wishes."

I think of Mrs. Hughes and her dysfunctional heart – out of beat, out of touch.

"You'll have to forgive your mother at some point, Ellen."

"I'm not a good forgiver, Dad."

Before he has the chance to continue, the waiter serves our salads. I'd rather have my dad marveling at my new Prada cardigan. I want him to continue observing my physical presence, the smile that I'm now finding hard to sustain. He, like many others, tends to look inside me, through me. But we're not looking at each other. I'm almost certain that our conversation is bordering on a fiasco. During the silence, he takes his first little bite of chicken.

"It's good," he says.

This is my opportunity to change the topic before he continues unfolding the past before my eyes.

"So, are you dating someone?" he says.

I knew it. Now I have pictures of lively cell samples in my head. Which guy could I possibly bring up? Which one is worth mentioning? Perhaps Jay? For some strange reason, I have Norman in my head. He was released the other day. In order to treat his temporal lobe epilepsy, Will completed an AMTR surgery on him last week. He's good so far. I haven't had a chance to say goodbye.

"Ellen?"

"Yes?"

Dad places a leafy vegetable into his mouth and chews delicately.

"Are you dating someone?"

"No."

"I don't know how you do it. If I were you, I'd feel lonely in such a big city."

"I don't feel lonely," I say. "I'm too busy to feel lonely."

Dad has grown old. There is an unfamiliar deep line on the lower part of his forehead, just above his right eyebrow. His hair is entirely gray. I didn't notice before. Over twenty years ago, I never would've thought that Dad could age at all.

"Ellen, you have always been a recluse. If you ever get lonely, I'll be surprised."

That's my dad.

"If anything, you only ever had one friend," he says, "but let's not talk about her. So, how's the training going?"

"Really good. I'm performing my first CT surgery in two days."

Mr. Whitley's operation, that is.

"CT..."

"Cardiothoracic, Dad."

"I know," he nods.

Long pause. He must be thinking of home.

"I saw your former consultant at the New Haven Hospital some days ago."

My heart rate increases, and I feel sudden cold perspiration on my palms as I let go of my cutlery.

"Oh, he's retired; what was he doing there? How is he?"

"He didn't look too good."

"Oh my God, he was a patient? What happened?"

He pauses for a while. I have instantly lost my appetite.

"You seem to care a lot about that fella, don't you? I was hoping you'd ask me why *I* was there."

"Conference, I suppose? So what happened?"

He puts down his knife and fork, his eyes signaling some kind of irritation.

"Your mother had a stroke."

"But you just said she was doing fine! You still haven't answered my question!"

"He'd had a stroke, too!" he says.

The silence and the angry look on his face make it hard to determine the result of the stroke. Dr. Dick is in his seventies, and thus he's more vulnerable.

"As you can tell, both survived. I mean, *he* survived."

I remember when Dr. Dick found me crying in the sluice room next to the operating theater. He had just finished a CT where I had been involved. The surgery had felt like a six-hour trance in which the color red was more dramatic and more beautiful than Mars. It was mind-blowing, breathtaking, and heartbreaking – a new kind of hematologic art.

"You did well in there," Dr. Dick had told me. "So, did it grab your field of interest?"

"You touched the heart as if it were…a little kitten."

He smiled.

"Well, that's how you have to view it, like a vulnerable little kitten."

"Will this help me heal mine?"

I felt like a little girl; I always have felt that way in front of him and my dad.

"It's up to you. Are you ready to enter that room again and be responsible for it?"

He pointed at the door that led to the operating theater. I suddenly began to understand that the true face of the world was behind that very door.

That was the last time I cried.

Dad drinks the rest of his water, which doesn't seem to cool him down. He gazes at his salad, seemingly debating whether or not to finish it.

"Do you remember my first school play?" I say.

He looks at me.

"I played the old witch. And Alicia, my classmate, was Sleeping Beauty. I was supposed to play Sleeping Beauty, but everyone pitied Alicia because she was so ill and fragile."

He looks down at the table.

"She touched the spindle and fell hard. Everyone thought it was good acting. You were the only one who realized something was wrong and climbed onto the stage. You called out her name, put two fingers on her carotid pulse, and then you shouted out *911*."

He remembers, of course.

"You used one hand for chest compressions, and you performed mouth-to-mouth resuscitation on her."

He straightens his napkin again.

"I remember I was very jealous," I say. "She got my role, and she got my dad."

I see a faint smile on his face.

"And then she revived."

"Why are you telling me this?" he says.

"Ever since then, Dad...I wanted to be you."

...And save a man your age.

I suddenly crave the chicken, so I continue eating my lunch. His smile grows bigger and has brought back his appetite as well.

I tell him about my work routine, my patients, and my excitement about performing my first heart surgery in which I am the surgical lead. I tell him about my involvement in different departments and how I assisted Will during neurosurgery. And then my beeper goes off.

"Work?"

"I'm afraid so," I say. "Maybe we could..."

"I'm driving back tonight."

We both rise from our seats to embrace each other. He is holding me very tightly.

"I am very proud of you, princess," he says.

I swallow hard. He releases me.

"Say hi to Mom."

The surprise in his dilated pupils compels me to turn away immediately and leave.

"Please come and visit us sometime."

CHAPTER EIGHT

Mother has just come back from grocery shopping. She is not alone; she has brought a stranger home. I told her this morning that I wouldn't be home this afternoon due to my final biology presentation on Mendel, genetics, and DNA. Mendel has helped me to view the world from a different angle, to understand why we are what we are. The presentation, however, was in the morning. I never told her that it was a competition. I have won the scholarship prize for a university and course of my choice. This is my chance to apply to Yale University. I don't want to be too far away from Dad.

I lied to Mother this morning so I can prove to Dad that she is cheating. He was angry with me when I told him about the stranger. I would never even dare to make Dad angry, not without a good reason. When I'm off to college, I don't want my dad to continue closing his eyes to Mother's lies. He deserves better. I know that once I'm gone, he will have less courage to confront her.

Here I am, home in the afternoon with Mother and her man. I see her and the stranger in bed. He has stronger features than Dad – broader shoulders and muscular arms. She is making lustful noises while he is on top of her moving rhythmically. I carefully slide the closet door more open, hold up the video camera and then press record.

I swear that I won't ever make such noises like my mother, but then again, I never make noises during sex. Boys have referred to me as "the corpse" before. Most of them came before I could even feel anything. My fingers have proven to be more effective lately.

Ever since I lost my virginity, my heart hasn't felt the same – I pin the lack of pleasure entirely down on that. I need to understand the language of my body better. I think it's talking to me, but I can't comprehend the signals, except pain or nothing. There must be a way to navigate and locate specific body signals, such as pain or pleasure. I'm sure all the answers are in the human cells. I can't wait to attend college and become like Dad.

I'm nauseated by Mother's screams as she comes. I don't remember her doing this when I used to catch her and Dad having sex. I must have been five or six, but I recall Dad's heavy breathing. I like it when men breathe heavily, especially against my ear.

I've been in the bedroom closet for over an hour, listening to their moist kisses and whispers – peering at the way their feet caress each other. I'm getting tired of holding the camera.

"Let's leave. I want to get out of Connecticut," Mother says.

My grip around the camera tightens.

Here are two people mapping out their future, and it's always the female who thinks ahead, leaving the man to dwell in the moment. There is tension in the air, filling the atmosphere with dissonant sounds.

"I'm not planning to leave my wife."

A sense of satisfaction rises from this bad vibe – my satisfaction. Madame Bovary has always been a whore and always will be.

Before bedtime, Dad usually completes some last-minute paperwork in his office. I'm in bed already when I hear him enter his office. I picture the way he stares at his video camera, how he slowly makes himself comfortable in the chair and hesitates to switch the thing on. He is undoubtedly overwhelmed by curiosity and a sense of perturbation. I hate having to put him through this, but I don't want him to pretend that everything is fine.

Fifty minutes, later I hear him leave his office, closing the door quietly. His steps lead him to my door; I see his figure covering the dim lights on the corridor. He enters my room. I pretend to be asleep, but I hear his gentle steps motioning towards my desk. He sits down and exhales.

"I know you're awake."

I keep my eyes closed; it doesn't make a difference whether they're open or not because Dad's looking at me with his back facing the window, which means I'd only see his silhouette.

"I'm so sorry, Dad."

"I know," he says.

I hold on to my duvet and tighten my grip.

"How did your presentation go?"

I thought he would never ask. A few hours ago at the dinner table, there wasn't much to talk about; each of us was preoccupied with something else.

"I got the scholarship, Dad. I'm applying for Yale."

"Oh my God! That's brilliant!"

He switches my desk lamp on. The rod cells in my eyes are in pain. I hide under the cover to save my eyes from the sharp halogen light.

"Why didn't you mention it earlier? That would've brightened up everything!"

"You didn't ask."

"I'm sorry, pet...I..."

"It's OK. I only wanted to tell you, Dad, alone," I mumble.

"Your mother deserves to know as well."

There is silence for a little moment. I hear him move the chair closer to the bed.

I slowly stick my head out and see his bright face; it's as if he hasn't watched my video at all. His eyes are flashing signals of happiness.

"I'm proud of you, Ellen."

Even though college is still months away, the big smile on his face evokes sadness in me. How will Dad cope without me? He pats my head before switching the lamp off. I hear him moving towards the door.

He says: "I'm not happy about you overwriting my ballgame, by the way."

"Parker, that was a hell of a lunch break!" Stuart says, irritated.

"I'm sorry. I was with my dad near Bellevue."

I follow him out of the wards towards the reception like a lap dog.

Stuart has been in an indescribable mood lately. Ever since he came back from his three-day holiday, he has changed. It'd better be temporary.

"I'm just telling you that Whitley's well-being is *your* responsibility!"

Mr. Whitley's air hunger has deteriorated. They figured a symptom of orthopnea early in the afternoon. He's unable to sleep in a lying position without getting respiratory complaints. As Stuart and I approach the reception, I see Miss Bobtail and Julia. And a very ugly woman, probably in her late fifties, rushes towards Stuart with both arms clenched as if nervous or hysterical.

"Is my Theo all right?"

She's wearing a wide silk top with three-quarter sleeves and a scoop neckline. Her collarbones look sharp. Her make-up application is striking: blue eye shadows, crimson lips, and dark rouge on her sharp cheekbones. That's Mr. Whitley's girlfriend?

"Yes, he is," says Stuart sternly. "Parker?"

"Yes, he's fine. I will treat him later today and…"

"Ah, my little baby…" she cries.

She makes her way towards Mr. Whitley's room. Her idiosyncratic movements and mesmerizing little steps make us all watch her without blinking. I pay double attention to her artificial buttocks. They are indeed well done and make her appear no older than forty-two from behind.

"Jesus!" Stuart says, tilting his glasses, "I need a coffee."

He turns towards the cafeteria and leaves.

"What's with Stuart today?" Julia says.

"He's been like this since his return from Connecticut," says Miss Bobtail.

I look at her.

"Connecticut? What did he go there for?" I ask.

That cool look in her eyes has returned. She raises an eyebrow as if to judge my lack of knowledge.

"Your supervisor doesn't seem to tell you much, does he?"

I ignore the question and instead hand Julia Mr. Whitley's updated documents.

"I'm sorry. I don't mean to insinuate anything," says the bobtail.

I shoot her a disapproving look and turn away.

"Hey! I mean it."

As I head to my office, she catches up with me. It's like having an annoying little cat glued at my ankle.

"Listen, he doesn't tell me much, either. So, don't assume he tells me everything."

"Well, you certainly know more than I do," I say.

"Yeah, true. Well, all I know is he helped out at New Haven Hospital. That's where you graduated, is that right?"

"Yes," I say, opening my office door.

Could he have gone there to see Dr. Dick?

The bobtail enters my office before I do.

"Wow, your practice room looks amazing. But it smells a bit strongly of disinfectant, don't you think?"

You are polluting my air with your irritating British accent.

"It's bigger than mine. Not quite fair, if you think about it."

"What's that supposed to mean?"

"You're a junior, aren't you?"

I interlock my arms as I approach her.

"I happen to be a fellow in General Surgery at this hospital."

She scrutinizes every bit of my face, her eyes rest on my lips, and then she turns away to walk around the room.

"I'm not interested in *General Surgery*. It's boring."

"And I thought building and connecting the CPB was boring," I say and snicker, although I don't mean to insult our former perfusionist, Alex. I do like the heart-lung machine.

She throws me a fierce look, but it disappears almost instantly. She runs her fingers along my nameplate to check for dust.

"You know, you should've applied to Columbia. The heart surgeries there are more intense," she says.

"Are you criticizing Stuart?"

"Oh gosh, not at all. I'm just saying…it's more exciting but very competitive. You might like it. We have seven CT surgeons. Drop by sometime."

It sounds tempting indeed, except I doubt I'd enjoy the high level of competition. If you learn a specialty, only one person should teach you. In fact, two. One to introduce the specialty's significance and a second to teach you how to practice it, help you implement and master that specialty. Could it be that Stuart and Dr. Dick are close?

"Maybe," I say.

Besides, I have no interest in finding out what the heart surgeons at Columbia Presbyterian are like if their perfusionists are as conceited as she is. Alex is a remarkable perfusionist and never acted like this. But Alex isn't a woman.

She moves towards the door. "Well, I look forward to seeing you in action. Mr. Whitley deserves the best."

"He does," I say.

She opens the door, but before stepping outside, she says, grinning, "I like you!"

I rest my behind on my desk and exhale. Stuart is right; I need to be more aware of my responsibilities. It's like I've not listened to his words at conferences. I wonder if Stuart is upset that I've not been paying him enough attention.

Dr. Dick must have been in so much pain. I wonder how he is now. I wish I had the courage to ask Stuart about going to Connecticut.

I won't ever forget my first encounter with Stuart here at Mount Sinai.

When I left New Haven Hospital for Mount Sinai, I wanted to show my enthusiasm by applying for a backup course at the School of Medicine.

Stuart had invited me for an interview. The day I entered his office, he had two glasses of champagne on the table.

"Congratulations, Dr. Parker. I'd like to welcome you as a team member!"

I don't think I'd ever looked that perplexed in my life. He passed me a glass.

"Pardon?"

"Let me put it this way, your resume is fantastic."

"You went to Yale, which means your consultant was Phillip – a genius, one of a kind," he said.

"Uh, yes."

"Well, I'm Stuart, your supervisor; nice to meet you."

It was very casual and surreal at the same time. He didn't offer me a seat or a handshake, and yet, I was standing there with a glass of champagne. I hadn't even participated in a competition. What interested me more was his connection with Dr. Dick, except that I'd never asked.

"I see you've applied for the Biomedical Engineering course – surely as a backup, but you don't have to. It'll bore the hell out of you."

"I think I'm going to take that course anyway."

"As you wish."

If it hadn't been for Dr. Dick's good reputation, I don't think I would have gotten that position effortlessly. I was the chosen junior surgeon out of one hundred and forty-nine top applicants.

Dr. Dick is a 1975 graduate from Harvard but ended up teaching at Yale University because his wife is a Communications teacher in Connecticut. He is indeed a genius and a very kind man at heart; I'm sure his wife is too, despite her strong religious views.

I sometimes used to fantasize about being together with Dr. Dick. Perhaps my heart would have healed, too. But my life has proven to be more complicated than that, and that's fine; hard work is essential if you want to reach your goal.

I remember the farewell BBQ at Dr. Dick's place; I had avoided most of the other surgeons. He noticed my reclusive behavior and said to me, "Ellen, a lonely wolf lady needs company. Remember to go howling with another wolf – one that's worthy of your company!"

Did he think that I was lonely? I hated the way he always put so much emphasis on the way I held onto unrequited love and a broken heart, but he was the only one I could confide in. I would never talk to Dad about heartbreak. He views me as the perfect daughter – someone indestructible and made of steel.

"It's not good and not healthy battling with reality on your own," he said.

I am alone in my office, enjoying a few more minutes of silence. Then I grab my pager hesitantly. I lean my body back slightly and begin to drum on the desk with my fingers.

"Dammit."

I start typing: "So you don't want me anymore?"

I type in the recipient's line, "Will," but my thumb hesitates to press the *Send* button. I do it anyway. I'm sure Norman still has Will's pager. Why did he leave without saying goodbye? I still have a bone to pick with him. Half a minute later, he replies: "I've always wanted you."

-

It's almost 5 p.m. I presume that Mr. Whitley's hysterical partner has left. I need to speak to Mr. Whitley urgently – alone. I'm having a date with Norman near Times Square at 8 p.m. But of course, I will cancel if Mr. Whitley needs me tonight. I'll probably return to the hospital after the date anyway.

Another aspect I dislike about ward rounds is entering a room where a visitor is present. Sometimes they are obstinate and insist on staying for the conversation between the patient and me. I'm sure his girlfriend is that type of person. Women don't grant you privacy if they think you're after their men. I want nothing but Mr. Whitley's heart; his heart is mine – every blood drop in his endocardium, every chamber, and every sound of the heartbeat…are mine.

I find him alone in his room. He's watching the evening news about Trump's recent scandalous rants.

"Hi, Mr. Whitley. How are you feeling?"

"Oh, Dr. Parker."

He turns down the volume.

"You should know me by now, strong like a rock, right?" he says.

"Indeed."

Never have I seen a more genuine smile, and it's because I am here. I take a seat next to his bed and stare at the screen for a while.

"In fact, you don't want to watch that; our politics have become a circus."

He turns off the TV.

"We all just want to close our eyes on the world, don't we?"

"Well, I don't," he says, "and I know you don't either."

Another smile transforms from his sweet dainty mouth, as he reaches out for my hand. I shouldn't have said what I did. It's something I would say in small talk situations. But we are closer than that.

"Dr. Parker," he begins, "last week you approached me so kindly. And you reminded me how important it is to stay healthy."

I press his hand.

"I have always hated how doctors tell me what's good for me. But you…"

He kisses my knuckle and places my hand on his chest.

"I know I have to let go. I have to let Angela go."

On my palm, the heartbeat feels normal, whereas the sound via the stethoscope suggests differently.

I'm going to fix your heart. This will be my cure, my new beginning.

Mr. Whitley's heart is more unique than mine ever was and ever will be. Here is my chance to pick up the pieces and make everything OK.

Someone knocks on the door and enters; it's Stuart. I let go of Mr. Whitley.

"Dr. McCormick, what a pleasure."

"Mr. Whitley."

Stuart's voice signals sincerity, but I can tell he is here to speak to me.

"My two favorite doctors," Mr. Whitley says. "God bless you."

"Parker, can we talk?"

"Sure."

I see a grin on that dainty mouth again as Stuart and I leave the room.

"Listen, Parker," he runs his hand through his hair and tilts his glasses. "You are a conscientious surgeon, and I know that. You know that."

He lowers his eyes as if trying to apologize for his previous grumpiness.

"Thank you, Stuart."

He nods.

"How is your father?" he says.

"He's good, thanks for asking."

He nods again and turns towards the staff room.

"Stuart?"

"Yes?"

"How is...Dr. Dick?"

He indicates no sign of surprise as if he has seen this question coming.

"He's all right."

There has been a slight delay in the subway. I arrive at Times Square at ten past eight. We have arranged to meet at a prominent Italian place called Carmine's, where the chefs are always very generous with Spaghetti portions.

I peer through the restaurant window to check whether Norman looks impatient, but to my surprise, I see Will sitting in a booth. He's drinking water.

"Shit!"

I stay outside and walk around the block and back to see whether Norman has arrived yet. He hasn't. I message him immediately saying:

"Hey, let's not meet at Carmine's."

Ten seconds later, a reply says:

"U kidding me, Elle?"

I cover my mouth with my palm. I lean against the window to think of a way out. Watching all fellow New Yorkers walk past makes me want to dive into the crowd and disappear – simply walk away. It seems like Norman had handed in the pager before he left.

Someone inside the restaurant knocks against the window. I turn around and see Will's big grin; there's something robotic about his smile. We are similar in person, so it can't be that complicated to get along.

"This is a gorgeous place," he says, sipping at his water.

"I...I don't feel like cheese tonight."

"No pizza for you then!"

He pours me some water. I never noticed that so many surgeons only drink water and coffee, and occasionally champagne. I sometimes let a patient's blood drop percolate on my tongue. Two-thirds of my tongue perceives how the taste travels through my facial nerves, and the sweeter it tastes, the more the glossopharyngeal nerve makes my throat and tonsils tingle.

"I thought you were going let me starve here."

"I probably would have."

He takes my comment as a joke. I scan the menu to ensure that they're still serving salads at this place. I always feel like a barbarian when I eat in front of a man on a date. Therefore, I have to order something light. But I've already had a chicken salad for lunch.

"You won't believe who I saw before I got here," Will says.

"Who?"

"Howie and Jules walking to the movies. They're most likely watching a chick flick now. Isn't that adorable?"

"Do you still believe that they won't be happy together?"

"Well, ugly couples are always happy, whereas beautiful ones always struggle. I guess Howie and Jules are ugly after all."

"You're such an asshole."

He is right, of course. Beautiful people have rivals, and this involves greed, envy, and jealousy. They also have a completely different perception of life because their narcissism is driven by power and control. I know what he is talking about.

The waiter comes to take our order.

"Heart surgeons first!"

I crave some red wine, but I don't dare say, and the outcome could be drastic. I order a Tortellini soup and he the homemade ricotta lasagna.

"You're good at pretending that you care about all these people, Elle."

"Pardon me?"

"In reality, you consist of nothing but dark inner faculties…"

I wonder whether he is trying to trap me, whether he is already knocking on the backstage door of the real me. He picks up his glass. His hands are manly and well-formed; the fingernails clean as a whistle.

"I find you interesting," he says.

I keep quiet; it's comforting to know that some people understand, and listening to him makes me feel less isolated.

"But we both know," he continues, "that fitting in is essential."

Will is like me with just one difference. How do I tell him that I have a broken heart to mend?

"There is only a pretense of being useful to the world, and truth be told, you're doing it all for yourself," he says.

I wonder about Will's heart rate during intercourse.

"What about you? Are you anything other than a cynic?" I say.

"Not at all. I have a gift, and it's called humor, which you don't have."

I roll my eyes.

"But I understand. If you can't make people laugh or piss them off with brutal honesty, then you'd better remain restrained."

"Is that what you think I do?"

"Yes. But tell me, what is it like not to have compassion?"

I see curiosity in his eyes where others would show only condemnation or disapproval.

"I naturally feel disconnected..." I say, presuming that that is what he wants to hear.

"Yeah...don't you hate it when patients share their emotions before surgery? I know that's part of the job. You've seen the way I operate. Most of my patients need to be awake. I have to talk to them, encourage them and be humorous."

And you are magnificent at it. I wonder whether he has any compulsive tendencies. Does he take anything from the patient for his own benefit?

"I'm a nihilist," he says.

I hold my breath for a moment. This is the last thing I would have expected to hear.

"And so are you," he continues. "You dedicate your life to the art of science, the physical beauty of human anatomy...even though there is no great meaning behind it all."

I watch him place a peanut between his teeth. With a few chews, he sucks the entire life out of it with his tongue and cheeks – pleasing the cranial nerves in his brain.

"You live by the concept of pleasure?"

"Exactly! We do! What's your favorite surgical toy, Elle?"

I laugh.

"I bet my forceps, hooks, and chisels turn you on," he says.

I see amatory intentions in his glowing eyes. I knew it was only a matter of time.

"A scalpel is a key to any human body," I say. "A clamp or a retractor keeps the door open for me. Scalpels of carbon steel are my most reliable friends. They help me enter a space deeper than the person's soul. It's all beneath the skin, inside the flesh, bathing in the red sea of life."

"Fuck me, Elle, that's so erotic."

"You know what?"

I lean over; his head approaches mine, his eyes digging their way through my soul. I say, "You hold the curettes and dissectors like my grandmother would hold her knitting needles."

We burst into laughter.

"Why are you laughing? I thought I had no humor," I say.

"You don't, but at least you're honest."

I figure that Will is not the person to ask about love. Maybe love is merely a chemical reaction. And you have to find the right person who carries the suitable chemical substance that corresponds with yours. Is Will the one? Is he the one to help me achieve the long-lost sensation of climax? I can't say I sense the chemistry; it might be a slow reaction or a missing ingredient, I don't know. The motion of electrons leads to a chemical bond, and this is how lovers meet. But these electrons are also capable of breaking the chemical bonds, which is how people fall out of love.

"I bet you steal your patients' hearts and keep them frozen."

Metaphorically speaking, he is right, except I don't steal them, I'm given those hearts; hearts that lack strength.

See Jay. See Bruce.

The only heart I am looking to steal right now is Mr. Whitley's, a genuine heart to steal and make my own.

"And how many brains do *you* keep in your basement, Mr. Cushing Jr.?"

If physical attraction has ever incited more than magnetism, then this is it – medical lust. Will has dispelled all my insecurities by highlighting who I am. The only thing he doesn't know is my intentions and goals in life. I'm doing all this for a reason, not for pleasure. Merely living for the sake of pleasure is nowhere near my ideal concept of satisfaction.

"I'm nowhere as crazy as that man. He was obsessed with brains."

"You're not?"

"I wouldn't say I am, no," he says.

"Then why did you choose this specialty?"

"It's the idea of control, Elle."

The smile on his lips makes me bite my lower lip. My foot slowly edges towards him; there is something even more magnetic in the air below.

"I am in control of the origin of brain signals. But because most of my patients remain awake during the OP, I need to communicate and maintain a high level of trust. Thank God I have nurses holding my patients' hands. I just do the talking and fiddling. And Jesus, I'm good at it!"

You are.

"You're a cocky bastard," I say.

He laughs again at either my humor or honesty. I suppose there is a lot to learn from Will, but I wouldn't necessarily dedicate my time to him. Nihilism is not what I am pursuing, but I like some of the ideas involved.

The waiter serves us our food.

With just one look at my tortellini soup, I perceive the dark side of life more and more clearly. The ring-shaped pasta floating on the soup's surface depicts skin with meat inside, but it's only Prosciutto – fine Italian ham, not human meat or human brain, although the chopped herbs and spices on the tortellini look like hair or stubbles. There are little heads in my soup. I suddenly have an array of my recent patients lined up in my head – all of them naked on the operating table. All these patients have added up to my inner chamber of collectibles – an unsettling area where my sense of self and balance still shake to every little movement. If anything, I'd be the one triggering an earthquake. But that chamber is the center of my existence, and I have to start taking responsibility. It needs to stay safe. It's my private property on which I build.

I place the first tortellini into my mouth. Will seems to be enjoying his lasagna. I wonder what he sees in it.

At Will's place, I realize that his notion of pleasure exceeds all my expectations. He is the closest physical connection I've ever experienced. My blood rush and hormone levels have roused into a kind of action that is unknown to me.

It's as if he had multiple limbs like a spider. And each limb has wrapped itself around my torso and is responding to each breathing pore of my skin. Maybe his saliva will turn into real cobwebs.

Each gland in our bodies is secreting a high amount of perspiration during this foreplay. We're both equally dominant, but since it's Will, the brain waves reader, I've decided that our efforts need to be reciprocal. I have always put great emphasis on how to satisfy a man, despite knowing that he won't bring me back the sensation of climax. But Will has awoken a different, a more intriguing part of my body, and I believe that I am close to discovering something. Our brains are joined like two connected computers, two sets of intelligence merging into something greater.

He inserts two fingers into me to conjure up a moan. The thrusts come quicker. Then I feel another finger creeping towards my anus.

"No," I say sharply.

He removes his slippery fingers and places them into my mouth. Our eyes are exchanging violent energies. I grab his penis tightly; on his knees now, he moves his lower body closer to my face.

"Elle, is it absurd to say that I feel connected to you?"

Our pulse is rhythmically at the exact same speed. I can hear and feel how our blood corresponds with each other.

I want to touch his heart.

I rise from the bed and press my hand against his chest. He reads it as "lie down." Maybe sleeping with Will is the only way to discover what my hemispheric control is doing to me. The rapid beating of his heart ensures that I am human, that he is human – we both are.

He supports my movements with hard thrusts, both of his hands grabbing the flesh on my hips.

Now reaching his climax, his eyes are strangely focused on me as if his climax doesn't matter.

Why is he looking at me like this? My heart rate decreases. I now remove my hand from his chest.

His hands are gliding over my pelvis, abdomen, and labia.

The movements stop, and I realized that I haven't been focusing on the sex; I've been too preoccupied feeling his heartbeat and my own.

Have I come?

I wish he would stop looking at me.

I climb down and sit at the corner of the bed with my feet touching the floor. My fingertips are shaking.

What is wrong with me?

I hear his breathing, and then he approaches me from behind. I feel Will's finger on the top of my spine. Slowly he draws his finger down, touching all 24 vertebrae, then stopping at the sacrum. He has sparked a curious chill in my body and goosebumps on my forearm.

"You can't feel orgasms," Will says.

For a second, I see black, and a sense of nausea envelops my head.

"What was that?"

"Gosh, I'm so sorry, Elle…"

Will swings his legs forward to rest his feet on the ground. Our legs are touching.

"What are you apologizing for?" I say.

"This is the most fucked up thing ever…"

I stand up straight, furious and confused.

"Are you calling me fucked up?"

"No! Of course not! Listen!"

I clasp my arms and press them against my chest. Throughout my life, I've never realized that my heart and brain are fucked up.

"I could feel your nerves," he says while stretching out four fingers.

"Your hypogastric nerve, pelvic nerve, pudendal nerve, and your vagus nerve," he says, pointing at each of the four fingers.

"But I received no brain waves as if those nerves didn't forward the sensation to your brain."

"You're full of shit," I say.

"I never told anyone about this. Come on, why do you think I'm such a good neurosurgeon? I can sense these signals."

I run my hands through my hair. I can't believe I just exposed a secret. I should have realized that he was no good.

Strangely, I cannot decide whether I am relieved or distressed.

"Besides, you were miles away," he says, "where were you, what were you thinking?"

I rub my eyes and walk away from him towards the closed curtains. They are made of fine velvet. My heartbeat has stabilized, and so has Will's; I no longer hear his heart crying out for me. I don't think it ever has cried out for me.

"I was trying to connect with you," I say.

"I felt connected at first…and then you shut me out."

"I didn't."

"What were you doing then?"

I begin to dress slowly.

"Well?"

"I was paying attention to your heart, I guess."

He shakes his head with a smile suggesting how he could be so blind.

"I should keep in mind that you're a heart surgeon," he says.

"You're using your brain too much, Will."

"It's kinda ironic…"

"What is?"

"An emotionless heart surgeon, in search of feelings."

I'm fully dressed while Will is still sitting naked and comfortable on his bed. We have disconnected again, despite being so similar. Every reaction has an end. Except that this was a quick one. How can I experience love if I'm emotionless? How can I move mountains if I have no feelings? Will is not entirely right, but he has discovered too much about me, more than what I'm willing to share with anyone. He is penetrating my brain so deeply I don't know how to get him out.

"Can I ask you something?" he says.

I'm about to leave.

"What *do* you feel?"

"Nothing, Will. Absolutely nothing."

I open the door, but he jumps up from the bed and closes the door again.

"Hold on!"

"What?"

He looks at me as if doubting me.

"You're just about to turn your back on a brain surgeon, dammit!"

I don't like what he is implying. I need to get out of here. My hemispheric control is at stake. My heart rate is increasing for no reason. How dare he say I emit no brain waves?

There is a sudden itch in my flesh. The next thing I know is I fling an arm around his neck and begin to kiss him hard on the mouth. He responds to the kiss with a growing erection then takes off my underwear before lifting me up.

This time I will focus; focus on the lower parts and my brain, but I hear our hearts again. I stare at his chest.

"Elle, I'm here. Look at me."

He lifts me further up and presses me against the wall before he enters me. We're no longer machines but human beings; in fact, we always have been.

"Don't think, you hear me? Elle?"

I kiss him again just to shut his mouth. I could suffocate him by clamping his nose shut. But I no longer see Will; I see Norman; whose seven-inch penis is impaling me.

I moan in pain.

"Ellen, what's wrong?"

I see Jay. He has already recovered from all his bruises.

"Ellen, don't leave me alone."

There is blood running down Bruce's face. He had cried before his death.

"Elle! *Elle!*"

The movements have stopped; someone's patting on my face.

"Elle!"

I look at Will; I touch his face just to make sure it's him.

"You were gone again."

"I was looking at you. What are you on about?"

He puts me carefully on his bed and then scratches the back of his head.

"Well, you weren't seeing me. I don't know who or what you saw in that spooky head of yours, but it was freaking me out."

I smile at his chest; I must have scratched him slightly because he's bleeding.

"Did you identify my brain waves?"

He is confused.

"Something angry and foreign. I don't know exactly."

I lie down on his bed. A sudden rush of tiredness has encircled my mind and body. It's like the chemical reaction has been halted or maybe it has been completed. I still sense no strong affection for Will. My heart is calm, no more excessive pumping of blood.

"Elle, can I do an EEG and a spinal analysis on you?"

Halfway asleep, I say, "No, I'm fine."

"Then how about get Stu to look at you or acquaint you with a first-class gynecologist?"

"Gynecology? Stuart?"

"You didn't know? You should know by now that all of us have had a shameful past. I'm an ear specialist."

CHAPTER NINE

I've never had many interactions with nurses at the hospital, apart from Julia. Nurses have a tendency to stick together and have little contact with the other physicians and surgeons, similar to the social hierarchy in high school, where the cheerleaders have a clique and little contact with other girls in their year. The male nurses are very quiet and remind me of hard-working college boys that never brag about their good grades. They always look after my patients perfectly. I've never minded this scheme at the hospital, but since Julia highlighted her string of concerns at the conference the other week, I've started to pay more attention to the nurses. There is a particular assisting nurse called Laura, who looks fragile and apprehensive. I often see other nurses send her off to fetch things, and she runs as if the world depended on it. The other nurses just giggle. There is always a black sheep in any social group.

As I'm heading towards the wards, I find Julia comforting Laura at reception. It's probably the nicest gesture towards Laura that I've seen so far. Laura is petite, slim, and quite pretty, but the stress has worn her out. I walk past reception and throw a quick smile at Julia.

Mr. Whitley looks lively. His eyes express an eagerness to live, a strong belief in success, and no trace of concern. It's only one day before surgery.

"Dr. Parker. It's always such a delight to see you!"

His high spirits dispel all negative energies; whatever they are, I do not wish to know. Luckily my cerebral hemispheres have recovered their equilibrium. Nothing will make this balance collapse today. I will try not to think about the lateralization of the brain, which will bring my deductive reasoning out of tact. My brain has always been bilaterally controlled. I didn't meditate this morning, as I fear that those jumbled images would reappear.

"Mr. Whitley, it's good to see you so happy. Has your girlfriend been around?"

"Oh, she's not coming until late. I'm just glad that I'll be spending this afternoon with you, Dr. Parker."

"There are just minor tests that we have to…"

He suddenly brings forward an urn, which I hadn't noticed was on the bedside table.

"What's this?"

"I have a favor to ask you," he says.

My eyes keep wandering from Mr. Whitley to the urn. I've just realized that my mouth is wide open.

"My son brought this for me."

He strokes the oval-shaped urn as though he had a little dog on his lap. I can see where this is going, and the word "no" is about to slip off my tongue.

"Could you take me to Central Park for a walk?"

"OK."

Wheeling Mr. Whitley into the Conservatory Garden in Central Park makes him seem like the grandfather I never had. I wish it were raining because I'm not up for this. But the sun's been shining vibrantly since morning. He is holding the urn tightly against his chest. From what I can read, this decision must have been tough for him.

"Angela used to help do the gardening here."

"I see."

We approach the Bessie Potter Vennoh sculpture illustrating a young maiden holding up a plate. Below her is a young boy playing the flute. Here Mr. Whitley asks me to stop.

"Have you ever read *The Secret Garden*, Dr. Parker?"

"I have indeed."

"This was our secret garden."

After twenty years, I can still see the blood on our lawn back home in Connecticut. And Dad wants me to visit. I'm not sure how convenient my visit would be. All these years, I'd wished my parents would move, but they never left Cheshire Village – a place that still haunts me in my dreams – the home that reeks of pubescent blood and disgrace. This is what I see in this peaceful garden.

Mr. Whitley rises from his wheelchair. I offer him my hand to help him balance while he holds the urn in the other arm. Upon standing, he freezes for a second, holding my hand tighter. The look in his eyes exceeds the depth of the Harlem Meer. He scares me. Eventually, his expression mellows with a nostalgic smile.

"I'm so glad that you are here, Dr. Parker."

I remember Dr. Dick saying the exact same thing to me in the operating theater. There was a lot of blood, and it was the first time I experienced Dr. Dick being tense. During a septal myectomy, the removal of a part of the aorta's septum, the patient was under cardiogenic shock. We carefully inserted an intra-aortic balloon pump (IABP), which led to over four hours of pumping, so we could increase the myocardial oxygen perfusion. The IABP was inserted conveniently not too far from the aortic arch, yet we were close to a renal failure and ischemia.

We had a sensitive body on the table – Mrs. Darling, a woman going through a divorce and menopause. Her kids had let her down, and she literally had no reason to live, but Dr. Dick didn't let that influence his job. The woman had signed the DNR document, but luckily the cardiac arrest never occurred. The entire surgery was an in-depth conversation between Dr. Dick and Mrs. Darling. A septal myectomy is a common surgery where complications rarely occur, but Mrs. Darling was deliberately impelling her cells to follow her will. Eventually, she gave in, and Dr. Dick succeeded like he always does.

"I'm glad you completed this with me," he had told me.

He remained close to Mrs. Darling afterward; a shame that the same never happened between Mrs. Hughes and me. All things considered, she did despise me.

Mr. Whitley opens the lid of the urn. His lips are whispering a prayer. As he raises the urn, I take a little step back. I don't want to be here; I don't want to witness how someone lets the love of his life go. I grab my mouth mask and press it against my face. He begins to scatter her ashes around the fountain. I take a further step back to avoid the dust. Even if the dust used to be flesh and bones, I no longer see a sign of it. The dust settles on the sculpture and floats on the water's surface. Before he turns back to me, I stick the mask in my pocket.

The sad smile on his face outshines his tears and facilitates the process of acceptance.

"Thank you, Dr. Parker."

*

Stuart and I are about to perform a valve surgery on Mr. Whitley. His respiratory disorders worsened overnight, leading us to start the operation now at 5 a.m. Nurses and thoracic surgeons were called in at around 4 a.m. The good news is that the bobtail has got caught up at Presbyterian with an emergency CT at the same time, which obligated us to call Alex for support. It's good to have a familiar face at the machines, especially for my first CT surgery. I sense a thrill building somewhere inside me. It's like I'm in my chamber of collectibles – each of them eying Mr. Whitley with jealousy because they know he's more special.

The operating theater is warm; it's full of high-status surgeons and supportive nurses that I respect. None of them will bother to listen to my conversation with Mr. Whitley.

After the anesthesia, Howard is now observing the procedure from the other side of the operating table, his eyes alert and sharp. At the back of the room behind him, six students are gaping at the anesthetized subject. Above them is a screen illustrating Mr. Whitley's chest. The nurse on my right passes me the instrument for the incision. I place the sharp end on the old man's sternum and slowly incise a fine seven-inch line down the center of the chest.

I suddenly hear the distinctive beat of his heart, which puts me inside a bubble of safety. It's like I'm in space but still breathing. No heart could ever generate warmth that is more sincere than Mr. Whitley's. This heart will heal mine and eradicate all accumulated impurity. I know it. This is the first time I believe that disrepair can be undone. I am replacing my heart with his.

I wish Dr. Dick was here to watch me.

To disconnect the heart, we allow Alex some time to set up the CPB. The heart looks incredible; it's big enough for two. When I was a kid, Dad used to tell me that the size of one's heart was the size of my little fists leaning against each other. Now it's just one fist. The sweet rhythm delivers peace of mind to Stuart and me – our threesome with Mr. Whitley.

"I feel cold. Could you hold me?" says Mr. Whitley.

I'm not surprised. The machine is draining the deoxygenated blood from his body.

I'm here; there's no need to be scared.

"Parks, what are you doing?"

I look at Stuart.

"What?"

He gestures at my hand, which is holding Mr. Whitley's arm. The thoracic surgeons are giggling behind their masks. I immediately let go of him.

"Stay calm and focus," Stuart says.

Howard and the nurses remain motionless like statues.

Just before I isolate the heart by applying clamps with the nurse's help, Stuart double-checks the machine's lung and the roller-pump with Alex.

By the time the heart is stopped with an electric shock, it feels like some hours have already passed.

Stuart finally signals that it's time to cut into the aorta. I realize that I am very fond of this old man, unlike previous patients who displayed no belief in their own life or me. Mr. Whitley knows that I'm not just a healing machine, and yet, for his sake, I want to be one; his kind heart deserves all the power that I have. Maybe I should not steal his heart. That would make me a criminal. How come I never thought like this before? I've been taking my job for granted. I've been viewing the job as a perfect alibi to fumble with someone's body. But I'm here to replace his aortic valve and provide him with a new life. His life, however, is not my life. I'm only here to do my job, to lead a persuasive and honest conversation. Nothing more.

"Do it," Stuart says.

Despite the heart's current immobility, I can still hear its hopeful murmur.

"Watch it. Find the left ventricle," Stuart says.

As I excise the aortic valve, memories of drawing broken little hearts shoot into my mind. Before I continue any further, I let Stuart decalcify the clingy ring of the aorta. He then measures it and compares with the nurse the variety of prostheses in order to verify the suitable substitute. We'll call the substitute, Bridget.

"Do you reckon I should propose to Bridget?" Mr. Whitley whispers.

I'm sure you'll make her a happy woman.

I remember that Bridget underwent a buttock augmentation, but he adores her, and she cares about him. Perhaps that is what counts. After cosmetic surgery, you can still love the person for who she is.

The opening of the right coronary artery resembles a beheaded baby bird. When disposing of the defunct valve, a part of Mr. Whitley has gone with it.

"Thank you, Dr. Parker," I hear him say.

I begin to stitch the valvular prosthesis onto the aortic ring. Stuart helps me widen the aortic opening, and thankfully the adequate dilation of the aorta isn't blocking the coronary arteries; therefore, no new implantation needs to be considered here. I think this is my lucky day.

Four hours later, the bubble of safety has popped, and the suture is done. My mind has gone blank, and my muscles are numb. I sense no victory or pride. Perhaps this is what some people feel after an orgasm – relieved and tired. But it is no orgasm. My brain is not connected in any way. Moreover, my attempt to fathom the warmth that I've felt inside that bubble is pointless. It's like trying to trap the wind. I need some fresh air.

Stuart follows me out of the operating theater. He tilts his glasses.

"Parker! Good job!"

Dr. Dick would have squeezed my arm. I give him a grateful nod.

"You'd better go home and get some rest. I'll do the report. I'll come to pick you up at seven, is that all right?"

I have to rewind this episode twice to make sure I have heard him right. My ears have accumulated a lot of surgical noise.

"Did you just say you'd pick me up?"

"Yes, I did," he says. "I reserved a table for two at Aureole. You know, near Bryant Park in…"

"I know where Aureole is."

"All right."

"But what's the reason for this?"

"Mr. Whitley insisted on *you* fixing his heart. And you did it."

It doesn't happen very often that people ask me to fix their hearts – which is why many words fall on my internal deaf ears. This time, these words are like a miracle. Though I still have difficulty in comprehending this transition from a broken heart to a healed heart.

In fact, I am not sure if the transition has taken place at all. I don't feel anything yet. Yes, it was a successful surgery in which I have put little broken pieces back together.

"So, would you rather have dinner with me or dinner with an old man who smacks his lips while chewing on a T-bone steak?"

I guess Mr. Whitley and Stuart must have mentioned me in their conversations during ward rounds. Mr. Whitley never said anything. Nevertheless, during the operation, Mr. Whitley and I had the most intimate conversation that we have ever had in our lives.

Walking past reception, Julia stops me with a big smile on her face that suggests congratulations.

"I'm so happy for you," she says and then passes me a sheet of paper. It's a fax letter.

"And so is this person."

The fax is addressed to me and simply says: "That's a happy kitten."

I can't rest. I was hoping that a bubble bath would slow down my heart rate and reduce the blushing on my face. Unlike most people, I take warm baths, instead of hot, as it cools down quicker. It's to make sure I get out in time before my skin starts to wrinkle.

Of all men, I don't understand why Stuart's shell is so hard to crack. Sometimes I believe that he spells out his intentions to me, but I don't know whether they are adequate or sincere.

Generally, the art of socializing is crucial in the operating theater – it keeps you awake; it keeps you interested in the patient whose life you are saving. The patient tells you his deepest secrets, innermost fears and reasons he wants to live. Stuart knows, and so does Dr. Dick. You know your patients' secrets and want them to feel safe on your operating table. You want them to build on their hopes and map out their future, as they will care a lot more about their life the moment they wake up from the operation.

The lukewarm water begins to slow my heart rate as well as cool my head. I stroke my labia with my fingertips, brushing along some stubble that I am about to shave off.

Why do people become more precious than anything when they're nothing but memories? Memories are so much more attractive when you romanticize them, even as they become less valid.

I take a quick cold shower to revive my senses and escape the hypnagogic state of mind induced by the bath.

I look at my ironed satin trousers. In all seriousness, I am hardly going to have a tutorial or a conference meeting with Stuart. My dress wardrobe is a mess. There are dresses from three years ago, which I have only worn once. There are long black Armani nightgowns with an amatory sparkle, and there's also a titillating red Hugo Boss dress. But they are made of silk chiffon, which represents the intrinsic magnet of attraction.

It's now 6 p.m.

Despite wanting to look stunning and confident, I don't want to give off the wrong intentions.

Green.

I have found my green evening dress by Ralph Lauren, which is suitable for little festivities and other occasions. It's an elegant one-shoulder dress rendered for timeless appeal; the fine cotton suggests decency and neutrality. I remember wearing it at Dr. Dick's barbeque shortly before graduation. He said that green made me look like a good girl; it matched my eyes, his lawn, his apron, and his green tomatoes.

"But sometimes these good girls are like poison ivy," he said.

"So, you think I'm noxious?" I said.

"No." He smiled.

Stuart is on time as usual. He is never late or early, except when preparations need to be done before an operation, then he'll be at the hospital three hours early.

"Green tomatoes!"

"What?" I say, confused.

"You look stunning and refreshed. Did you get your cat nap?"

"I wouldn't call it a nap. More a near-death experience in the bathtub."

"Hell, Parks, do you know how many bathtub deaths we have in this country each year?"

I picture submerging into the tub and drowning as the result of being transported by a beautiful thought. That's a kind of drowning where agony is absent. But I didn't go that far.

He is wearing Ralph Lauren, too: an elegant brown button-up shirt suitable for casual occasions. On the outside, we match like wood and leaves. And Fall is close. It's weird that we're dressed like this. Besides, I don't often see Stuart without a lab coat, except when we happen to finish work together, which is rarely the case.

"Let's put death back on the waiting list, shall we?" I say.

He hands me a bottle of Schramsberg – one of the finest sparkling white wines and probably the most voluptuous chardonnay that exists.

"Since you're no longer a junior," he says.

"It's one of my favorites! Thank you."

"I've never tried this one; haven't had the right occasion, yet."

"Well, that's very kind," I say.

His eyes are fixed on the bottle.

"Aren't you going to open it?"

I rarely invite guests into my apartment.

"Sure."

After two glasses, Stuart has become giggly and light-headed. While we're walking down the staircase, he randomly talks about how much he liked blowing bubbles as a kid. The bubbles of the sparkling wine have done it to him.

Stuart drives a modern black BMW from the Z-series – almost too somber and gloomy for him. The car is a manifestation of Stuart's inexplicable nature and deep charisma – it's the sort of car Al Capone would have chosen.

In fact, I have never been to Aureole, although I eat out often. I do let men invite me for dinner at their house, and only sometimes do they ask me out to a fancy restaurant, but I've never been to this one.

As we arrive, a handsome waiter, probably an undergraduate in his early twenties, walks us to our table. Stuart immediately orders a bottle of Veuve Clicquot, which reminds me of the type of champagne that people drink at polo matches. That is a good one-hundred-dollar bottle.

As he holds up his champagne glass, I find myself staring at his fingers. Stuart has ordinary, strong hands that reflect determination, precision, and control, but also gentleness. I can tell by his champagne-drinking etiquette. He places his palm courteously at the base of the glass. It's the way I would hold mine if I were a man. I pinch the stem of my glass with my index finger and thumb.

I remember a palmist saying to me that ordinary hands are full of wit and astute insight. That's Stuart in his own weird kind of way.

"How is Mr. Whitley?"

He laughs.

"Jealous, of course."

The waiter passes us the menu. I could swear the waiter has a hard-on.

"Green tomatoes."

Stuart is looking straight at me.

"What did you say?"

"I said that Mr. Whitley wished he was in my place."

"Who knows, I might go out for dinner with him, too."

"No, that was not the deal."

He slightly slaps my upper arm as though I'm not part of this insider agreement between him and my patient.

"What the hell did the two of you agree on?"

"Isn't it obvious? I mean, you chose to go out for dinner with me already."

"Is this a game or something?"

"Come on, Ellen. We would never play games with you."

He sounds sincere, and...did he just call me by my first name?

"All right then, Parker...good work!"

Again, he raises his glass of champagne; I do the same.

I am under the suspicion that Stuart is about to get drunk. He has consumed a fair number of tipples so far.

"So, what do you think of my black beauty?"

"Your *what*?"

"My bike...?" he says.

"You have a motorcycle?"

"Oh, I came with the car, didn't I?"

Before he takes another sip of his drink, I immediately reach out for his glass and put it out of his reach.

"What are you doing, Parker?"

"You don't seem to be good with alcohol. Not that I care about you getting wasted, but remember you have to drive me home!"

"I'm fine. The cops have never stopped me."

I think I've met Stuart for the very first time as if the previous Stuart McCormick has never existed.

An awkward silence hangs in the air for a while, so I stare out of the window where I see a little girl holding a string attached to a heart-shaped helium balloon.

"Green..."

"What?"

"Either you have a terrible attention span, or I'm boring the hell out of you," he says.

He doesn't appear to be offended; instead, he grins very sharply, a grin that I've never seen on him before.

"Who knows?" I smile back at him.

"Phil was right about you."

Something hits me hard inside – glaciers crushing my bones. My eyes must be flashing SOS signals.

"I don't understand. You talked with Dr. Dick about me?"

"Of course. Otherwise, you wouldn't be here having dinner with me."

"Tell me more. It's like you told the whole world about me."

His cheeks have turned slightly rosy.

"Don't worry—just Phil. And Mr. Whitley," he says.

"So, what did Dr. Dick say?"

"He knew that you were applying for a position at Mount Sinai, right?"

"Yes, I mentioned it to him once."

"Well, I guess you have no idea that he'd sent me a glowing reference?"

I am shaking my head, but I begin to understand – everything – everything that made me wonder about Stuart, his attitude towards me, and his hidden kindness – all that has coherence.

"He said you were wearing a green dress at the BBQ and that you were a looker."

"What?"

"I'm joking! He was talking about your skills, of course."

A big lump has developed in my throat.

"Are you all right, Parker?"

I look at the ice bucket in which our bottle is kept; a cold drop of water is drawing a line down the neck.

"Why did you never tell me?" I say.

"I'm telling you now, aren't I?"

"What did he write about me?"

He shakes his head with a rejecting smile.

"I'm afraid it's confidential information."

"Is he all right?"

"Yeah, fragile, but recovering."

For a minute, I am unable to utter a word.

"Tell me something about you, Stuart," I say. "Why are you no longer a gynecologist?"

He looks surprised. I let him take another sip this time. Then the good-looking waiter comes back intending to refill Stuart's glass. I stop him.

"Later, thanks."

"Oh, let's order, I'm starving!" Stuart says.

He quickly browses through the menu card.

"Please, could I have the buffalo tenderloin tips? Thanks very much."

"Sure," the waiter says. "And you, ma'am?"

"I'll take the salmon fillet, please, but no rice and no sauce, thank you."

"Would you like extra vegetables instead?" he asks.

"That'd be nice, thank you."

As the hot waiter walks towards the kitchen, I could swear shiny sweat pearls are standing out on his forehead.

Stuart smiles at me as if he has caught me in the act.

"Interesting to know that you appreciate clean food," he says.

"Just trying to separate carbs from protein. I'm also looking to become a pescatarian."

"I don't like fish," he says.

"Why is that?"

"The smell."

He narrows his nostrils and fiddles clumsily with his napkin, unfolding and then placing it on his lap as though ready for immediate food.

"I suffered from hypothyroidism as a teenager," I say, "I went to a health resort in Florida where I spent most of the time on the beach. They would serve fish and broccoli. Once, we had oysters, but I didn't touch those."

"Why?"

"Those creatures were still alive. It was like watching people squeeze lemon juice on the vulvar vestibule. The muscle contracted, and then they sucked it in..."

Stuart bursts out laughing. I slowly move the glass of champagne away from me.

"The food had a fresh seawater smell," I say. "Everything smelt of the sea. I used to bathe there a lot."

Stuart refills my glass and then his.

"This is highly entertaining. Please continue!"

I look at the bubbles in my glass but refuse to consume any more of it.

"I'd rather you told me what's so interesting about the science of female genitalia," I say.

I can tell by his facial expression that he wants to hear more about vulvas and labia look-alikes.

"Well, thanks to you ladies, we men have found a home," he says. "I thought I might be able to fix this home, heal it when it's sick and take care of it, enable happiness."

His cheeks are still rosy. He glances at the champagne, but as soon as he catches my eyes, I shake my head. I don't think he has told anyone about this before.

"Well, I kind of doubted myself," he says.

"Did you have to prove something to yourself?"

"Yes, myself…and Phil."

I haven't a clue how often this name has been said out loud today; this recurring person from our past appears to be an unfinished project waiting for its evaluation.

"He always wanted to become a gynecologist himself, but he met his wife too soon. Then he no longer had any interest, except that he'd infected me with the same idea. So, I opened up my own practice after graduation. I got to know my ex-wife back then. She was aroused by the way I used the vaginal speculum. Apparently, there was something about the way I inserted it. However, she wasn't the only one who felt that way."

I suddenly burst into laughter, and everyone in the restaurant begins to stare at me in surprise. I have never heard anything more hilarious and preposterous in my life, and it's coming out of Stuart McCormick's mouth, which makes it even more absurd.

"And let me guess...She caught you satisfying a dirty hooker, and eventually, a rumor went around that you were inadvertently sleeping with your patients!"

For a second, it seems like I have said the wrong thing in the wrong tone, but I am right. He laughs along with me. Suddenly I find myself playing with my tongue inside my mouth. I gulp the rest of my champagne down my throat. However, some sadness etched on his face, a hidden message that he refuses to say out loud. He is not looking at me, either.

"It sounds like you have experienced the same thing," he says, at which point I almost choke on my drink. My laughter fades; his comment comes like a shock to my face.

"You all right?"

"Yeah, just don't make me laugh," I say.

"Well, I guess the rest is self-explanatory. End of story."

"No, wait a minute," I say. "What has Dr. Dick to do with this?"

His firm eyes indicate a lack of interest. But since he has been filling me in about more or less everything, he might as well give me the entire story. I watch him straighten the napkin on his lap and stroke the bridge of his nose.

"In his view, a married man shouldn't stare at other women's vaginas. It's not that he didn't like it, but it was for the sake of his wife. To me, this is a matter of trust."

"True."

"Even if trust is evident, it's still a very provocative thing, he used to say. And we are men after all."

"It still doesn't explain why you don't like fish."

"I lied," he says, "I am a man, Ellen."

Eventually, the waiter arrives with our meals, but my appetite has gone.

After our meal, Stuart is still tipsy but not entirely drunk. For the love of God, I really shouldn't let him drive; after all, he still believes he picked me up with his motorcycle.

"You really need to ride my black beauty sometime!"

I refuse to comment on that one, as it evokes some bestial dreams that I have had.

An awkward silence between Stuart and me has evolved into something very daunting and somewhat sexual. We seem to be experiencing a mutual impact on our hemispheric control. I can hear my own heartbeat's disoriented rhythm, which is not similar to Mr. Whitley's but more intense. My palms are sweating. For a moment, I think I've just imagined Stuart's regular heartbeat, but then I notice that he has switched the radio on. Before I even get to process the sound, he has switched it off again.

"What do you see in a heart, Parker?"

"Disrepair."

"That's a lie."

The more I think about inviting him into my apartment, the more I am deluding myself that nothing will happen. As he stops outside my place, we both keep silent for a while.

"Thanks for dinner," I say.

"My pleasure. Well, thanks for the company. But please don't take everything I say so seriously."

"I never do, don't worry."

"Ouch!"

My smile doesn't feel like an ordinary smile; it's not a smile that people get to see often. Sometimes I tell that woman in the mirror to stop looking at me.

I suddenly notice Stuart's head moving towards mine, but it's too dark to see his lips. I tilt my head to the side. I feel his warm lips on my cheek for a second, and then he presses his cheek against mine and whispers, "You did it."

The tip of his nose brushes against my neck as he moves away.

I step out of the car slowly. I close the door behind me and wave swiftly before I turn my back on him.

I hear him roll down the car window, but I am not turning around. My entire body is about to paralyze.

"Keep up the good work, Parker!"

CHAPTER TEN

The next day at the hospital, I bump into Will and Stuart, who are walking together. I can't imagine anything more awkward than friendship between heart and brain in human form. To my surprise, they look like brothers.

"Congrats, Elle, you're officially a heart surgeon," Will says.

Apparently, I transcended into another being – one of a higher status than before, and all this through hard work.

"Mr. Whitley wants to see you. You'd better go," Stuart says.

Will gives me a cheeky grin, whereas Stuart is hiding a smile. It's almost like a hundred-and-eighty-degree love triangle. For a second, I feel some kind of inner balance.

As Stuart is about to tell me something, Julia appears with an urgent note, and together they head towards the wards.

Will begins to walk a slow circle around me like an

observant cat. His nostrils are flaring.

"You smell different, Elle."

"What do I smell of?"

Now standing close behind me, he says, "Like Stuart."

My arms freeze.

"Like a heart surgeon," he says and pats my upper arm tenderly. Just before he walks away, he says, "I'm always there if you need me, OK?"

"Thank you, Will."

I knock on Mr. Whitley's door. As I enter, I find him with his girlfriend, Bridget.

"Ah, here's the superstar plumber," she says, approaching me with small, quick steps – her high heels making clacking noises.

She encircles my hands with hers and kisses both of my cheeks, which are now marked with greasy lipstick. I hear Mr. Whitley laugh with joy.

"Thank you, Dr. Parker, for everything! I hope Theo behaved, as I told him."

Why is she so nice to me? Is the ecstasy in her voice a sign of gratitude? Maybe she is only pretending.

"Ladies, please can I have your attention?"

Mr. Whitley looks good. The blood has returned to his face; he's no longer cold, that's because I was the one to hold him in the OT.

"You little attention seeker! Can't you see I'm thanking her for saving your life?"

"I just need two more minutes of attention. Please come over here."

There's always something about happiness that brings out the most foreign of sentiments in me. Most of all, it saddens me. It's like I'm in my chamber of collectibles, and one of my possession decides to leave me forever because he has found his own happiness. And I am not able to share this happiness. For the first time, I don't know which mask I am supposed to put on.

"Dr. Parker," he says, holding my hand.

His warmth fails to heat me up this time.

"Thank you," he says.

I can tell that he's not necessarily referring to the operation but to the Bessie Potter Vennoh sculpture in the Conservatory Garden. I see the urn reflected in his pupils.

"Because now," he continues, "I can do this…"

From underneath the pillow, he removes a ring box and presents it to Bridget.

"Oh, Lord!" she says.

Here comes her peculiar idiosyncrasy, hysteria mixed with ecstasy. I think she's about to hyperventilate. He opens the case to present a small silver diamond ring.

"Bridget, you bring sunshine to my heart."

I brought sunshine to your heart.

"You light up my days, and I want this to continue until the two of us forget each other's names."

She chuckles and weeps.

"Will you marry me?"

She lets out an orgasmic scream that could tear apart the thin membrane of a child's eardrum. After the short moment of happiness during the surgery yesterday, I can no longer fathom it. If only I knew what else is required to understand and feel this happiness. Perhaps Will is right. The lack of sensitivity defines a nihilist. What's the meaning of all this happiness anyway?

Stuart and Julia storm into the room to check if everything is OK. Bridget is still squeaking as she shouts:

"Yes! Yes! Yes!"

"I love you so much," Mr. Whitley says to her, and they commence a round of kissing. I smile self-consciously at Stuart and Julia as I leave the room.

There is somewhere else I need to be – my office, my territory. There are a few appointments, no major ones. Mr. Whitley probably didn't even notice me leaving. It's good to see him happy. If only he could tell me how I did it, how I succeeded in conjuring such great happiness.

I need the restroom, but I don't want to run into anyone.

After checking the corridor, I see that the coast is clear. The staff restroom appears empty. I look under the doors to double-check, but I see two feet with a relatively long distance between each other, signifying that the legs are splayed out, reminding me of a shooting position. I imagine a male hunter sitting in the exact position, holding a rifle with his legs spread out and heels dug into the ground.

I quietly tiptoe down to the toilet at the other end. I doubt that person has heard me coming in at all. I lock the door quietly and place my hand in my trousers. I try not to make any sounds while inserting two fingers. Why are there no noises from the other end? No urinating, no excreting – nothing.

As usual, I barely notice that I am coming. And yet I let out a little sigh just for the hell of it – like all these women do.

I feel angry, the kind of anger I used to feel when former boyfriends broke up with me. Back in the day when I was at college, I used to repress my vaginal discharge so I wouldn't be moist enough for decent penetration. It's easy. You think how much you hate the person on top of you. That way, I keep the excitement low and the body's natural lubrication unavailable. The result was blood. The penis would rub against my sensitive cervix and scratch open a wound. It was a self-induced blood bath during which I lost my virginity again and again. They thought they were hurting me. I, on the other hand, thought I was falling in love.

Suddenly I hear a bang at the other end of the restroom.

I decide to wait.

Nothing.

Quickly I open the door, listen again, and then walk back towards the other end of the restroom. Who can it be? Perhaps I have imagined the sound.

The dreadful-looking woman in the mirror catches my attention. I grab some paper towels to wipe the lipstick off her cheeks, and then I add more volume to her hair.

A slightly reddened area on the side of my nose beckons me closer to the mirror. Turning back to the locked door, I bend down and see that the two legs are now tightly pressed against each other, diagonally, indicating that the head is leaning against the wall. I see foam dripping onto the floor.

I bang against the door, shouting: "Hello? Who's in there?"

It's locked.

No response. Panic is not good for the blood pressure, and mine has increased in the last few months. I remember that all staff has a master key for the restroom to check up on patients who lock themselves up in the toilet.

My hands are shaking; I can't grab hold of that little key in this big bunch.

When I finally manage to unlock the door, I see Laura sitting there, unconscious with a foamy mouth.

I slowly drag her from the toilet and lay her down on her back in the recovery position, and then I shout down the corridor for help. Carefully I tilt her neck so that her chin and throat form a ninety-degree angle. I feel dirty for not having washed my hands, and I'm touching her all over the face. Her mouth is still foaming.

Finally, Sarah, Stuart, and some others come in. Stuart kneels down beside me.

"There is no pulse," I say. "Get me a mask!"

The vomiting has stopped.

"Dr. Parker!" a nurse shouts and throws a CPR pocket mask to me. I begin to compress Laura's chest fifteen times, followed by two breaths through the pocket mask. Stuart, who is now across from me, places two fingers on Laura's carotid pulse.

"Pulse is back, but no breathing," he says.

I administer two more rescue breaths, and suddenly Laura begins to cough up the remains of her vomit.

Everyone's looking down at Laura, apart from me. I

need to get out.

I leave the staff restroom instantly, leaving them to take care of her. My hands are filthy and trembling. I squeeze a handful of sanitizer on my palm. I'm not surprised about the current rash on my face; it means I need to recover my composure. I haven't meditated in a while, either. Have I got hydrocortisone in my office?

As I make my way down the hall, I glance into the waiting room. There, I spot Joe, the sales assistant from Prada.

"Oh, hello!" he says.

He doesn't seem to notice my distress and smiles at me.

"Hi."

"How do you like your shoes?" he says.

I notice his severely injured hand, which has been poorly bandaged. There is beautiful blood seeping through.

"Oh my God, your hand!"

The blood has completely thrown me off focus.

It turned out that Laura was addicted to MAOI, an antidepressant formerly banned in this country. I was right after all about her anxieties, but I didn't approach her or tell anyone about it. I merely saved her life instead.

I pity her. She is in her late thirties and in good shape but has failed to come to terms with her husband's suicide. It has been two days, and she never thanked me for saving her; in fact, she can't even look me in the eye. I'm glad that Julia is willing to deal with the rest. Her role is to play everyone's older sister.

The entire scenario has struck me somewhat, but I'm not sure in what way. It's the whole idea of me touching myself while she was dying on the toilet. People have been praising me for saving two lives in two days.

Who will I save tomorrow? And again, there is no sense of pride or victory, just an expansion of emptiness inside. What am I doing wrong? The whole concept of giving and not receiving is supposed to make one feel better about oneself, but it's not. Am I merely pretending that I'm one of them? I've been spending too much time blending in.

I'm glad to have bumped into Joe, who reminds me that there is a routine in my life—a routine that recovers my equilibrium.

I'm on my way to meet him at Jams for lunch. I took a blood sample of his while disinfecting and stitching his wounded palm. I analyzed the bloodstained band-aids, too, mainly because I like the smell of dried blood. Once it has coagulated, it emits a distinct metallic smell.

I knew that there is a reason why he is bald; why he looks so pale and tired. I remember his poor adrenal functions. They could be the result of vitamin deficiencies or some kind of stress-related mental issue.

He is O negative; this explains why he likes eating meat. It was him who told me about the juicy steaks at Jams.

I found his fingerprints on the sticky part of the band-aids, too. Perhaps I should check whether he has ever been convicted of any crime at all. That'd be another way to explain his baldness and his funny looking ear lobes. I did an autopsy module at Yale, where I worked with people in forensics. They enlightened the class about the nature of criminals. You can ostensibly identify a criminal by the ears. If the ear lobes are attached to the head, rather than hanging down, the person is most likely a criminal.

Joe's earlobes are thin and attached to his head. His blue iris has turned paler than the last time I saw him; I can't decide if he is handsome or not. But he is still a very charming gentleman. He has offered me a ten percent discount on my next visit to Prada.

This restaurant is actually where I first met Bret Easton Ellis, who created my favorite protagonist of all time – Patrick Bateman. I immediately had a crush on

Bret, who was merely nodding at everything I said. But I think I turned him off as soon as I started talking about *The Monk* by Matthew Lewis.

Joe is three minutes late, which means I only have forty-one minutes left for lunch.

"Hi Ellen, sorry I'm late. My boss..."

"It's ok, Joe! Shall we order?"

I look at my watch and then I call for the waiter. I have some examinations to run with patients in less than an hour.

"How's your colleague? Laura?"

"Oh. She's in rehab."

While talking about our jobs, I catch myself playing with my pocketknife. He has such a pale complexion that I want to break his nose just to add some color.

"Your hand looks better," I say.

"Yes, thanks again for looking after me. Stupid glass accidents."

I grab hold of his hand to take a closer look at my nice sutures. His head and heart line have been severely altered.

He smiles weakly; he always smiles weakly. I'm trying to figure out which kind of vegetables would help strengthen the smile. Meat eaters usually have color in their faces, except for Joe. Why? Zinc deficiency?

"Do you eat spinach?" I say.

"Yeah, sometimes. Why?"

"Just wondering."

He orders potato chips with beef and steak sauce. These are salty – which also means *tasty* – for O negative people. He also insists that it's not cooked with onion. If we have a child together, he will probably be O negative since O-types most likely dominate A-types.

Children – I immediately let go of this thought. I shouldn't think that far, ever.

"Ellen?"

"Yeah?"

"Oh, nothing, it's OK."

"Come on, tell me."

Instead of answering me, he plays nervously with his chubby fingers. I enjoy his company; he's counting me back into the rhythm of my routine.

"OK then," I say, "I'll get some salad. Do you want some?"

"Yes, please. But no onions, I'm allergic!"

As I walk over to the salad table, I suddenly notice the Norman look-alike sitting alone by the window. He's wearing sunglasses. The dark shades catch me with the same seductive and demonic smile as last time in Times Square – the hallucinogenic crash scene. Then he holds up his bottle of Asahi beer and mouths:

"Cheers!"

There is a band-aid around his index finger. I remember pricking his finger there. At this moment, all sounds vanish, and there is nothing except the two of us. There is something strange going on inside of me. Something is alluring about the sight of this man that I have never even spoken to.

I hurry back to Joe and put the salad in front of him.

"You OK? I thought you wanted some salad, too?"

"No. I just have the main course!" I say.

I taste Asahi beer in my mouth, although I've never tried it before. I don't even drink beer. For a moment, I believe that this is a dream.

Perhaps it wasn't Norman. Perhaps...

At this very moment, Joe starts choking.

"Oh shit!"

"Help!" Joe gasps.

Ever since Mr. Whitley's successful surgery and his engagement to Bridget, I've realized that happiness is no longer on my wish list; to gain and preserve happiness is to be unaware of its existence. It should all come naturally. Though, right now, I can't think of anything beautiful that is inherently human and leads to enlightenment – neither in behavior nor thought.

Joe is too embarrassed to talk to me. I thought I'd accidentally put onion in his salad, but there was no onion. He had a green cherry tomato stuck in his throat. I leaned his body forward to give him some back blows and then followed up with some chest thrusts until he finally spat the green cherry tomato out. It was covered thickly with saliva.

I saw some evil spirit at that restaurant. And it wasn't Norman.

The work dynamic at the hospital has changed. First, they marveled at me, praised me as a pivotal surgeon at Mount Sinai, and the next, they walked past me as if I were a mannequin wearing an out of fashion Chanel dress.

Or maybe I've been looking too long at people's reflections in the glass door. Somehow the outlines of my face are not clear, and my body shape is somewhat distorted. Why do I look so opaque through the glass, whereas others don't?

One clear figure is walking towards me from behind. There is a smile on Will's face – his winks still express amatory tendencies, but there's no longer a physical spark between us. Sometimes he places his finger on my spine and draws a quick line. I wouldn't be surprised if he still wants me naked on his table. Perhaps I should succumb to his tests. What is there for me to lose?

"Elle, you've been sitting here for a while."

And you're the first to talk to me.

"Drinking coffee."

I stare at the full cup. It's no longer hot.

He sits at the table. The warmth that his body omits feels good.

"Blending in is a hard job, isn't it?" he says.

I look at him, surprised.

"Pardon?"

"Do you remember when I told you we were the same, except that I was the better actor? I was damn right. You suck at blending in."

I shrug at his comment.

"Is that all you can say to cheer me up?"

"I'm just saying that I understand how tough it is to mask one's real face." His eyes emit concern. "Control is not always in our hands. Sometimes we need a break," he says.

Mother and I don't often go to the grocery shop together. She prefers going alone. She was on the phone with someone before; it sounded like she would meet that person. When I asked her where she was going, she said, "Grab a few bits and pieces from the grocery store." Since I have nothing to do, except for school revision, I invited myself along.

She doesn't talk much and seems uncomfortable with me strolling next to her while she is pushing the shopping cart.

So far, there are bread, bananas, and peanut butter in the cart. We still have plenty of that at home.

As we walk down the dairy aisle past the refrigerators, she shivers.

"Have a look 'round at what we might need," she says, passing the shopping cart to me. "I'll grab something from the deli. I won't be long."

I watch her turn into the spice aisle, taking a complete detour to reach the deli section. We have plenty of turkey ham, and cheese – no need to buy more.

The refrigerators are blowing ice-cold air against my legs, which feels nice. I almost want to abandon our cart of unnecessary items, yet I find myself pushing it for her.

I wish Dad was home more.

Approaching the meat section, I come across a small in-store hot dog cart promoting Thuringian sausages. A small line of people has started to build, and it won't take long for the smell of sausages to lure everybody else since it's free for the next half hour. You can have the sausage on its own with mustard, or diced and dunked in curry ketchup, or in half a French baguette. An older woman asks for the baguette. The server cuts off the top and uses a heated metal spike to punch a hole into the baguette. The spike is warming up the inside. Half a minute later, he removes it from the spike and places some condiments inside, followed by the final insertion. The Thuringian sausage slides in smoothly.

Before I get the chance to watch the woman take her first bite, my mother catches me off guard by dropping some ham into the cart.

"I feel like some real ham," she says.

She takes over the cart again and moves toward the cashiers. I don't understand why she chooses a slow-moving line. At the cashier next to us is the woman who has already devoured her French-style hot dog.

"It was so nice and juicy!" she says to her friend, "you should've tried one."

I catch my mother exchanging eye contact with a man, who is three rows down at the other cashier. He is tall, dark-haired, and fair – perhaps of Russian descent or some different Eastern European background.

"Didn't you want anything from here?"

"I thought I did," I say.

"Did you try a free sausage?"

"No."

"They are really nice."

The sight of her tongue cleaning her teeth inside her mouth makes me twitch.

The female cashier is slow; she types in the wrong codes for several fruits and vegetables, leading to voids for which she needs the manager's key. The customer ahead of us is irritated.

"I think Dad won't be home till late tonight," I say.

"You know he's busy."

She has never been good with eye contact unless she is angry and has to make her point clear.

"Can you drop me off at the library on the way back?"

"Sure!" She sounds happy. "You have to do some more revision, right? I love the library. It's a much better place if you need to concentrate."

The tall man with the fair skin collects his shopping and heads towards the exit. I don't even need to look at Mother to know that she is eying the exit door.

More and more people are eating Thuringian sausages now. I have no appetite left for anything, not even dinner.

After dropping me off at the library, I say, "Enjoy your ham."

-

The bobtail has been caught up at Presbyterian and will attend her first heart surgery with me next week as far as I know. And Stuart probably won't even be present this time. We have decided to take turns in heart surgeries.

I'm busy most of the time. The most recent operations have lacked a lot of soul. My patients have been unaccountably dull, uncharismatic, and hollow like the dead. That way, it's impossible to have memorable conversations in the OT. There is no story to unfold in those bodies, and even if there were, it's nothing but meaningless small talk. I am not evolving, and my heart is still in two pieces.

I'm in my office, and for the first time, I feel like a complete stranger that has never stepped a foot into this room before. Like waking up from a ten-year-old dream, I touch my dusty nameplate and wonder who would ever waste time carving my name into metal.

Stuart enters my office. He must have knocked, and I didn't hear it.

"Hello, Stuart."

"Hi, Parker."

As he lowers his eyes, I expect unpleasant news. It is now that I remember him wearing contact lenses on our date and even a little bit of hair gel. How could I not notice?

He smells intriguing.

He tilts his glasses.

"I need to speak to you."

"What is it?"

I want to get down to the point immediately.

At my desk, Stuart picks up the photograph of my father and me. He smiles.

"Your old man looks like me."

"You wish," I say.

He places the photograph right next to his face to prove that Dad and he have the same smile, which I cannot deny this time. Stuart is copying Dad's smile rather well; both of them have smile wrinkles and manly mouths.

"I feel like he and I have a lot in common," he says.

One corner of my mouth rises up into a half-smile.

"Being a good father to a little girl has become a crucial aspect of my life, you know that, Parker? This is why I can relate to that cocky smile of his."

He rests half of his behind on my desk.

"I realized how much it meant to Helen for me to attend her school play. It felt like her performance depended on my presence."

I can't look at him for some reason.

"Why are you telling me this?" I say.

"Because that kind of life is different from the life we live here, Parker. What we have out there is a lot more precious, and we mustn't lose contact with it."

There is nothing out there.

"What are you implying, Stuart?"

"You've not been well. You're overworked."

"What makes you say that?"

"Parker, your holidays have been accumulating since last year."

"So cancel them."

He laughs and says, "That's insane."

Seeing him walk from one side to the other of my office irritates me, but I can smell him better that way. His scent pats my brain like the smell of Dad's coffee.

"As your supervisor, I'm telling you to take a week off. For starters. I might even add another week on top of that."

Has he noticed the rash on my face? I've been putting on more make-up than usual lately.

"You mean it, right?" I say.

"Yes, I need you to rest."

"This is absurd."

"You're tired, Parker."

"I can't afford to be tired, Stuart."

He laughs. "You're drinking more coffee than I do. Mind you, I drink decaf."

"No, you don't!"

"I've always been good to my heart. Have you?"

I'm speechless.

"Parker, you are fully awake during operations, fully focused, but once it's over, you're not just exhausted, you're shattered."

As I walk down the hallway towards the elevator, I avoid exchanging looks with colleagues. Still, everyone is glancing at me – the burned out bloodsucker that has intercourse with accident patients. I take the stairs to the first floor. I can't tell whether I'm walking down into my release or into hell. I walk to the reception where Sarah and Julia are talking.

"I'm off to the Bahamas. See you guys next week."

"Ellen!" says Sarah.

She follows me out of the hospital.

"Are you all right? You're not really going away, are you?"

"If it's not the core of a heart that I'm going to, then I guess I'm not going anywhere," I say, hurrying towards the subway.

"Please wait up. I have to tell you something," she says.

"If it's about Jay, no hard feelings."

"Are you sure?"

She has finally stopped following me.

"I'll call you!" she shouts.

I've spent the rest of the day at home – unable to meditate, unable to relax the uptight shoulders. My beeper lies nearby, quiet.

The landscape of Connecticut shoots into my head. It would only be fair to go home for my father. It's strange to believe that home has made and broken me at the same time, whereas New York has fixed and built me. If all American dreams were based in New York, I would write a book about it. At least I am more optimistic than John Dos Passos. Back in Connecticut, when I was younger, I was obsessed with the big city as portrayed in films and literature, which were about finding fulfillment. But I never knew my pursuits until later, when they emerged from biology books.

And now I realize that all I want is peace of mind.

I was attracted to the city because my super-ego was hungry for perfection. With my talents and qualifications, I knew that the city would feed my needs. That's only because I know my way around.

But now...

Something strange is happening to me. I hear my dad pronouncing the term "recluse" in my head. Ever since my career began, I've denied my true self in public only to bear other people's burdens, which they put in my hands. Then again, I want their physical burden. Sometimes I wonder what their burden would feel like on me, on my body, *inside* my body.

How did they feel during intercourse? For Bruce, it must have been like being blindfolded. How would Norman feel having a convulsion during sex?

All my life, I've always known what I wanted. I would like to believe that I still do, except that I am now unsure about where my search is headed. Peace of mind doesn't happen within a snap. I saved a heart, and I slept with a brain surgeon. What's next?

The past seems to be catching up and putting my life in a state of disorder. The disrepair is now stretching beyond my ability to fix it.

I wonder what Dr. Dick went through and which segment of his cerebral artery was to blame for the stroke. I would like to go to Connecticut to see him. New Haven brings back good memories, unlike Cheshire Village, where my parents are.

Sarah calls me in the evening. Whenever I see her face in my head, I picture her at a Californian pool party juxtaposed with a picture of myself on the catwalk in Italy.

"Hi Ellen, what are you doing?"

"Putting my thoughts in order," I say. In actuality, I am sorting through the expiry dates on my hemp milk.

"I'm calling to make sure you're OK. I hardly ever get a chance to talk to you at work. Are you all right?"

"Yeah. How is Jay?"

"He's fine. Strong bones."

As a matter of fact, Jay makes love like a virgin. His innocence in bed was unbearable.

"Good."

"Hey, I know you two had relations," she says.

"Why does it matter?"

"Listen, do you want to come out?"

I imagine myself on the dance floor, picturing men who will not leave me alone during a good song, laying their dirty paws on my behind and swinging me towards their groin.

"Sure. Why not."

"Great! Oh, by the way, Stuey said you should turn your pager off because no one will be beeping you for a week."

This is going to be a big challenge, as we are hardly going out as friends. I've never really experienced New Yorker nightlife before. I barely even went partying at Yale.

I plan on wearing my wine-red Prada dress, which is suitable for occasions like this. It's a sleeveless dress with a V-neckline, high side slits, lined interior, and equipped with a concealed zip fly closure at the back.

Nowadays, men don't look at women's clothing. They look at eyes, sometimes even hair, and get turned on by the way women smell.

While styling my hair, I notice that the woman in the mirror has aged.

I'm overdue for some meditation sessions and breathing exercises.

Sarah and I have arranged to meet at the City Music Hall, from where we will head to the clubs. I see her in a black Armani dress, accompanied by a young, handsome man. I see myself as Napoleon in 1815 during his surrender. She never mentioned bringing a date.

"Ellen! You look gorgeous!"

"Thanks."

Black is used to allure, whereas red defines sin.

I smile at the young man, but his eyes are glued to my body. He is about six foot three and has a crew cut making him look tough, but his big brown eyes convey something else.

"This is Zach."

"Hello," he says.

"He just saved me from a thief! Some asshole tried to steal my purse and escape!"

I look impressed, but I also smell something foul. Could she have brought him along as a date to make me look bad? She is holding her purse tightly against her chest now.

"I thought in return we could invite him to come along."

"Sure."

For a casual guy that saves women from thieves, Zach is dressed rather formally: black pleated trousers with a hint of silk, leather shoes, and a white Tommy Hilfiger shirt. Either he is timid, or he prefers to let Sarah do all the talking.

"Right, guys! I feel like dancing!"

"*Dancing?*" Zach blurts in astonishment.

Sarah and I stare at him, stupefied. I can tell by the look of Sarah's eyes that her reaction is genuine.

"Yeah, where did you think we were going?" she says.

"I've no idea. For a beer or something."

"Of course. To a club. Where we can *dance*."

Zach hesitates. "Um, I don't think so!" he says.

"What's the matter with you?"

"Are you twenty-one, Zach?" I say.

"Yes."

"So what's the problem? You got no ID on you?"

Sarah seems no longer fond of his presence, but this is what she gets for inviting him along in the first place.

"It's because it's a *dance* club."

"Honey, maybe you should go home," she says.

"But I thought we were hanging out!"

"Didn't I just invite you along?"

"Hey kids, stop it already!" I say.

I turn to Zach, looking him in the eye.

"Well, young man. Why don't you want to come for a dance?"

He throws an anxious glance at Sarah and then looks at me again. His face approaches mine as he whispers, "I'm scared of dancing."

"What?"

"I've got chorophobia."

I immediately turn to Sarah: "OK, how about you go first, and I'll catch up?"

"What?"

"I won't be long. I'll talk to Zach. I'll give you a call!"

"Ellen!"

We are walking down W Fiftieth Street, past Starbucks and other little shops. I know that Sarah won't have a problem going on her own; she will find some company in the club.

Zach and I aren't talking. I'm wondering how to crack his big shell knowing his problem – one of the oddest I've ever encountered. I'm familiar with all sorts of phobias.

"So, Zach...where is your friend?"

His face turns white as he looks at me.

"What friend?"

"Come on. The one who tried to steal Sarah's purse? You can tell me."

He hesitates. His eyes reveal uncertainty like a child scared of revealing his imaginary friend to his parents.

"He's called Fred. He's gone home because I got a date."

"Hey, didn't you say you wanted a drink?"

I don't believe that he is twenty-one, so I buy him a

coke from a fast food place, and we carry on walking down W Fiftieth Street toward Fifth Avenue. I notice security guards sneering at Zach, but he doesn't seem to pay attention to them.

"Are you lonely, or do you just want to screw someone?" I say.

"Excuse me?"

I always thought that the youth nowadays were brutally honest, but I guess I'm wrong, or I'm probably dealing with the most peculiar kid in New York.

I step in front of him, bring my face close to his.

"Answer me truthfully, buddy!"

"Screw...someone," he mumbles, eyes fixed on my lips.

To kiss him would be like kissing a spring blossom; there is over ten years difference between us.

"Do you feel old?" he says.

"Excuse me?"

"Oh, nothing."

"Wait a minute, what did Sarah tell you?"

His mouth is open, but he utters nothing.

"Hey, you've obviously realized that I am *not* stupid, tell me!"

"She said you need someone to pump you up."

I keep quiet for a while, momentarily regretting choosing this stroll.

I actually think that he looks more like sixteen or

seventeen.

"Well, then! Let's pretend you are my patient and let's have a little chat about your fear."

"Are you a doctor?"

"I said, let's *pretend*!" I catch my breath. "Chorophobia, is it?"

"Yeah. It's quite worrying when it comes to socializing."

He drinks his coke with big gulps.

I've never noticed how many people go shopping late in the evening. J. Crew and Banana Republic are full of people browsing. On Fifth Avenue, we turn right towards Rockefeller Centre.

"Tell me the story."

"Well, it's my mother's fault."

In all seriousness, the last thing I need is someone telling me about their mother. I'd shut him up if it weren't already feeding my interest.

"She used to be a dancer... a terrible dancer. She lost at every dance competition. She would make me watch her practice all day long. Even at night. She would force me to be her partner sometimes, and I would freeze."

"Why was she so bad when she used to practice so much?"

"Some people aren't made for dancing, you know. Just like you're not made to become a doctor sort of thing."

I play with the pocketknife in my purse.

"And besides," he says, "she had no rhythm, and she was in her forties when she'd started."

"She must've had a really dull life before that..."

His eyes are fixed on the can.

"Then she became nocturnal and only danced at night. She kept me awake. Imagine a lady in white with long black hair and no expression on her face. She was a zombie, a dancing zombie."

What a preposterous night.

"Do you suffer from nightmares?" I say.

He throws the empty can in the air and kicks it across the street.

"Sometimes."

"Tell me?"

"No."

Zach's posture has become more rigid now, and his eyes have turned into slits.

"Why? I'm sure your dreams aren't as crazy as mine..."

"You want a bet?" he says.

"Why not?"

"You start!"

I take a deep breath.

"Ever dreamt about an ax slashing you between your legs and finding it pleasant?"

He gulps.

"And also, ever dreamt about carrying a bag full of men's testicles, which you throw onto your bed to sleep on because it feels like a waterbed?"

He drops his jaw.

"Wow," he says. "Are you a murderer?"

"What?"

He keeps quiet, and I see a confidence in his eyes that conveys psychosis.

"Come on, you're not just gorgeous. We have things in common."

He kisses me violently, but I push him away.

"What are you doing?"

"I'm sorry," he says, "but you look like a model, and I've always wanted to screw one."

Next, I find myself pressing my body hard against his; I kiss him then bite into his lip.

"Ouch!"

He pushes me back.

"What are you *doing*?" he says.

"Nothing."

He grins ominously at me as he licks the blood from the corner of his mouth.

"I get it."

He drags me into an alleyway and sucks on my lips again, more violently; he squeezes both of my breasts – licking his way down to my neck and collarbone.

A sudden image of his dancing zombie mother shoots into my head.

"You're not going any further than this!"

"But you're enjoying it, aren't you?"

He wipes the blood from his lips, whereas I suck the rest from between my teeth. He tastes a tad too sweet for me.

The probability of having intercourse is low and undoubtedly absurd. Also, every time I close my eyes, I see dancing zombies. What use is his blood on my lips when I'm in the street with no microscope? I only have a pipette but no lab-on-a-chip. By no means will I invite this stranger to my place. I should've realized that he's been talking about his mother in the past tense.

"Come on, I saw the way you looked at me earlier," he says.

"Don't be a fool, Zach!"

He grabs hold of my arms tightly and presses me hard against the brick wall.

"I won't let you go."

I should be concerned, but for some reason, I am not. I grin at him, yielding to his sloppy kisses. He rubs his penis against my body, and I find my hips responding.

The kisses have stopped.

"What are you doing?"

I put my arms around him so that I can move him

along with me to an imaginary beat.

"Get off me!"

In my head, I'm dancing to some Industrial beat without hearing the actual tune.

"Stop it!"

His eyes are wide open, and I notice a nervous twitch and an upcoming panic attack. I try to think of a more upbeat song and start dancing to Depeche Mode's *Personal Jesus*. I move my bottom back and forth steadily, holding both arms up in the air. He releases himself from me. I don't dance often, but if I do, I lose myself entirely – eyes closed and body as light and transparent as that of a jellyfish. I'd initially planned to steal Sarah's show on the dance floor with this move.

The moment I stop to look at Zach's face, he has disappeared.

I can't get hold of Sarah on the phone, so I head back home. I'm never concerned about walking in the dark on my own, but since that peculiar incident with Zach, I'm not too sure what might await me there. I stroll past the Louis Vuitton shop – the brand that has always attracted Asian tourists.

Now walking on Fifth Avenue again, I see a gentleman coming out from the Rockefeller Center. He bears a huge resemblance to Norman. His suit looks suspiciously like Armani.

What is he up to?

If I don't follow him now, I will never know who he really is. Maybe he's gone back to cocaine and is now catching some fresh air, unless he has assigned himself some dirty duties. My heart is pounding. I want to confront that person – no matter what. Suddenly he cuts into a blind alley, so I begin to run.

It is so dark at first that I trip over a filthy bum sitting there against the wall with his legs spread out. He screams and blatantly pours his cold coffee onto my Prada outfit.

"Fuck!" I say.

Next, I find myself laying into him, hitting him several times on the shoulder until he starts to cry, "Please have mercy!"

"Son of a bitch."

Sister Fury grabs hold of me again. The last time I saw her must have been when I was a teenager suffering from anger outbreaks. My former pediatrician used to pin it down on a mental disorder, whereas now, as I look back to those days, I call it a psychological crisis due to my problem of dealing with my grown-up emotions at the age of thirteen. Unlike troubled teens, I knew exactly how I was feeling. I just had no one that listened to me.

The veins are throbbing in my head. I forget where I am.

The crying sound of the bum drags me back into reality. His hair and beard are long and disheveled, not to mention dirty; his body is emaciated, skeletal. I hit him like he was a person from the past – my pediatrician. I remember hitting her in the head when she tried to inject me with tranquilizers. Her medical assistants had to press me down. They didn't believe me that I was heartbroken; they thought I had a school crush or a nightmare.

The bum is too scared to look me in the face now.

A sudden eerie emotion floods through me, and my hands start to tremble. This man must be in his late fifties. The smell of urine and sweat begin to penetrate my brain.

"I didn't do anything, I didn't do anything," he repeats. He sounds like a baby that has wet itself, like a hungry, sick kitten – the heart frequency weak – very weak. Now I smell the coffee.

"I'm sorry."

I throw a fifty-dollar note at him to stop the whining. I taste blood as I lick my lower lip. I must've bitten myself. After using my hand sanitizer, I grab my phone and dial Sarah's number.

"Where are you? I'm coming."

CHAPTER ELEVEN

Despite my lack of experience of New York nightlife, I think it might not be a bad idea to give the night another shot. Surgeons usually only go to bed before midnight (if lucky) and wake up at 5 a.m. to start work or at least prepare for work.

Before I meet Sarah at the rooftop bar, 230, I use my pocketknife to tear the lower part of my dress off to get rid of the coffee stain.

It takes a while to reach the top, and you have to line up at the elevator. Once you're there, you wonder if you've entered some kind of a fancy outdoor restaurant. It's beautiful. You're on top of a building whose height is almost that of a standard New York skyscraper.

At the rooftop garden entrance, I find many people drinking champagne, socializing like it's the end of the world.

Although I don't fit in here, my appearance says I belong. I look like these people, though, we may not think the same way. Most of them are probably Wall Street people.

The soft beat ambient music in the background smooths out all the unbearable voices in the air.

"Ellen!"

Sarah grabs my shoulders from behind. Why does she act like we're friends?

"Finally! What did you do to the boy?"

"He's a kid. I sent him home."

"Well done!" she says, "Hey, your colleague is here."

"My...who?"

She leads me to the garden's West Deck, where I see Miss Bobtail chatting to some smartly dressed men. Judging by her casual body language in their presence, I can tell that she and the men already know each other. She glimpsed at me fleetingly.

"Ah! Look who's here!"

"She finally made it," Sarah says.

These are the last people in the world that I want to tangle with. They are all surgeons! Their ingenuity is chiseled into their doctor's hands.

The bobtail stares at the lower part of my dress.

"Either your dress was made this way, or you've been in a fight with a tramp!"

Some of the men laugh, probably at her dialect, except for a handsome one who says, "Come on,

Immy, she looks stunning. Are you going to introduce us or what?"

She raises an eyebrow and smiles.

"Well, she's actually *my* friend," Sarah interrupts, "Ellen, can I introduce you to the perfusionists Pete, Harry, Si, and...you're not a perfusionist." She points at the handsome one with the curls.

"I'm Garrett, the thoracic surgeon," he says and reaches his hand out to shake mine.

Sarah and I take a seat while the bobtail continues her scrutiny of me.

"Can I get you something?" Garrett says and already raises his behind to fetch me a glass. I smile at him.

"Red wine, please. That would be terrific. Thank you."

Sarah nudges me slightly with her elbow, suggesting that I should ask him to get two glasses.

"Congratulations by the way," says the bobtail. "She's now officially a heart surgeon."

"Oh, you must be the one that Stu is training," says Si.

My face hurts from smiling; the flesh on my cheekbones is heavy and pressing against my eyeballs.

"Stuey's the best," says Sarah, "better than the ones you have at Presbyterian!"

For a second, there is laughter, and then Garrett arrives with my glass of wine.

"I'm sorry I couldn't assist you at your first responsible surgery," Bobtail says. "As you may know, we have a lot more heart surgeries at Presbyterian, and we lack perfusionists despite these wonderful men here."

The perfusionists begin to cheer.

"I'm sorry I was on holiday, Immy," says Harry.

"Well, luckily Alex helped out," I say. "He did a brilliant job as always."

"I heard your patient proposed to his girlfriend after the surgery."

"He did."

Two of the perfusionists laugh.

"Goodness, that's cheesy," says Pete.

"It's romantic!" Sarah blurts out.

While Sarah and the perfusionists delve into the topic of what's romantic and what's not, Garrett moves closer to me.

"To be honest, I didn't think that you were a surgeon when you entered the garden with Sarah. I thought you were a West Coast friend of hers," he says.

His eyes sparkle as if he has just dug some gold.

"I'm from Connecticut."

I can't explain the sound of pride in my voice.

"I see! Interesting."

"Why?"

"I don't know. Just not what I'd have expected."

"I've never been to California," I say.

"It's like saying you've never been to Italy."

"Well, I have. I did modeling there."

His eyes brighten up. Si and Harry overhear the term "modeling" and look over at me.

"Who was a model?"

"Ellen," Garrett says. "Wow, I can't believe that we have a modeling heart surgeon among us. This is astonishing."

I look at the bobtail whose lips widen into a straight-line signaling frustration. Until this moment, she was telling Pete, Si, and Harry about how she had recently tackled a severe hypoperfusion.

"There were rumors about that, actually," Sarah says.

"Show us a walk!" Si says.

This is the last thing I need. All I want is to sit and marvel at the beautiful flowers. It's as if Ophelia had spent years creating this garden of escapism. She knew what the world out there was like. But these flowers reflect life. If you find them beautiful, you will automatically see some beauty in life.

"Leave her alone, guys. This is a roof, not a runway," Sarah says.

"Which designer did you model for?" says Miss Bobtail.

I open my purse and then throw the tainted piece of fabric on the table. With the dirty brown color fused with the red, you can still tell it's from my dress.

"Ugh, it stinks!" she says.

Si reaches out for it. As a doctor, you would not express disgust at any kind of smell. The color of that piece of cloth is the color of dried blood, which smells like coffee.

Si finds the inside label and pronounces: "Prada!"

"I don't believe you," the bobtail says and finishes her champagne.

"Come on, Immy! Look at her, would you believe that she is a surgeon?" Garrett asks in my defense.

"Maybe she isn't, and she's dreaming this conversation," she says.

"Jealousy alert," Harry mumbles into his palm, making others laugh.

"Hey!" Miss Bobtail says, "I mean it. You can't be both. You're either one or the other – a doctor or a supermodel. But if you're a doctor, you have to be one hundred percent committed. You are born to be one, or you're not!"

I look at her earnestly. Her words take my breath away. Maybe it *is* a dream, and my deepest desires are floating to the surface, showing me a life that I could have had. There is always a choice, and I made mine years ago.

"You are right, Imogen," I say. "I lied. I didn't model; I was offered it, and I declined."

She rolls her eyes and shakes her head.

"You are fucked up," she says and gets up from her seat.

I think about what Will has taught me about humor and honesty and how you can combine them successfully with one another. I guess I still don't have the hang of it, but at least I'm honest. She walks away from the group.

"Don't worry about her. She'll calm down," Garrett says.

I didn't realize that she was as dedicated to medicine as I am. Our interest in medicine is measured in terms of how much we value our job and the effort we put into it. We show confidence in our actions.

In my life, I opted for medicine, which was the right decision. It was the only way to grow as a person. A modeling career would never mend my broken heart, and I wouldn't be any different from a crack whore sleeping with her photographer, agent, or designer. Though in the end, you may find many depressed and disoriented people in other industries as well. We all get sucked into a downward spiral in one way or another.

In our job, despite the pressure involved, we look at the benefits that we give to our patients. What we get in return are self-validation and even acceptance. Life and death are in our hands. But there is more to it. Not only do we receive a patient's gratitude, but they become part of our developmental process as surgeons, which makes us who we are.

The Bobtail knows.

"Ellen? Ellen?"

Sarah's voice echoes in my ears.

"Yes?"

"She is not worth it."

"Bear with me a second," I say and rise from my seat.

I'm sure I saw her walk towards the north side of the roof. I fight my way through the chattering crowd, feeling each word jolt through my mid-ear.

It's late. I'd better go home soon.

As I reach the northern part of the garden, I lean against the railing, but she is nowhere to be found. On my right, I notice a marked-off area with a small sign saying: "Construction Site. Please steer clear."

I walk past the forbidden part of the garden, through the canopy of a low-hanging palm tree in a pot, and then turn right into a corner where I see Imogen resting on a wooden beach chair. She has loosened up her bobtail – her brunette hair now hanging down. Between her fingers, she holds a cigarette.

"Are you lost?"

I stare at a pot filled with earth, wondering what seeds have been planted underneath. Around us are more earth-filled pots and some sprouting plants. This garden is like a newborn child.

"No," I say.

There is a long break. Only the laughter from around the back disturbs the awkward silence. I can smell the last summer breeze. Fall is just around the corner.

"My parents sacrificed a lot for me," she says, "without them, I wouldn't have made it to where I am now."

There is something American within her British accent now.

"But like you," she says, "I fantasized about other dream jobs."

"Like what?"

She smiles.

"I wanted to be Audrey from Twin Peaks."

We giggle.

"Have a rich dad and fall in love with an intelligent FBI agent. But that was twenty years ago. Do you regret being where you are now?"

"No," I say.

"Good. You know, I made my parents happy pensioners. That's worth the effort, right?"

"Sure."

She lets go of the cigarette bud and gently steps on it.

"What are your parents like?" she says.

It's on the tip of my tongue to tell her about my dad's successful career as a physician.

"Very supportive."

She nods.

"It makes you feel bad sucking your parents' bank accounts dry at first. I think about that sometimes during surgery. I watch how the reservoir fills with blood. The responsibility to keep it oxygenated keeps me going. The idea of the patient trusting me with his blood…"

Her right hand rolls into a fist. The fist rests peacefully on her chest. I sense an emotional beat, a heart that only beats for the ones she loves.

She looks at me.

"Does it sound bad when I say I consider the blood mine once it's in the tank?"

I shake my head.

"Well, at least for a while," she continues. "But I know that I have to return it at some point. All you do is borrow happiness, take care of it, and hand it back."

Throughout my life, I have always felt some kind of paralysis just from thinking differently from others, but we're all the same – the other may just be a better actor than I am. I understand what Will meant about always be who you are. He uses honesty and humor to mask his indifference, whereas Imogen uses metaphors to hide her guilt and selfishness.

It's only natural.

Her eyes, which, in the past, have always undermined my potential as a surgeon, now seem kind.

"I trust Stuart's skills," she says. "He is the best heart surgeon in New York."

"I know."

It feels like being back in High School where I attempted to make my first friend, but I will not succeed.

"Stu is like a brother to me," she says. "I'm sorry I doubted you."

"It's OK."

She rises from the beach chair and comes towards me. I assume that she wants to return to the others, and I step aside. To my surprise, she halts in front of me and fixes her eyes on my face.

"Why do you hate women?"

"What?"

"You despise them," she says.

"It's not true."

Her eyes are resting on my lips. Our faces are almost touching.

"You like to think they don't like you," she says, "so you hate them."

Her Britishness has returned.

For the next hour, I tell Imogen about Mr. Whitley's surgery. Sarah has been dealing exhaustively with the perfusionists, who have ceased to show interest in her pathology skills. She shoots me several looks indicating boredom and neglect. Garrett listens to my OP stories as if hoping that I'll switch back to talking about modeling. He still doesn't see me as a surgeon.

We head towards the elevators at 1 a.m. Imogen is with her tipsy fellow perfusionists, messing around with drunken words, giggling.

Garrett has taken his chance to walk with me, leaving Sarah behind us, all alone.

"So, Ellen, where are you off to next? Fancy a cocktail?" he says.

I smile at him, wondering what his blood tastes like and how he would suck the air from my lungs.

"I'm sorry, Garrett."

"No prob," he says, "I'm free tomorrow."

I shake my head.

"I'm busy, and besides…"

I wait for Sarah to catch up with us. Her eyes express confusion as she looks at us.

"It was supposed to be mine and Sarah's night out."

Together in the cab, Sarah still hasn't cheered up. Perhaps she regrets asking me along.

"Thanks for taking me out," I say.

It takes her a while to answer. The driver stops at the traffic light.

"I've always had this feeling that you don't like me," she says.

Although I'm staring straight ahead, I can tell from the corner of my eye that she is looking at me, waiting for a response.

"Maybe it's because I don't like anyone."

"But you seem to like Imogen."

I giggle. I don't understand why it's important to her that I like her. I've had relations with her boyfriend. Other women would stay away from me.

"She and I just terminated a war," I say.

"Really? What was that about?"

This is the Sarah I know – inquisitive, nosey, like your little sister.

"I don't want to talk about it."

Judging by her irregular breaths, I know that she has something significant to share, but she keeps her mouth shut.

After a while, she says: "I didn't really fit in tonight with my pathology background. For them, I was just a lab girl."

"And I was the model. Come on, why do you care about what they think?"

"You're right, I guess."

We're on Park Avenue now; I'm close to home, close to my bed. It's time to get rid of this dress.

"You love your job," I tell her.

"Yes, I do. Too much."

I look at her.

"I love my job, too. There's nothing wrong with that."

"You don't understand," she says, lowering her head.

"What do you mean?"

She fidgets with her hands like your annoying little sister after misbehaving.

"I collect the specimens, you know – the benign ones. I have a couple of malignant ones, too."

"Why do you keep them?"

"Because there's not enough good in the world."

I realize that my entire body has shifted in her direction – my eyes examine this brand-new person that I've never really known. All of a sudden, Sarah mirrors the same quality that I saw in Imogen.

"So, you collect benign specimens, like tissue samples?"

"Yes," she sobs. "Sometimes, when I feel depressed, I even cook them."

My jaw drops.

"And I eat them!" she says, sobbing.

The driver looks into the rear-view mirror but luckily hasn't been following the entire conversation.

I wonder how much of Scott's benign thyroid lobe she has consumed.

*

During a late-morning jog, I find my feet running down Fifth Ave towards the hospital. Standing across the road, I see returning patients and other guests coming in and out, as well as fellow employees. I have disguised myself well behind my Prada shades and Huskies hat.

I stretch my hamstrings and pick my workout playlist.

I see Sarah leaving the hospital with Jay – hand in hand.

As they cross the road, I go behind the bench and retie my shoes. I hold the loop of my shoelace and feel a little cramp in my palm. I can't remember how to tie my shoes.

Someone casts a shadow over my body. The smile of a very familiar man drags me back into reality. I take off my shades and smile back.

"Mr. Whitley."

He offers me his hand. A sudden rush of warmth spreads through my body. I feel how my own heartbeat jumps into the same rhythm as his.

"Miss Parker! *Dr*. Parker! What a surprise."

He carefully pats the surface of the bench with his hand, signaling for me to sit down. "No, no, Doc, your foot!"

I place my foot on the bench. Mr. Whitley ties my shoes like my father used to when I was three or four. No one has tied my shoes ever since.

"How are you?" I say.

"Oh, splendid, thanks very much! You're so kind."

He always expresses more gratitude than I can take. Patients like him overestimate my actions. However, it's good to see him happy and in such good shape.

"So, you've come for your weekly check-up?"

"According to Dr. McCormick, I can come every fortnight, but Bridget insists I come every week, you know."

"She must care a lot."

"I keep telling her that the fairy has healed me, so there's no need."

I smile.

"I don't think she'd like hearing that on a regular basis. You'd better not talk about me so much in her presence."

He looks older than I remember: his hands are still dry and reddened, his dainty mouth kissable, and his bright eyes keep him young and vigorous.

"Listen," I say, "I haven't had lunch yet. Do you want to join me before you go in there?"

"Oh, Miss Parker, I would love to, but I can't."

Stuart comes to my mind, the wine, the fish talk, my green evening dress, and the black beauty that I've never seen. If two men have closed a pact, there's no way of re-opening the sacred deal.

"I'll only ask you once," I smile.

"Dr. McCormick says you're on vacation, but I'm happy to see you here."

"Please don't tell him you've seen me today, OK?"

"My lips are sealed, dear."

"Thank you."

Just before we part, he says: "He is the only man who deserves someone as wonderful as you, Miss Parker. And I wouldn't dare betray a friend like him!"

I have no idea what he is talking about, so I feign an understanding smile that possibly mimics anguish.

He waves goodbye before he crosses the street. I know that I won't see him again, and it saddens me.

I put my music back on. The song *One Caress* fills my ears.

An inner voice tells me to go for a long run around Central Park and Theodore Roosevelt Park.

I obey that voice.

There is not much to do when you live in a dull place like Cheshire Village. Mother isn't home, and Dad is at work, but Mother says I'm old enough to look after myself, whereas Dad says I'm not. In other countries, children work when they are twelve, and some even work when they are ten. I am in between, so I'm not sure what I'm supposed to do. Mother says I have no right to complain, but I never complain. I like spending time alone. I can secretly play with her tampons. She says I'm not old enough to use them, and they could ruin and hurt me. I guess I'm old enough to at least understand that she is talking bullshit. I don't like sanitary towels because you feel dirty underneath, and I am not dirty. I insert an ordinary tampon into my vagina and another small one up my bum. I want to know what it's like inserting a suppository by myself. A year ago, whenever I had a fever, Mother would take me directly to Dr. Hymen, behind Dad's back. I hated it. Dr. Hymen is a witch and hates me, but I hate her more.

I'm beginning to panic. I can't get the tampon out of my behind, and it has gone tight. I'm scared of tearing the string when I pull. It's itchy. I sit on the toilet, waiting for my behind to loosen. It's not happening. Perhaps I should try to squat.

I suddenly hear the doorbell. I jump down from the toilet and run towards the front door. Then I remember Mother saying that I shouldn't answer the door. I should pretend not to be in. But I've been running towards the door so loudly that the person has surely heard my approaching steps.

"Hello? This is George from next door. I have a couple of your letters delivered to me again."

I hesitate at first, and then he says, "Ellen? Little Ellen? Are you there? Your mom's car isn't here, so I'm guessing she's left you on your own again."

I still hesitate.

"That's not nice, is it? I can keep you company if you want?"

My hand is on the handle. I slowly open the door and see George, who is over six feet tall. I stare at his face, and then I move the door back until he can see me entirely. There is a sudden change of expression on his face as if there is something wrong with me. I notice that I have no panties on. My long shirt only just covers my bottom. My pair of leggings is in my room.

I'm blushing, trying to stretch my long shirt downward. I feel the strings of my tampons brushing against my legs. George quickly nudges me into my house and closes the door behind him.

On his knees now, he says, "Ellen, are you all right?"

I utter no words. He looks concerned. We are currently the same heigh, but he isn't looking me in the face; he is looking at my body.

I feel his hands caressing my arms. He is moving up my neck and face and slowly slides them back down to my hips. Two of his fingers are resting between my legs. He draws my legs back a little so that he can get hold of both strings. He pulls one tampon out of me; it's tainted with some blood.

I feel embarrassed.

There is also something happening inside his trousers. I have seen something like that before when watching the boys in my school.

I don't know how, but he manages to pull the other tampon out, too. We are breathing in the scent of my blood and my butt.

I am even more embarrassed now.

Before I have the chance to register what is happening, he has already laid me down on the floor, spread both of my legs open, and entered me with his tongue.

The parquet floor is cold. I imagine a bat licking a cow's wound.

I sigh and cry at the same time. His stubble is tickling my soft and sensitive skin. Both of his hands have rested on my chest.

I am wet below; it could be juice, it could also be blood or his saliva. He seems to like it. His tongue is moving fast, and I hear licking and sucking noises.

The next I feel is something large and hard crushing into me.

From upside down, I glance at the bamboo stick sword, which is hanging over the electric fireplace in the living room. My mouth is wide open – I try to scream, but he covers it with his palm. Both my hands are grabbing hold of his big arms.

"Oh, Ellen...sweet Ellen."

Sweat pearls have accumulated at the sides of his head.

I feel nothing down there after the sting.

I hear terrible thrusting noises. I watch him make these funny up and down movements while his big body is over mine.

It smells like blood, metallic blood. I think of rusty doorknobs, tools, and chains. His breath smells like cherry, but it could be wine.

I look him in the face again, but he isn't looking back at me. It's the first time I ever been so close to someone, and they're not paying attention to me when I need them. I need him because I feel scared. My grip on his arms has loosened up. I carefully press my hand against his chest and feel his pounding heart against my palm. His warm cherry breath is tickling my ear, his eyes fixed to the ground, as if deep in thought, but he is not looking at me.

He's gone, and I'm wiping the floor. There is so much blood, and I won't stop bleeding onto the floor. It hurts when I try to insert a new tampon, and it hurts when I move my inner thighs the wrong way. I step into the garden and watch the blood run down my thighs. I'm scared, and I don't know what to do. My mother walks out into the garden and stares at me in disgust.

*

I have been running the six-mile route counterclockwise starting from the hospital – past Harlem Hill and the Jacky Kennedy reservoir. Now I find myself at the Columbus Circle, which means I'm about to leave the runner's loop.

I'm losing my focus. Also, my watch has stopped ticking since five minutes to twelve. I look up at the town clock. It has stopped too.

There is an eerie silence. The car engines are off; the entire city has come to a halt.

A blockage of cars in the circle stops everyone from moving. And all the cars upfront on East Fifty-ninth Street are lined up in front of red traffic lights that are not turning green.

I take off my sunglasses to observe people in their cars and people lining up at food vendors. The sun and some drops of sweat blur my vision for a few seconds.

I take a deep breath through my nose, inhaling the weak scent of my aloe vera deodorant. Usually I would smell hot dogs and roasted peanuts in this area, but I smell nothing but myself.

As my vision recovers, I see how they are all staring at me resentfully without blinking. I perceive a thousand eyes.

If only people were cells.

I run down East Fifty-ninth Street until I reach Madison Avenue and take a left.

The city is made of endless veins like a functioning human body. This is why this city never sleeps. The human body never sleeps.

Here I find the same thing as before – motionless cars, dark gazing eyes.

Just as I reach the Michael Kors shop, I see blood washing down the entire avenue, coloring the street with a metallic red. The smell makes me hungry.

As it hits my feet, I look up to see a naked replica of me crucified against the building next to the Michael Kors shop. The crown of thorns has pricked numerous wounds around the head, and the flowing blood has dyed the hair slightly ginger. My replica looks tortured and exhausted, almost dead. Its eyes are closed.

The flowing blood on the street is coloring the soles of my sneakers crimson.

From the top of the building comes a figure crawling on all fours like a spider; it is the Norman look-alike. He approaches my replica and scrutinizes it. As his head moves closer, he places his tongue on its shoulder and licks his way along the clavicle and down my replica's left breast.

I taste blood on my tongue.

He punches his fist into my replica's chest, making it cry in agony. I touch my own chest, gasping. The green eyes fade into gray as the Norman look-alike rips out its heart.

Aren't we lifeless objects without our hearts?

He rubs the throbbing heart against his face, covering half his cheek with blood. At the same time, he is tongue-kissing the pulmonary artery.

I observe my replica come back to life. It raises its head and stares right at me with its gray eyes.

Then the Norman look-alike raises his eyes and looks at me too.

"Look."

Both their lips move, but I hear only Norman's voice.

"Your heart is fine, but you are not. She is not."

He throws the heart at my feet into the flowing blood. Its rate equals my own.

But it can't be.

No.

I turn around and begin to run.

I head for Park Avenue, where I believe it's only two turns away from my apartment.

My head is spinning. My hands are shaking.

"You're just running away..." Norman's voice whispers.

I must have entered a maze. I can't find my apartment. This area appears so familiar and is yet so mystifying and illusory that even my instincts fail me.

I turn back to Fifty-Ninth Street and then right onto Lexington Avenue. After a few more turns, I finally reach my apartment.

Out of breath, I notice a black motorbike parked in the drive. Someone puts his hand on my shoulder.

"It's only me!"

Stuart.

My breathing is heavy, and I have a stitch in my side.

"Are you all right, Parker? Are you being chased?"

The concern in his eyes indicates the warmth that I have seen before in my father's and Dr. Dick's eyes.

There was so much blood.

"I went for a run."

I peer through the entrance door and see on the wall that it's almost five o'clock. How have I been running for so long?

"You look exhausted, Parks."

I wonder how much of my make-up has smeared, or is it my ponytail or the sweat? There is no blood on my body or shoes.

"There is a little rash on your skin," he says, pointing at a spot in my face.

I cover my face up immediately with a piece of tissue and head towards the door.

"Allergy, hay fever...nothing serious."

I turn towards his motorbike to divert his gaze.

"That's the black beauty?"

He smiles.

"Yep. It's a Honda CB. Looks good next to your Civic, doesn't it?"

I have a Honda Civic Sedan, which I hardly ever drive. I sometimes forget that I have a car. It's almost due for its annual checkup.

"Listen," he finally says as he tilts his glasses. "The reason why I quit my previous job was that I proved myself unable," he swallows, "to fix those homes. Each home is different, and...I'm no architect."

"What are you talking about?"

"I just need one home."

"What?"

He stutters.

"OK, whatever," I say.

He tries to keep his cool by frowning and folding his arms analytically like he does at the hospital when examining x-ray negatives.

"Stuart, why did your ex-wife really leave you?"

He exhales. "I wasn't always there for her," he says.

"Is your daughter with her mother?"

"Yeah."

"She should be with you," I say.

"I'm a busy man, as you can see."

I wonder what would have happened if my parents had separated. My dad probably wouldn't have had the time to look after me, meaning my mother would have had full custody. Perhaps that was one reason why Dad decided not to confront her. He didn't want to lose me. Moreover, he didn't want to be alone when it was time for me to go to college.

It amazes me how quickly I have recollected my senses, how rapidly I have recovered from that madness just now. Reality can be messed up sometimes.

"Listen, Parks, no hard feelings about me sending you on vacation. I think you need it. Everyone does."

"Yes."

I wonder if he is waiting for me to invite him in. I think of the underwear and CDs lying around—the unmade bed and cracker crumbs on the couch. Usually, everything is tidy before I leave the apartment. This is what vacation does – disrupt my routine of sanity. More interestingly, what has led him to stop at my place after work to tell me all this?

"I'm tired, and I need a shower."

On his next step forward, I feel his lips on mine. They are warm and smooth, transmitting a deep spark into my brain, conjuring up a tingle down my spine and a prickling sensation in my stomach.

Two types of emotions are effervescing within my body, and I can't decide which one is stronger.

"I want to help you," he whispers.

I take a step back.

"What did you say?"

He seems confused about my reaction, my sudden rush of anger and irritation.

"What do you mean, you want to *help* me?"

"You're obviously insecure about who you let inside your home," he says.

"*What*? Listen, what do *you* know about me?"

I think everyone up to the tenth floor must have heard me.

"I just…"

"What? You think I want to let you in because you're currently homeless and looking for a new home to fix? You have no idea who I let in!"

Little Ellen, are you there?

He looks hurt. I have never seen him disconcerted before.

"Why are we talking about wombs anyway?" I say.

I turn my back on him and put my hand on the doorknob, ready to go inside.

He grabs my shoulder and turns me towards him. Next, he presses my body hard against the glass door, kissing me.

I can't resist the new kind of warmth spreading into my heart. It's so transparent and real for once. But I don't seem to be able to fathom it. I'm slipping again. I'm slipping.

Inside my apartment, I insist on having a shower first, but he follows me impatiently into the bathroom.

The warm water opens each pore of my skin, washing away my salty perspiration. Stuart places a hand on my chest as if checking I'm alive – a like-minded heart reader. He lifts me up to enter me. I close my eyes.

"Stay with me, look at me," he says.

I place my hands on his chest to calculate his heart rate.

"One hundred and twenty-six," I say.

"One hundred and thirty-three…" he says.

I close my eyes again.

"Parker, look at me."

"You know my heart rate," I smile as the warm water runs down my cheeks.

"Listen to me." He slows down the thrusts to tease me; he has now my full attention. "Listen to yourself, listen to your body, but not in there."

He gestures to my head and says, "count your heartbeat for me and keep looking at me."

His hazel eyes reflect so many perceptive insights of my heart's faculties, not the dark faculties around it, but the irretrievable core, the core that was once me. I can see myself again – pure and in love; I am not alone. He is looking at me.

"What's a heart to you?" I say.

"It's the making of you."

He speeds up again, my eyes not looking away, not for a second.

"One hundred and forty-four…"

"One hundred and fifty-two," he says.

I don't know what else this is, if not love. It's the heart rate that an athlete reaches during his high-intensity anaerobic exercise.

My body has gone soft; I'm light as a cloud underneath the winter sun. Goosebumps have sprung out on my limbs.

After a kiss, he increases the speed again, and I let out a genuine sigh for the first time.

While playing with an unused lancet, I realize that there's one thing I've forgotten about. I don't even know Stuart's blood type or if he is at risk of diseases. He is too deep to be an A-type, too straightforward, and determined to be AB. In my little pocket mirror, I notice that the redness on my face has vanished.

When I hear movement on the other side of the bed, I hide the lancet underneath my pillow. Stuart puts his arm around my belly. The spark is still setting each cell in my blood in motion. Is this the chemical reaction that I've been longing for? Is this going to last? I turn around to look him in the face. His eyes are closed.

"You fell asleep," I say. "You should quit drinking decaf."

He smiles and opens his eyes.

"I don't drink coffee."

"Liar."

His smile widens. He brushes a curl away from my face.

"So, what did Mr. Whitley tell you today?" I say.

"How did you know he came to see me?"

"Maybe he and I went for lunch?"

"Liar," he says.

"He's my patient."

"He may be your patient, but he is my buddy."

Mr. Whitley is my buddy too, but men view friendship from a different angle: loyalty is all-important in male bonding.

"Can I ask you for a favor?" I say.

"Sure."

Underneath the blanket, I pass him a round-headed vaginal speculum. He laughs.

"I told you the truth. It's no myth."

"We will see," I say.

I lie on my back while he leans his body over mine, his right hand holding the sterilized speculum underneath the blanket. He laughs again.

"I'd rather perform cunnilingus," he says, "can I please?"

"No."

He spreads my legs wider apart and slowly places the instrument against my vaginal wall. I hear how my vaginal moisture kisses the tip of the instrument. As he inserts it, he leans over, so our cheeks touch.

CHAPTER TWELVE

Jay is no longer pursuing me, which on the one hand, is a relief, but on the other, I do miss his boyishness. In fact, he called me up to discuss Sarah's current mood. I suggested meeting for a coffee, as it gives me an excuse to get out of the apartment.

I'm sitting outside the Italian place Via Quadronno in the Upper East of the city, sitting in the sun. Seeing him approach me on crutches fills me with discomfort. The surgery was over three weeks ago; at least he is recovering well. The smile on his face no longer expresses longing but kindliness and appreciation.

"Hi, it's nice to see you," he says.

"It's nice to see you, too. How are you doing?"

"Good, it's no longer painful."

"I'm glad to hear."

We order some mineral water. The day resembles the one we had in the park three weeks ago. It was sunny but uncanny.

I sneeze.

"Bless you. Are you all right?" he says.

"Yeah, the weather has cooled down."

Fall is only a few footsteps away. He glances at our drinks as though experiencing the exact same chill. After a long pause, he says, "I'm in love with Sarah."

"I know. And believe me, her feelings for you are reciprocated."

"I know," he says.

The silence resumes. I take a big gulp of my drink just to bring in some movement. People have been acting strangely lately, and my current sixth sense is predicting something unpleasant. It may be Jay himself; maybe he is due to another accident.

"There are two things that I need to ask you." He drums his fingers on the table. "First, I want to propose to her. Second…"

"She has been acting strangely?"

"Exactly!"

I wonder why he has turned to me over this. That evening on the roof garden was the first time she and I had ever hung out together. Just because she slept on my couch doesn't make us friends.

"What's the matter with her?" he says.

Besides, I don't know anything about her – her blood type, medical records, or prescribed medication. She is unknown to me. Her habit of consuming organic matter is certainly odd; it may even count as cannibalism. It's not like a kid biting its fingernails or the skin around it.

"I think she's just stressed from work."

"But she loves her job," he says.

"So do I, but apparently I was so burned out they sent me on vacation."

He looks deep in thought. "Perhaps I should give her some personal space."

"We had a nice night-out a while ago. It helped her loosen up. I think you should take her somewhere nice."

"I will," he says. "Thanks for being a good friend to her. I do want to make her happy."

I can taste something rotten on my tongue. Maybe life is devoid of all happiness. And all we strive to live for is to maintain the idea of happiness. But love...This is something that I need to figure out, something I have to remember – to re-develop my memory's photo negatives.

Many years ago, I decided to keep those memories in the back of my head for future reference. I knew that by the time I'd reached the peak of success, I'd still be unfulfilled.

I remember how Dr. Dick questioned the look in my eyes. How, in the OT, they shoot a sharp and cold look at the patient's organs, as if I were to eat them alive.

"It's like you're completely gone," he said. "Knives and needles are multiplying in your eyes."

"That's just me concentrating."

Some wrinkles in his face twitched. His mouth revealed uncertainty as if signaling that the next sentence was bound to hurt me. If only he'd known that he'd be the last person to hurt me. Then the indefinable lines faded like the creased bits on bed linen underneath a hot iron. An unexpected giggle cleared the air.

"Very well, just don't forget to talk to your patient, too. You're too robotic," he says.

"So, you think I operate like a machine?" I said.

I knew that this was not what he'd intended to imply. There was something else on his mind. In fact, I find the idea of teasing more inappropriate than an insult. But humor is like a brick wall in my mind.

"Come on, Dr. Parker," he said, "you know what Dr. Calvin thinks of her robots."

He was lucky that I was familiar with some of Asimov's literature. In Asimov's world, some peculiar people are more in love with their creation than with their fellow humans. Sometimes they get so attached that they believe their creation is more human, authentic and more realistic than any human touch.

It is now that I understand what I have become – something which Dr. Dick had been trying to protect me from.

"Earth to Ellen! Earth to Ellen!"

The image of a stainless-steel robot recedes into the distance, but I don't want it to—it's all I've got to define my handiwork.

"Look, Jay, Sarah's fine," I say.

"She has been doing so much overtime lately, I hardly see her. I want to make sure that she's OK and not avoiding me for some reason."

It's on the tip of my tongue to tell him that Sarah has an eating disorder, just not of the ordinary kind. A regular person like him wouldn't understand a surgeon's point of view.

"I'll talk to her, OK?"

"Thank you."

At the other end of the avenue, I see the Norman look-alike again – in the same dusty trench coat from the underworld. He is walking towards Madison Avenue. It's the second time that I've seen him first; it's usually vice versa. Not that it matters, but each time his presence comes with a nauseating aura, and it feels like the atmosphere is losing gravity.

"Jay?"

"Yes?"

"Are you mad at me?"

"Why would I be?"

His eyes now dedicate their full attention to me, but I can no longer find the past sentiments he had for me.

My mineral water has gone stale and warm. That's what I get for declining ice every time I'm offered water.

"I don't know."

The Norman look-alike has now turned right into Madison Avenue without seeing me. Maybe he has found a new victim to tantalize. But I won't let that happen. He and I still have a bone to pick. I won't let him walk away from me like that. Have I been making him wait too long?

"Jay, I have to go," I push the chair away from the table.

"What's the reason for your early departure *this* time? Is there something about me that bothers you?" His tone of voice reflects pain and irritation. The metal part of his crutch is reflecting sunlight onto my face. Behind me, kids are shouting and playing.

I feel nauseated.

"No," I say, "you're a good man. You always have been."

He looks at me in surprise, unknowing that this is my first candid compliment. "Sarah is lucky to have you."

I rise from my chair to dodge the reflection of the sunlight. There is a stabbing sensation in my body; I'm not sure where.

"Can I ask you one thing before you go?" he says.

I nod, but my eyes are fixed on the street beyond Madison Avenue.

"Did I ever mean anything to you?"

Suddenly there is a sound of breaking glass followed by a ringing in my ears. And time has slowed down. The world now strikes me as an expressionistic canvas painting with thick blurry lines and distorted faces. A red road emerges from the center of the canvas and stretches into the sky. Another one starts at my foot and connects with my body.

I see a distorted version of Jay rising from the chair. The tinnitus is amplifying in the center of my head, between my eyes, splitting my brain in two.

Within the noise, Jay catches me. The red road reaches my face, and I see red everywhere. I look at Jay and utter one word, but I can't hear myself. A warm hand is placed on the side of my stomach. There is a sensation of pain on the right side of my stomach and waist. I'm choking up groans that I can't hear. I taste the sweetness of my blood as I cough; my mouth halfway fills up. To avoid choking on my blood, I let it flow out of my mouth.

The last thing I hear is Jay calling out my name, but the sky has turned black.

This is Cheshire Village – boring as ever. I often write letters in the garden, leaning against the wooden fence, staring at the sun with my eyes closed. I wonder why everything is red when I stare at the sun through closed eyelids. I will have to ask Dad when he comes home from work. He knows everything. The other day I told him that I'd woken up in the middle of the night and seen an enormous neon cobweb with tartan patterns on the ceiling. I asked him what that pattern had meant. He said it was only a dream that I had brought into the real world. The pattern depicts the membranes behind my eyes. I didn't ask him what membranes were. I looked the term up in the dictionary. I find the anatomy of the eyes fascinating.

"Stupid cunt."

I hear George in his garden. He has just slammed the backyard door shut. I hear the ignition of a lighter, followed by a heavy exhalation and a groan. The other day, I drilled a little hole through our fence. Dad forgot to put back his tools after building the birdhouse for our garden. I peep into the garden, where George walks back and forth, looking distressed. He has probably had an argument with his wife, Maureen. I don't like her, although she likes me. They don't have children of their own. When I asked my parents why they said it was a personal matter and we would not get involved. I don't think George likes Maureen, but I think he likes me. A few months ago, at a barbecue party, he pushed me on the swing, and he stroked my head. That means something. He is younger than Dad but just as tall. George is a handsome, slender man with strong arms. But I don't think he lives a healthy lifestyle. He ate three burgers at the barbeque. Dad makes me eat fresh vegetables at least five times a week, and I like it. Ever since going to that health resort in Florida, I've grown to like broccoli, cauliflower, and Brussels sprouts.

George told me that I was quite tall for my age. I said that I wasn't as tall as my dad yet. And he said he hoped I would never be that tall..

George has such attractive features – full lips and green eyes. His hair is dirty blond, which shines through the hair gel. I often watch him work out on his gym equipment in the garden. But he hasn't been exercising much. He used to do one hundred push-ups every day. I remember him telling me that he used to be in the army. Knowing a soldier is like knowing a celebrity.

He looks unhappy, though. Obviously, his marriage and his unhealthy diet are the culprits. Or perhaps it's his job.

He is a stockbroker in New Haven, so he is always either hyped up or tense. I'm almost sorry, but Dad says that the working world is a tough place, and you have to be prepared before entering it. I should suggest meditation to George.

Dad practices it every other day. All he does is sit cross-legged with eyes closed. Since Dad knows I'm pursuing the same career as his, he keeps repeating that I need to work hard and pay more attention during biology class; in a few years, there'll be chemistry as well.

I'm sure George has worked hard in his life, but he doesn't seem to be at the right place. And Maureen is too stupid to show decent support.

He picks up a bottle of cold beer and gulps it down quickly, draining it dry. Then he inhales the last puff of smoke from his cigarette and flicks the stub into the bush. Eying his recycling bin, he throws the empty bottle in. The sound of glass hitting glass makes me twitch. The sound continues to ring in my ears, making me dizzy.

A strong breeze is blowing the pollen my way. I sneeze behind the wall.

Immediately I cover my lower face with both hands. Hearing no further sound, I look through the hole again. George is approaching the fence with a questioning frown on his face.

"Little Ellen, is that you?"

I rapidly lift myself from the lawn and dash back into the house. I realize that I have left my letter at the fence.

Through the blur, I see a distortion of frizzy hair.

"Dr. Parker, it's me!"

I recognize Dr. Liddy's voice. I rub my eyes and open them to see Dr. Hymen bending over me; I shake in fear.

"Dr. Parker!"

When I refocus, I see only the frizzy head again. The blurry face of Dr. Hymen slowly re-shapes into that of Dr. Liddy.

"What happened to me?"

I touch my body, check on my limbs, face, torso. There is a bandage around my stomach.

I taste the NSAID on my tongue and in my gums, smell it in my nose. But I've no recollection of what happened, except that Jay and I were sipping water and then...

"You've lost a lot of blood."

I try to raise my body but feel overwhelmed by a sense of nausea and tiredness.

"You'd better lie down, Dr. Parker."

"How come you're in the ER unit?" I say.

She points to someone at the other end of the room; it's Scott, the musician, sitting comfortably in the bed with a graphic novel in his hand, his thyroid no longer swollen.

"Hi," he says, smiling.

"We urgently needed a blood transfusion yesterday, and he was there. He said you knew each other and had the same blood type."

This kid – seventeen years of age and still in need of a pediatric supervisor.

I now have innocent blood in my veins. What is it like to be innocent again? And how much do I trust Scott's blood? After all, he's sleeping with the pink head whose blood is unknown to me. Still, I can't help feeling rejuvenated and relieved. The sight of Scott is pleasant and comforting.

I notice flowers on my bedside table.

"What happened?" I ask Liddy.

"You had a terrible glass injury."

No kidding!

"According to Mr. Adkins's statement, a little girl accidentally stabbed you from behind with a sharp piece of broken glass."

"Accidentally?"

"She and her brother were playing ninja," Scott says, smiling.

I wonder what that little girl looked like. It felt like no accident. There was something in the air when it happened.

"When you recover, you should consider pressing charges against the parents of the girl."

Who is she to tell me what to do?

"The girl needs to be locked up," I say, at which her eyes bulge.

Scott laughs. I decide to laugh along, and Liddy's eyes soften.

"Be happy she didn't pierce through your kidney. It was close!" she says.

"She would've got mine then," Scott says, still smiling, as though enjoying Liddy's complete perplexity.

"I got to go," she says.

"Wait," I say, "who did the suture?"

"Dr. McCormick washed the wound and sewed it shut."

Before I could ask her about the flowers, she has closed the door behind her.

"Don't tell me you like her," I say to Scott.

"Are you kidding me? She's worse than my former nanny."

Scott and I stare at each other. I usually have a big aversion to looking people in the eye for long. It's like they are ready to take something away from me, but Scott is different. He used to be a part of me. I realize it now.

"I knew that sooner or later, I'd see you again," he says.

"Just one question."

"Yes?"

"Do you and your lady friend use contraception?"

Shyness is etched all over his face; he blushes as he delves into the pages again.

"I can't believe you're asking me this."

"Why?"

He puts down the graphic novel.

"Because it hasn't happened yet, OK?" He sounds disgruntled.

There is no card evident next to the bunch of Leucanthemum; I wonder who would send me flowers.

"In fact, she is becoming impatient," he says. "But…I don't want to do anything wrong, you know."

"Why would you do something wrong?"

"I don't know!" He raises his voice in agitation.

I look at him and admire his innocence. I feel the gloomy shadows of my past hanging over me, and I don't want him involved at all. I want him to be safe. He shouldn't be here.

"Hey?"

"Yes?"

"Do you have bad memories?" he says. He looks at me earnestly, like a grown man. "I'm worried about you, Doc."

I can smell the flowers – the scent helping me to unravel the images in my head. But all I see are the photo negatives, not the actual photographs of the past.

"I'm OK," I say.

"I hate to say that, but I don't believe you."

At that moment, someone knocks on the door, and Stuart enters the room.

"Hi," he says and nods at Scott.

"Scott, your girlfriend's in the cafeteria. I got her a hot chocolate, and there's one for you, too. You reckon you're all right to see her?"

"What is *she* doing here?"

"I can tell her you're still dizzy from the blood transfusion if you want," Stuart says.

"She doesn't *know* I'm at the hospital."

Stuart shrugs his shoulder unknowingly. Scott slowly moves his feet to the ground and grabs his nightgown. It's only now I notice that his lips are slightly blue. I wonder how much blood he has donated to me.

"Are you sure you're OK?" Stuart says as he leads him towards the door.

"Yeah. Did she look pissed off?"

"Just a bit."

"Oh, Christ."

As soon as Scott has stepped outside, Stuart closes the door. Three days ago, he stayed at my place. Seeing him as my supervisor in his lab coat turns the memory into vagueness, and the image of the shower scene recedes into the distance.

"Maybe I shouldn't have sent you on vacation. How are you feeling?"

I nod.

"You're better off in the hospital than outside in the big world."

"Remember it's you who told me not to lose contact with the outside world."

He takes a seat next to me, unsure of what to do with his hands. It is the first time I see Stuart McCormick's determined hands fiddling about.

"Let me have a look."

I pull away the blanket, exposing my naked legs. He lifts my gown up a little bit to check the firmness of the bandage.

"It's not too tight, is it?"

"No."

Stuart's hand covers mine for a few seconds, then he releases it as though scared of something.

"You'd better press charges against that little girl's parents. This is unforgivable."

"It's nothing to do with parenting. It's the girl."

"But she's just a child."

"Children are evil, Stuart. Besides, she had my blood on her hands. She won't ever be the same again. Assign her to some counseling, therapy, I don't know."

His face darkens; I remember that I am talking to the father of a girl.

"If Helen had done that, I'd have taken the responsibility."

For a second, I see my dad in Stuart's eyes. Then he grins. "Besides, you talk as if your blood was evil."

"Well, who knows?"

I am tired and nauseated all of a sudden, despite the new blood rushing through my veins. I think my blood cells need time to welcome a long-lost member of the family – Scott.

"However, you seem to have a lot of admirers," Stuart says.

"Admirers?"

He is eying the flowers. His attempt to maintain his usual cocky attitude is failing him big time. Fighting the urge to question me about those "admirers" and pretending he doesn't care is killing him.

"The flowers are from your stalker friend."

"What, Norman?"

"So, he is a friend now?"

"I haven't seen him since he left the hospital. That was over a month ago."

He nods disbelievingly.

"What's the matter, Stuart?"

He laughs. I wish the good old Stuart McCormick would return and feign callousness like the expert he was. But unfortunately, he is no longer that person. For now, I can hear his heart more clearly than before.

"Nothing, except that you received a rather extraordinary gift from a former patient called Todd Wilson, flowers from a stalker, and out of the blue that kid turned up in your most critical hour to donate his blood." He takes a deep breath. "Don't get me wrong, I like that kid. He saved your life. But this is all too weird."

As for me, this is too much information.

"Are you and Jay close?" he says.

"No, why?"

"Just wondering."

Speaking of the devil, Jay and Sarah enter the room, followed by Julia, Howard, Will, my personal scrub nurses, and other people from our department.

"Elle, one-nil for the Halloween kid!" says Will.

Do any of them actually care about me?

I see Dr. Liddy smiling at the door, but as her smile fades, a haze of sadness covers her face.

According to Jay, the last thing I said before fainting was "Georgie." When he asked whether it was my little sister, I said maybe with no further comments.

Scott left early this morning. Yesterday his lady friend attempted to drag him home, but Dr. Liddy advised her to pick him up in the morning since he still needed rest. He'd asked to sleep in the same room as me, but he wasn't particularly talkative last night.

"She doesn't want me to see you again," he said.

"If you care about her, you'd better promise her."

"But..."

"Be good to her."

He didn't say anything to this, and when it was time to say goodbye, there were no words, either.

Looking at the daisies still in bloom makes me miss Scott even more, but at least I know he isn't alone. If this room were a garden, I wouldn't have to worry about the daisies. This room offers no scent of life. They will only wither away in my presence.

Norman left no card, no contact number. How did he even know about this?

Stuart was right; he shouldn't have put me on annual leave, especially now, because a significant number of photographs have popped up in my head. I must have developed them somehow. And like a forensic photographer, I am dwelling in the red room, searching for answers. If I'd been working, I wouldn't have stepped into this mess. I'd be focusing on my valuable collectibles in my chamber. The OT is my main focus. My sanity.

If Mr. Whitley had agreed to go for lunch, I could have squeezed more information out of him. In fact, I don't feel anything anymore. The image of Mr. Whitley has faded away, along with all the other following heart surgeries. The operation became like any other.

When Stuart brought back that ancient feeling, I thought I was saved, but I'm not. I can't feel anything that lasts. Perhaps we are only meant to be happy for a little while. What really happened in the shower, I can't explain. And it hasn't happened again.

Ellen Parker, formerly made to pursue a heart surgeon's career, is now dealing with an unfinished project from the past. If my life story has ever had a plot, it will begin here.

There are three purposes in my life, after all. To mend my broken heart and to feel an orgasm again. And three—I don't remember.

A gentle knock on the door pulls me back into the unpleasant world of definable noises. I watch the door handle bend down slowly.

Then something incredible happens. I see my younger self enter the room: I have long blonde curls, fair skin, and meadow-green eyes. I have blood on my hands.

I blink a few times and see a young girl with short blond hair, timid-looking. The blood has gone.

Behind her is Dr. Liddy, who accompanies her into the room. Fascinated by that little girl's beauty, I hold my breath. Carefully Dr. Liddy removes her hands from the child.

"This is Laurie."

She is so young but no longer innocent. I look at her hands of guilt – there are a couple of band-aids on her right palm. Where will she be headed in her yet distant future?

Her hands and body are trembling like a kid's in a fairy tale when confronted by its stepmother. I wonder where her protective brother is. I've always wanted a brother.

Laurie approaches my bed hesitantly. She glances back at Dr. Liddy, making sure she hasn't left. I wonder what it would be like to wrap my hands around the girl's neck. How easy would it be to twist it?

Come closer…

She stands still at arm's length. Kids have always looked at me as if I were not one of them; even at Laurie's age, I wasn't one of them.

Laurie glances at Dr. Liddy again, who gestures her to proceed with her little apology.

"I'm sorry," she says in a squeaky little voice.

My eyes examine her from top to bottom, her hunched back indicating fragility that might improve if her parents remind her to stand straight. She is about four feet tall. I wonder what her father's job is and whether it is worth pursuing.

The awkward silence is waiting for me to fill the air, but I let it drag on.

"Come on, Laurie. That's not all you have to say, is it?"

I'm sure she's able to talk for herself.

Laurie blushes as she looks me in the eye. I imagine devouring her tender cheeks, how smooth and juicy they feel on my gums while chewing and sucking the sweet blood that goes down the back of my tongue.

"I…" she says.

I hold my hand out, reaching for hers. She hesitantly grabs it, and I pull her body towards me. Her eyes bulge in fear; her heart rate increases. Staring at the glimmer in her iris, I suddenly see my former backyard in Cheshire Village. But I see no hint of blood, no taint of suspicion.

I begin to stroke her little hands. I've stopped paying attention to Dr. Liddy, whose face is creased by fear.

Her hands are soft, smooth, and free from foul play.

She is a child, isn't she?

Yes, she is. Not all children are like you, Ellen.

I lean my face towards her and smell cinnamon in her hair, which is overwhelming my nostrils. I remember the smell of glue and gasoline from back in the days.

"Have you ever played with a boy's penis?" I say.

"Dr. Parker!"

Liddy quickly drags the girl away from me, as if protecting a child from an abusive parent. To the girl, it's like I've spoken in a foreign language.

"Unbelievable!" Dr. Liddy says. She nudges Laurie towards the exit and slams the door shut. I feel hungry.

The door opens again with full force as Dr. Liddy enters. She slams the door shut behind her. "I can't believe what you just said to the girl."

"Girls that age talk about things like that every day. You just never know," I say.

"She's only nine years old!"

The pollen daisies' pollen has reached my nostrils, but I suppress a sneeze, which leads my eyes to water.

"Old enough to feel attracted to her father."

Her face tweaks in disgust. "I never knew you were so repulsive, Dr. Parker."

It's on the tip of my tongue to mention Sigmund Freud, whom she would have studied too, but I am not going to.

"We are all familiar with disgust, aren't we? At her age, I was masturbating while riding my bicycle. The saddle would massage my clitoris, and all of a sudden, there was this beautiful feeling, which I didn't understand. Do you know what it feels like, Dr. Liddy?"

She shakes her head in slow motion, looking confounded. Either she is lying, or she is crushed by the truth.

I sense her heart rate decreasing; she is not breathing sufficiently.

"Are you feeling nauseous? There's a chair."

Instead of sitting down, she remains stiff nearby the door.

"That girl is sincerely sorry," she says.

"I know."

"You want her to get in trouble?"

"No," I say.

"Then why…"

"Why do you care about children so much?"

In her unexpected smile, I watch her plunge into her own fantasy world where children draw sunshine and rainbows, but this image crumbles away as soon as her smile fades into the blank.

"They remind me that happiness exists; they remind me of who I wasn't."

Join the club.

"I think that the parents are always to blame."

"Were you abused?"

She covers the lower part of her face with her hand to suppress a sigh of sadness and nods heavily.

"You?"

"No," I say.

I wonder whether she used to be a good-looking child and whether her frizzy hair used to be beautiful curls. Probably. But you can't imagine what sixty-year-old women used to look like when they were young. Strange. It's like they've never been young. This is the first time that I've seen this unusual sadness on Dr. Liddy's face, which denotes the sorrow that I have seen before on my neighbor's face back in Connecticut – a woman unable to have her own children.

She cries. "So, are you going to accept the girl's apology?"

"Why do you care?"

"Don't make her suffer."

"She seemed fine to me," I say.

"Now, perhaps. But in a few years, she will realize what she's done, she will be plagued by demons."

Demons.

"Trust me," she continues, "if her parents had paid more attention, this would never have happened!"

I don't believe her parents are at fault. Thinking about my parents makes me miss their company, Dad in particular. It was always Dad who lightened up the dark, Dad who had encouraged me in difficult times, Dad who gave me a reason to live. Perhaps he knew about my dark inner faculties, which was why he pushed me into medicine. But medicine is merely a prop. I am at the peak of my career, and everything has happened so fast.

"OK," I say.

"Oh, thank you! Thank you! I'll go get her. I'll get her now."

"Dr. Liddy?"

"Yes?"

"Please tell her parents that I won't press any charges."

CHAPTER THIRTEEN

It wasn't love…

During my recovery, I spent a lot of time thinking, looking at photographs in my head. I understand now why you can't just throw away the negatives. You can remove an appendix, but powerful pictures of the past, in whatever form, will remain with you for good. There are mental and physical scars, and you will find that the physical ones, which come in various shapes, are easier to remember. You know for sure that the incident really happened. You can't deny it or push it away like a mental scar.

Stuart left me a sweet one on my waist area. It looks like a centipede.

I have never learned how to live with those images; I have spent years studying them, figuring out how best to fix them, filter them because I do not, and I cannot accept them. Once I have, then what?

Despite reshaping the past and memories, they say your feelings will always tell you the truth, no matter how well you try to veil or modify them.

But…I have no feelings.

The only way to come to terms with these images is to accept the truth that you've been denying.

As a qualified heart surgeon at Mount Sinai, I've begun to question the purpose of my life, as it seems, I know nothing about the meaning of existence.

Like the Brothers Grimm, who re-wrote the original fairy tales, I have tried to cover up and embellish the truth with the idea of love – a happy tale without ever looking at the origin from which this story has sprung.

The lucky people like Jay for instance, to whom the secrets of life are unknown, aren't aware that there is a so-called truth. If one denies the truth, he denies himself. The truth is not God, neither is there a purpose to the world, but it's you alone. It's the lines on your hands, every single hair on your body, the sixty thousand miles of veins beneath your skin. The cells are the real people who walk down the road of life, every minute, every second. As a human being, you are merely the product of those inner faculties – in other words, your thoughts and feelings. People have never really come to an agreement on what these things are good for. The red sea is producing life inside us. It communicates through pain to signal that something is wrong.

I did not press charges against Laurie's parents because they are not at fault. It was not Mom and Dad's fault that I am heartbroken.

I decided to extend my vacation to dedicate time to myself, as these girls with crimson hands wouldn't go away. Never has the sight of blood terrified me but seeing blood on hands that can be saved from guilt weighs me down with pressure on my neck and pain in my stomach.

It's terrible how holidays have a tendency to turn you into a zombie. The idea of not wearing a lab coat and mouth mask leaves each day purposeless.

At the breakfast table, I am no longer hungry. Sometimes I buy a ready-made pie in the morning just to remind myself of my perfect incisions. If only the mushroom sauce was red. It's soothing to identify signs of my patients on the table. In each dish that I prepare, I see someone that I have operated on. Soup, for instance, brings up images of abdominal surgery in the ER. When I order chicken feet from the Chinese, I see Todd Wilson's hand, which is now bedded down in my freezer. After his mother's death, he found his hand again in a special separate freezer. So he thought of me.

I never knew how nice it is not to be forgotten.

With a little effort, I managed to find Norman's address in the phone directory. He lives in Astoria, which is one of New York's most European parts. Come to think of it, I think Norman is of Irish descent. His former drinking habit suggests it.

I walk down the popular street market, which reminds me of New England, and this is another reminder of past-related knots still to be untied.

Norman rents an apartment in a building where no security guard is in charge of the occupants' safety – an impossible place for anyone like me to live. You don't even need to ring the doorbell to access the building. There are Polish-speaking kids playing card games at the doorstep of this nineteenth-century building. In central New York, I'm usually familiar with them playing betting games, and in those bets, they'd put either their hashish or parents' money on the line. No one pays attention to kids anymore. I never have.

Standing in front of apartment number thirty-three gives me a stark reminder of my age, which suddenly doesn't seem as young as before. That's seven years from forty. I haven't planned my life that far ahead. If I measure my life expectancy in terms of my health, I guess I will live past sixty, but I don't know if I like this biological supposition.

Norman opens the door and stares at me with surprise.

"So, how did you know what my favorite flowers were?"

His apartment is small and plain, and cleaner than I expected. There is a little reception area, which is simultaneously the lounge equipped with a kitchenette. There are two separate rooms for bath and bedroom to offer a little discretion. It smells like he had coffee two or three hours ago.

"I've been living a healthy life, Dr. Parker."

"I'm glad to hear."

He opens his fridge to get two bottles of mineral water.

"First, I did it for you."

"And now?"

He smiles. "I'm doing it for myself."

I smile back at him. This must be the kind of life I'd be living if I weren't a cardiac surgeon – find someone to live for.

"Where do you work?"

"In a betting agency," he says, "not betting, however."

"Not even tempted?"

He shakes his head as he places the bottles on the glass table. The sound of glass on glass evokes a sensation of pain in my waist area; I sense a blood rush around my suture.

"How's your injury?" he says.

Paula C. Deckard

"That's another thing I want to ask you about. How did you know?"

"You must think I'm some kind of psychic. I assure you I'm not."

He passes me a glass. There is a band-aid around his index finger.

"Life comes with plenty of coincidences."

Looking at him now, a clean, healthy man, I envy him. How could he change from what he was to what he is now? Is it a matter of discipline, belief, perhaps even surgery?

I grab the bottle and rub it with my right hand until Norman says, "Stop it, please."

"What?"

"I take it your injury has healed," he says. "Little girls are evil, aren't they?"

I cringe.

"You must think I follow you around, but I don't."

I don't believe him.

"But then in my head, I saw you holding a piece of glass."

"I wasn't holding anything!"

The tremble in my voice has almost evolved into something dramatic.

"Ellen," he says. "I...see...you."

"Pardon?"

"Sometimes I see a young girl who looks like you."

"You're not making sense."

"Well, you saw me, too, at my accident. You said I was smiling at you while, in reality, I was unconscious in the car!"

There is something uncanny in the air, something bad.

"Something extraordinary happened at the car accident," he says. "I guess I did see you."

I know he did.

"In my dreams, though. But you were little."

"Little?"

"It wasn't just you. There was somebody else. Someone evil."

"Who?"

"I don't know," he says.

"Was it a woman?"

"I don't know. But there was a garden."

I swallow deeply. Now his eyes express some sort of revelation as if he knows all the answers to my questions.

"Have you seen the spiritual version of me again since then?"

I nod. I imagine the two of us on the swing in my former garden, me on top of him. For some reason, I can't imagine myself older than ten, my hands stroking the stubble on his face and feeling happy.

"Are you stalking me by any chance?" he says.

"Are you crazy? Why would I do that?"

"Well," he says, rubbing the back of his neck and then scratches his head. "Ellen, admit to me that you need help. And I will help."

"Why would I seek help from you?"

"Then why are you here?" he shouts. I flinch like a child in front of its teacher. I see myself climbing down from the swing.

Taking a sip of his water, he moves to the sofa, where he takes a seat, facing away from me. The smell of disappointment is similar to the scent of rue. I remember we had some in our garden. Dad didn't like it. He must have removed it by now.

"You've put me on a spiritual path, Ellen. And I'm thankful. There is only one thing that I have to eliminate, and it's that child's misfortune."

It's *my* job to take care of that girl.

"I don't need help," I say.

"The fuck you don't."

Moving to the window, I brush my finger along the dusty jalousie. Norman has a nice view; you can see a part of the Astoria Pool and the Hell Gate Bridge.

Carefully I place the cold glass of water on the floor and begin to rub my hands.

It's cold.

"Maybe you're not asking for help, but the little girl is. So why do you reckon you still see that spirit?"

"I don't know," I say.

He is staring big holes into the air.

"Maybe she wants to be saved from that bad spirit of yours," I say.

He chuckles.

"If you ask me, I reckon the little girl and the man are the same people, except that the girl's the baddy."

"So, you and I are the same people. But am I really that bad?" I say.

Finally, he rises from the sofa. His eyes fixed on my body as he approaches me. I never noticed how his dainty lips resemble Mr. Whitley's: they express a sincerity that fills my body with warmth.

He squints at me.

"I'm nothing like you," he says.

He turns away from me again, this time unsure about where to go.

"I don't deny who I am," he continues, "at least I no longer do."

"What makes you think I do?"

"You're a liar."

I move backward, accidentally knocking over the water with my heel. The sound of glass hitting concrete resonates in my ears, triggering a kaleidoscopic vision for a few seconds and then a stinging headache. The sound of the fading carbon dioxide is like acid eating its way through a solid surface.

"When did I lie to you, Norman?"

"Don't you see that I'm worried about you?"

I don't understand why people have to pretend they worry about me. The day I taught myself self-reliance was when Dad had decided not to leave Mother. I begged him to because I would've chosen to live with him. I was angry with him, in fact. He was the only person in whom I could confide when I doubted my future and when I needed his guidance the most, even when he was busy trying to save his marriage. Mother was such a wreck, whereas I was young and ambitious. Why would he choose her over me?

When I won the biology scholarship competition, I didn't tell either of my parents about it – not right away. I knew that Dad would have sponsored me with his savings, but I realized how crucial it was to count on myself. Even those closest to you won't always prioritize you, not even in your darkest hour. You need to be ready to stand on your own. They may tell you how worried they are about you, but there is this empty sound between those words, a hollow echo of meaninglessness.

"I'm not a liar," I say.

"There you go again."

Neither of us has bothered to pick up the glass. The water keeps on running.

"So if the little girl that you see is me, then why isn't she coming to me instead?" I say.

"Do you really not know?"

I imagine Norman in a patient's gown on a patient's bed. That way, he'd be easier to talk to.

"If you can't tell me why you're here, I have to ask you to leave, Ellen."

I wonder why I am here. "Thank you for the flowers," I say.

He exhales some desolate air like a parent about to give up on his child.

"They were my first," I add and move to the door.

He says nothing.

I haven't heard from Stuart since I left the hospital. Does he really believe that Norman and I have had a relationship?

Arriving at his place at 7 p.m., I find myself staring at his door through the car window. Stuart lives in Midtown East, close to Hunter's Point.

After twenty minutes of waiting, a woman arrives with a little girl in the backseat. As the woman steps out of the car, I see long dark hair, long legs, and firm breasts underneath a tight long-sleeve shirt. The little girl jumps out of the car, running towards Stuart's door to ring the bell. She has long blonde hair, which will turn brown in a few years. In the womb, the girl's keratin levels must have been strong, but as the years go by, her genes will adapt more and more to what her parents have passed on to her.

She jumps Stuart as soon as he opens the door. The happiness on his face reminds me of what I used to see on Dad's face when I was that age. That was long before my schoolteacher Miss van Carr sent me to the school psychologist. From that time on, Dad's happiness was not quite the same anymore.

I turn the ignition, ready to head back home. It has started drizzling.

When I release the brakes, I see a puppy on the street, staring at me with fright.

I've never liked animals. If it had been a cat, I wouldn't have bothered hitting the brakes; but there is something about the eyes of dogs, a kind of sadness that stirs something up in me.

It doesn't take me long to figure out that the dog is a Border Collie – apparently a trendy farm dog breed in the United Kingdom and Australia. How does a sheepdog get lost in the center of New York? Shockingly enough, they get up to twenty inches high, weighing approximately forty pounds once fully grown. Having taken him home, I figure that it is a mistake to keep him because I live in an apartment where he won't be able to be as active. Within two days, this creature has triggered several anger outbreaks. Concerned about my personal health issues, I consider abandoning him. But again, it's those eyes that stop me. Despite peeing against my bonsai plant, chewing garbage, and excreting under my bed, I hold him, as only then is he free from anxiety. I've never been allergic to animals, but there is a small rash on the side of my nose.

By day four, I carry him down the stairs towards the exit. I put him down on the ground near the car park and say, "Go. Get the hell out."

I start pointing at the street, but he just stares at my finger. As I come closer, he starts wagging his tail.

"No, no, no, you're getting the wrong idea, buddy."

I shove him lightly towards the street, but he gets more anxious, shaking like aspen leaves. I see a neighbor staring suspiciously at me from the balcony like I'm about to kill it. The dog then pees casually against a bush.

"Good boy!"

I hold him up in the air and look into his innocent eyes.

"Now, what do I do?"

Buddy is asleep on a pillow that I bought for him. I believe he deserves better, but I enjoy his presence for now; he keeps me busy.

I informed Dad that I'd be coming for a visit soon. Unfortunately, they are not looking for a pet, and besides, they are moving to a new house. They are moving closer to New Haven, which surprises me because my parents love Cheshire Village. According to Dad, they've found a lovely place to grow old in. Apparently, the atmosphere in Cheshire Village has changed. There has been a murder of some sort in the neighborhood.

Having done more research on border collies, I stumble across a website of a farmer in Connecticut. His name is Hank Chrome, a forty-four-year-old widower who owns a little ranch in Redding in Fairfield County.

The picture shows a handsome man with a genuine smile. Not even the death of his wife has brought him down. He breeds cattle and other animals, such as pigs and goats. His photo albums present his entire farm, his barn, animals, and nearby fields. Although it all looks lively and vigorous, it makes me think of a circus parade.

Then I notice pictures of his well-trained border collie, who has passed away. I imagine both of them jogging across the field together, something Buddy certainly won't be doing in New York City.

I admire Hank for being the guardian of so many living creatures. I've always thought animals to be more challenging to deal with than humans. How do you even know when an animal is sick? Being specialized in the functionality of the human body, I've always wondered what it'd be like operating on an animal, which is still alive. I'm sure the structure of an animal's anatomy and physiology is interesting, but it had never crossed my mind to become a veterinarian, except when I was a child.

I examine the pictures of the pigs on Hank's website. They are looking at their master like retards. No, animals certainly don't function the same way we do.

I compose an email to Hank, introducing myself to him as Helen. Then, I try to figure out why I'm doing this.

I stare at Buddy and realize that I no longer want him to go.

I ask Hank for advice about bringing up a puppy that poops, pees, and chews in the house. I've never really had pets of my own. Dolly was Mother's pet and bled to death after the dental surgery that I gave her. I also believe that I broke a cat's neck once, but it came back to life for some inexplicable reason.

I take a picture of Buddy to attach to the email. I act like a bum who uses animals to seek sympathy and attention. Anyway, it seems to work because Hank writes back immediately. He must be lonely.

Hello Helen,

Thanks very much for your email! You make me feel like a fully certified animal specialist and dog trainer, which I find rather funny, but it doesn't change the fact that you have put a smile on my face.

Well, Buddy looks like he is less than five months old, right? They are very vulnerable and clingy during this period and need extra care. After a few more months, he should be fine. I hope you have a big yard for him to play in. Border collies are very active dogs and never bored; they refuse to simply sit around watching you, especially a puppy at that age! I'm sure that you are a patient person and will make an effort to keep him good company. You must've got Buddy for the same reason as I got my wonderful Jacob fifteen years ago. Believe me, you won't regret it.

Feel free to drop me another line in case you need more help.

Regards,
Hank

I write back, this time telling him the truth about where I found Buddy; I tell him where I am from and that I live in a two-bedroom apartment with no yard outside except for the car park which – once everyone has removed their cars in the morning – can be huge. I have no idea what a border collie is doing in the middle of New York.

What am *I* doing in New York? I should be at my parents' house in Connecticut.

In his next reply, he simply asks me to add him on Skype, only if I am OK with it. At first, I am hesitant, but I create an alternate account, and then I add him.

It's getting late now, but there are butterflies in my gut, which refuse to go away. I wonder whether Hank has any medical conditions. He is typing.

Hank
"Hello there."

Helen
"Hi."

Hank
"So has Buddy been keeping you up at night then?"

Helen

"Not really. He goes to sleep before I do."

Hank

"Well, this means he'll be up before you tomorrow and probably more active than ever :)"

Helen

"How about you look after him until he's potty-trained?"

Hank

"I wish I could, dear, but my animals need to be looked after."

There is a little pause, and I don't dare to start a new topic since my last post was slightly direct. But I'm glad that we're not video chatting, although he would bring me closer to my home state.

Helen

"Perhaps I can look after them. I assume they are all grownups, aren't they?"

Hank

"I presume you're not good with little ones, are you?"

Helen

"I'm not good with myself, so what can you expect?"

Hank

"How old are you?"

Helen

"Please give me a description of how you imagine I look like and how old I am."

There is a very long pause, and finally, he starts typing – for minutes. After almost five minutes of typing, a long text appears:

Hank

"I have this image of a blonde lady with short curls; she is in her mid-twenties or early thirties, bright eyes and a firm expression on her face, which indicates confidence and determination. However, when she receives a compliment or sympathy or observes her little puppy, her face softens. And because she lives in New York City, I bet she is either a lawyer or a businesswoman. Or maybe she's in advertising, sales, or marketing. Her team members are envious, because she is more successful and receives attention from her superior. Nevertheless, she seems unhappy, but I can't exactly tell why."

This is it. I turn my camera on and hope that he will do the same. Now I can see my own face, still slightly made up but a little faded. I can't help but smile – exposing a small hint of embarrassment.

"Thanks for the compliments," I say.

He keeps silent for a while, making me feel exposed. A few minutes later, he turns on his camera. I see a hurried face as if he has been rushing around.

"I'm sorry. My cam wasn't plugged in, and for some reason, I had to reinstall it."

I would use this as an excuse to reapply my make-up. However, it is a forgivable lie showing effort – making an effort to look good for me. He doesn't look exactly like in the photo, but somewhat older and a little sad.

"You look stunning," he says.

I take the camera and slowly lead him across my lounge to the pillow on which Buddy is still sleeping.

"You'd better not wake him. You'll regret it!"

CHAPTER FOURTEEN

I see Bruce hiding behind the advertising pillar, which is illustrating Prada lingerie. I am arguing with Jay outside the hospital, except that I can't hear him speak. He's talking in a different dimension. Each word makes a noise like the sound of a pebble thrown into a lake.

Next, I'm in a salad bar with Joe, who seems to be talking to himself. Norman, wearing black shades, is standing near the buffet with a peeled onion in his hand. He smiles and then bites into it brutally.

He comes to sit at the table across from me. My sense of sound has returned – the bubble has been broken.

"Hi Ellen, I came because you asked for help."

I suddenly feel like I have shrunk: my feet are no longer on the ground, my arms not long enough to reach across the table. He takes off his shades, and instead of human eyes, I see two small breasts popping out of his eye sockets.

"I can feel you!" he laughs, stroking the nipples.

I realized that it's not Norman, but…

He puts his shades back on. "You're not a good girl. You're a disgrace to your parents."

I am eight years old, crying with uncontrollable sobs and a runny nose.

The waiter arrives and serves me a dead kitten.

"You see what you've done?" the man in the shades says.

The dead kitten's stomach and lower abdomen are covered in blood. I didn't do it, I didn't do it. It was an accident.

"Accident, you say?" He points at my bloody trembling hands.

"You sliced it open!" he says. "This poor little thing!"

I wipe the blood onto my white skirt and sob harder. I've almost forgotten the painful sensation of crying. Why am I in this little body?

This is not me.

"Is this how you will operate in the future?"

I shake my head repeatedly.

"THIS - WON'T - HAPPEN – AGAIN!" As each word comes, he hits his fist on the table, and each time I see a different male figure: Dad, then Dr. Dick, Norman, and finally Stuart.

"You're a good surgeon," Stuart says, and we're both looking at the pumping heart on the plate between us.

I'm no longer a little girl, but a grown woman with a career, a purpose: to live life with a daily task, covering my hands in blood.

But strangely, Stuart's hands are clean. Despite the taint of ruin, he reaches his hand out for mine.

"You have to trust me, Parker," he says.

But I back off.

Tender licks behind my ears wake me up almost instantly.

It's Buddy.

Then I notice the gross smell in my room. He has defecated on my bed.

The concept of a vacation is to go someplace. It's the first time I desire to leave New York, at least for a little while. My hospital withdrawal is at its most intense when I find myself doing nothing productive except for petting a puppy. I've started analyzing my blood after each meal out of pure boredom.

According to Hank, Buddy needs to be fed several times a day. He also suggested going for some walks, for instance, around Central Park, but dogs aren't allowed in some areas. Apart from fitness, the many walks are also to tire him out. Hank is helpful, patient, and considerate.

He and I have been talking for over a week, but the struggles with Buddy are ongoing. The rash on my face keeps coming and going too. I fear that it could be an early stage of rosacea. As a child, I was on antibiotics for a while, which had stopped it from developing. City people, in general, seem to be more affected by this chronic skin disease.

Hank suggested that I came to Redding in Connecticut for a visit, as life in the big city can drain you from the inside after so many years. Redding is less than an hour away from New Haven, not too far away from Cheshire Village, and less than two hours away from Manhattan.

*

The car is ready to go. The bag is packed with casual clothing enough for at least three to four days. I wonder what else I might need for this little weekend away. There are a couple of lab-on-a-chip devices in my handbag, although I'm not sure how handy they will be.

Buddy is hidden away in a dog kennel on the passenger's seat. I'm also about to feed him some tranquilizers to ensure the prospect of a peaceful trip.

It's funny how rarely I use this car. I've always preferred to walk or at least take the subway to certain places, especially during off-peak hours. Everything I need seems to be within walking distance—the convenience of living in a big city.

Just as I turn on the engine, I see a text message from Stuart asking if he can come and see me. I message him back saying that I'm on my way to Connecticut. At least he knows it's my home state, my parents are there, and Dr. Dick is there.

According to my maps app, Redding is about ninety minutes from here in this current traffic. All I have to do is follow I-95 until Norwalk and then head north. If I were to go to New Haven, I would have to continue on I-95 past Bridgeport and West Haven and take exit forty-seven. I have to remember to head north this time, because I am not going home, not directly.

However, going to see a stranger living on a farm suddenly strikes me as weird. A former ex-boyfriend from college used to live in Redding. I visited him once but have no recollection of what Redding was like. Telling myself that I am heading towards New Haven makes the whole trip easier. At least there is some familiarity to lean on.

After traveling six miles north from Manhattan, I take I-95 N. I love the drive on the interstate during off-peak hours. From here, it will be around fifty minutes until Norwalk.

It's sunny. The air is clean and fresh this afternoon.

One thing about Connecticut is that the people appear to be friendlier and more outgoing. They randomly greet you on the streets, which New Yorkers wouldn't. I wouldn't, either, not even in my hometown.

The last time I felt nervous and foreign was when I traveled to Milan. But this is my home state; why should traveling here make me feel nervous? I don't know. Perhaps it's the idea of visiting a stranger – a virtual person. It's also unclear where I'm staying. Maybe I should look up some nearby motels in Redding when I reach the next gas station.

Buddy is still asleep.

I find myself cruising around in Norwalk, where numerous signs indicate I-95 N to Oak Street, which eventually connects to New Haven. I'm about half an hour away. Driving past the city hall, I decide to head towards the harbor to spot some boats. Now I'm a little further away from the interstate and, for some reason, somewhat at ease. I see groups of people sitting outside some trendy restaurants advertising specials of seafood and lobster.

The closer I get to the water, the stronger the sea breeze becomes. The salty smell of the sea reminds me of Florida without the heat. It's slightly cooler here in

Connecticut, too. I remember that I tend to get allergies during ragweed season – the sneezes were unbearable. It used to be intense when I was a kid. I've not had any symptoms since living in New York.

Dr. Dick likes the sound of my sneeze. He calls it dainty, as apparently it resembles that of a child. Monks believe that the moment of sneezing fills one's conscience with clarity. But to me, it's just a second of vigorous muscle contraction in the chest. Other people feel it more in the face or in the throat. It might be a fascinating human reflex, but I dislike the late notice the body gives me.

Either the red lights in this town seem to last forever, or my sense of perception has changed – things have slowed down dramatically.

An old couple is crossing the street. The man's walking stick falls over, and a little girl crossing to the other side picks it up for him. The elderly couple shoots the girl a look of gratitude in the middle of the road.

People are very aware of their surroundings and their fellow people here; in New York, it's easy to be too busy and preoccupied with one's own business. Instead of seeing things as they really are, they see what they want to see. Many city people are captives to disillusionment and delirium, and I have chosen to be part of it. I hope that Connecticut towns will never change and never become like New York City.

At least here, I believe that meditation will be more practicable. I should have made a better example of my dad when I was younger.

Buddy whimpers.

I begin to follow the signs indicating US-7 N on Danbury Road, which will lead me to CT-107 N towards Redding. I'm less than eighteen miles away from Hank.

-

Hank is about six foot three inches tall and slender. At my arrival, he emits a warm charisma. His brown hair is slightly gelled – his face shaved and dominated by his beautiful blue eyes, which are brighter than on the webcam.

His smile broadens as he approaches my car. I get out and make sure I don't slam the door too loudly.

"You found my farm. Welcome!"

Before I get the chance to stretch my hand out to him, he kisses me on the cheeks three times – twice on the right. I almost blush.

"Oh, are you Dutch?" I say, a little dumbfounded.

"Sorry! Yeah, my grandmother was."

"That's nice!"

"It's nice to meet you, Helen," he says.

It has happened so quickly. I can't tell how much of an air-kiss or cheek-to-cheek kiss it was in the end. I don't think I have felt his lips on either of my cheeks.

"Here's the little man!" he bends over to take a look at Buddy in the kennel.

It is unusual being greeted like this by someone that I meet for the very first time. However, to Hank, I'm not Ellen. Perhaps Helen has a purpose yet of being discovered.

Hank has a blue truck in his parking lot, a Toyota Tacoma. Right in front of it is a huge timber-framed red barn. I've always wondered why so many barn sidings are vertically constructed. It must have been built in the early nineteen hundred; the open-hinged doors look fragile and rusty. I see a large hay wagon inside the barn.

Next to the barn is a big modern farmhouse equipped with a metal roof of solar panels. Judging by the size, it has at least five to six bedrooms and a spacious attic. The porch looks like it could fit fifty people.

"Does he want a drink? He must be thirsty."

He hands me a cup and fills it with water from his flask. I place the kennel on the ground and open the cage door. Buddy drinks so fast he almost chokes.

"I like the barn."

"It's very old and unstable. It'll make it through another winter, and then I'll have to tear it down and rebuild it. I'll need tongue-and-groove boards to sheath the walls better. For now, I can only hope for a mild winter."

I hear a horse's nickering and look over to the fenced yard, which is perhaps thirty-five square meters big. A blonde horse is swishing his tail while his mouth roots around in the grass.

"Oh, that's Dexter, my brother's horse. I have more space for him to roam. He'll have to go back into the shed during winter. He doesn't like the barn because I have pigs, cows, and a little hen-house in there."

"Horses do love their freedom," I say. "So, you own this farm with your brother?"

"I own it now. My brother is a rancher and a sharecropper. I just let him use my land."

He grabs some dog biscuits from his pocket and feeds them to Buddy. When looking at this vast land, I find my eyes resting on the dog carrier.

"You'll like it here," he says. "The first thing city people notice about our state is the fresh air. It gets windy, though. But thank God there were no hurricane warnings this year. I was pretty worried."

"I heard it gets bad here sometimes," I say.

We are sipping coffee on his porch. It's only two o'clock in the afternoon, but it feels a lot later. Perhaps I've been on the road for too long, or it appears to be late because I haven't been out much lately. And coming here was a very spontaneous decision, which makes me wonder why I am here.

"I really love living in the country while everybody else strives to live and work in the city. All I need is right here."

"I guess not everybody owns land like you do," I say. "And everyone has a different idea on job and lifestyle."

"Is that why you live in New York?"

For some reason, I have Cheshire on my mind. Even though it belongs to the New York metropolitan area, it has never felt like it. New York is an entirely different story. Cheshire was recently ranked as one of the best places to live in the States. To me, Cheshire mainly makes me think of my parents' house and our garden.

"Pardon?"

"You said New York offers variety," he says.

His hands are large but gentle.

"But you know what," he continues. "Most of my friends are farmers or ranchers. It's not much of an adventurous life and surely not a place for the creative-minded. People nowadays, especially the youth, hate hard work. They wouldn't take over family businesses. They don't want to stick around."

Buddy is exploring the field by sniffing the ground as if following a trail, and surprisingly it leads him to Dexter. He becomes scared and alert.

"Decadence and apathy are big issues at the moment," he says. "People have their heads up in the clouds. They just don't know how to appreciate what they've got."

For a farmer I find him rather articulate and insightful. His accent is like mine – softly rhotic.

"I'm sure it's more complicated than that," I say. "And yes, variety or possibilities broaden their chances of getting what they want."

He smiles.

"Have you always wanted to be a physician?"

"Yes."

"You must've worked very hard to get there."

Dexter doesn't like Buddy's presence and keeps turning his back on him. Buddy is still alert and curious about Dexter.

"Well, people here aren't as happy as they appear to be," he says.

"What about you?"

He remains silent for a while, then says, "I've always wanted to take over my dad's farm when I was a kid.

But you know, once you have what you want, you get bored, despite the work that keeps you busy."

"Are you lonely?" I say.

"Well, I watched a lot of high school friends leave."

His face saddens a little.

"I guess the search for the American Dream is still an attractive one," I say.

"The modernists have already proved that the American Dream doesn't exist," he says.

It's like I'm back at university – in a workshop with literature students, either realists or cynics. The tutor is merely sitting at his desk, listening with an inscrutable smile.

"Why do you believe in what those writers say?" I ask.

"Because that's the truth. When you don't know what to do with your life, you go to New York or California...it's a gamble."

This sounds familiar.

"Did you study literature?"

"No, history. And look where I am?" he smiles.

It's on the tip of my tongue to tell him that there has never been a better place for me to live apart from New York. I know who I am; New York allows me to camouflage my inner self and deal with it in silence. It's not self-denial, which happens to most people who come to the city to fulfill their dreams. However, the odds of success are low if you have no social status, educational qualifications, or decent family background.

"So you think I'm gambling in New York?" I say.

He thinks for a while, or at least he pretends, refusing to look at me.

"No," he says.

Buddy hops onto the porch to seek our company. Hank strokes him gently on the head, his hand now not far from my leg.

My phone vibrates, and I grab it from my bag. Stuart is calling. I dismiss him.

"I hope you're hungry," Hank says.

I feel sick to the stomach for some reason.

By the time we go inside the house, it's almost 6 p.m. I've only just become aware of the quiet environment – the absence of sirens, filtered conversation, and the sound of thousands of people walking through the city center. The last time I felt this way was in Milan. I remember having my lunch in the park, where I was observing a toad in the pond. It didn't move for the entire time that I was eating. Then a little girl and her mother walked past. Excited about the toad, the girl hopped towards the pond, and the toad jumped into the water.

Why am I not with my parents or Dr. Dick?

"I was hoping that you'd like to stay. So I've prepared a room for you. Take a rest. I'll prepare dinner. I'll show you around tomorrow morning."

The inside of the house is massive, with a high ceiling. Only a married couple with big plans would have bought or built a place like that.

He has picked king-size bedroom for me, decorated with fine velvet curtains, a thick embroidered carpet and an expressionist painting illustrating a herd of horses.

At the end of the bed is a large treasure chest on the floor. It's locked.

"You really live on your own?"

He has cooked lamb chops with vegetables and mashed yam. I'm not surprised that farmers like him have a healthy diet. There is nothing about his physical feature that would imply any vitamin deficiency. Seems like he consumes enough good fatty acids that add luster to his good-looking face.

"Yeah, but every other week I have my pals come by for a few beers and poker."

I seem to have entered a world where stereotypes have their own reality. He describes to me a typical men's night. I suddenly find myself having an ordinary human conversation; it is no longer just about anatomy or relieving pain.

Is this the world of Helen?

Hank's lamb chops taste more organic and tender than the rubbery ones I once had in a New York restaurant. I'm one of the few people that can taste the blood when eating medium-rare red meat.

One part of me is dying to prick Hank's finger with the lancet that's in my pocket, but Helen is telling me to wait and adapt to this healthy type of social convention. This is what people do when they like each other, she says.

"Helen..."

The name has me stumped every time he says it and makes me question my identity. Despite the insecurity, my voice seems to respond to him.

"This is very tasty, Hank," I say, gazing at the food, actually not that hungry.

"Thank you. I like cooking for people."

Men who cook most likely make their wives put on weight. I see Helen, pregnant with twins walking towards the television in the living room to rest while Hank is doing the dishes. As Helen smiles at this image, my eye twitches.

"Listen," he says, "I don't have guests often, and I want to make sure you feel at home. If there's anything you need, just give me a shout."

"Everything's good, Hank. Thank you."

Buddy has just finished his rice and chicken in the corner of the dining room; he sits up and burps. I don't remember him ever burping after the wet food I fed him in New York. I honestly wonder why he hasn't died on me yet like a plant would.

"I don't go away often," I say.

"More reason to enjoy your vacation."

"More importantly, we have to sort that fella out." I nod at Buddy. "I'm sure he's better in your hands."

"Have you ever had pets, Helen?"

"No."

We agree on training Buddy in the morning.

CHAPTER FIFTEEN

The kitten doesn't like me. When Dad found her this morning on the doorstep, he thought it would be a good idea to wake me with her. But instead of a pleasant wake-up call, the kitten scratched my head. When I come back from school, I find her staring at me as if I weren't a part of the family. We have decided to keep her in Dolly's rabbit cage at nighttime.

After brushing my teeth, I to go to bed and find that Daddy has placed the kitten in my room. Her evil eyes are scrutinizing me.

"Hey princess, look, you have company tonight."

"But cats rob little children's breath, Dad!"

"Don't be ridiculous. I've told you not to read horror books, haven't I? She's just a little baby; give her a chance to get used to you."

I never used to be scared of the boogieman, candyman, hollow man, or the postman, but that kitten... This is the first time I've had a living creature at the end of my bed. Dad gives me a kiss good night, then turns off the light in the hallway.

The kitten doesn't make any sound until 3 a.m. when she wakes me with her pitiful meowing. I switch the night lamp on and notice that her head is stuck between the bars of the cage.

"Shut up. You're going to wake up my parents!"

Carefully I try to push her head back in.

I don't know what I have done, but all of a sudden, her whine stops, her eyes close, and her head hangs down.

"Kittie?"

Two seconds later, she opens her eyes and forcefully pulls her head back. She continues to whine even louder.

"Shut up! Shut up!"

I grab underneath my bed and find the pair of surgical scissors that I stole from one of Daddy's colleagues. I hate this creature. I never realized that animals could even express anger, agony, or anguish.

"Shut up!"

I stick the pair of scissors multiple times in the cage, turning and twisting violently.

"Shut up! Shut up!"

The sharp end of the pair of scissors has entered the flesh. I hear a small groan and then feel no more movement. There's blood on the tip of my surgical scissors.

I hear no one down the hallway or squeaking of coil springs.

It's dark inside the cage. Touching the blood, it looks like cranberry juice from concentrate. Her whine is still resonating in my ears; I hit my palm against my head a few times.

Before undoing the hook of the cage, I wait a little longer. Maybe the nine lives myth is real after all.

Then, I undo the hook and hold the cage upside down, so the kitten's body falls onto a magazine. I got her in the stomach. She is not coming back to life.

I remember Dad saying that I will make a wonderful doctor. In fact, I want to be a surgeon. Looking at the kitten's motionless body, I feel like a veterinarian during an operation. The wound needs to be sewn. Maybe her third life will commence after the suture. I will get thread and needles. But first, I have to sanitize my hands.

I still haven't grown accustomed to the lack of noise in the countryside. It's almost too quiet for me.

My hay fever is back, which is unusual because I last had it as a teenager. It got better year after year as I grew older.

We're close to autumn, and I don't feel well enough to leave my room. Sneezing every other minute with a runny nose, I don't want to face anyone. My anti-allergy pills are back at home in the mirror cabinet and probably out of date since I don't need them in New York. I'm embarrassed and can't face Hank like this. I'm sure he has heard my sneeze attacks. My eyes are swollen, along with rashes on both sides of my nose, spreading across my entire face. It's not the dust mites in the mattress, as Hank has provided a protective cover. I blame myself for being so ill-prepared. Didn't I know I'd be spending time in the countryside?

I have brought nothing but moisturizing cream on this journey. When have I ever been so terribly equipped? Worst of all, I have no opportunity to check my blood regularly. I've left my needles, tubes, and microscope in New York. And what's the use of a lancet with no analysis device?

Who is this ugly swollen person in the mirror?

I hear a noise outside: Hank's Toyota pulling down the yard. I hear Buddy, the cause of all my troubles, scratching gently against my door. He whimpers at the lack of response. I start to walk around in the room to check that there is no specific allergen that has triggered this attack. I feel as though the stability of my immune system is at stake.

My eyes rest on the large children's treasure chest at the foot of the bed, dusty and unlocked. It only appears locked. As I open the box, I find kids' toys: string-operated dolls, Matchbox cars, and numerous stuffed animals, which have never been played with before.

For some reason, this room gives me the creeps. I open the door and find Buddy wagging his tail. The hallway is huge, but it looks like there are only two bedrooms. The other rooms must be downstairs. Certain that the other bedroom is Hank's room, I open the door and find a king-size bed, a framed photograph of his wedding, and a large wardrobe. The room is somewhat less spacious than mine but looks comfortable and cozy. His former wife bears a resemblance to me, except that she has a rounder face, but we almost have the same blonde curls and smile.

Helen wonders what it'd be like settling down with Hank and leaving New York behind for good. New York – where my life has lost its purpose to grow any further. Helen views Connecticut as her true home.

I take a quick shower before Hank comes back and lock myself in the bedroom again. About half an hour later, he returns and knocks on my door.

"Helen, please answer me?"

I lean against the door and say, "Hi, sorry, I'm not feeling too good."

"Well, I got you some pills which might help. I also got some eye drops, nose spray, and ointment, if you need them. I'll leave them by the door, OK?"

"Thanks."

I listen to him walking down the stairs. Then I observe him from the window watering the ground; maybe he is trying to reduce the pollen count in the air. I take the pills and go back to bed, as antihistamines always make me tired.

I wake up at half-past eight in the evening. Feeling a lot better and more rejuvenated. I open the window and breathe in the fresh chilly air like I did when I arrived. The rash has gone, but my skin is dehydrated.

I brush my teeth and put on some moisturizing cream before leaving the room. I find Hank downstairs in the living room watching television with Buddy. On TV is a rerun of Tom Colicchio's show on the American way of cooking.

Is this really what lonely men watch nowadays?

"Hi," I say, and only Buddy seems to hear me. He jumps up, wagging his tail.

Hank turns around and says, "Hey, are you OK?"

"Yes, thanks for providing me with antihistamines. You saved my life. I was a little embarrassed."

"I didn't know you have hay fever."

I notice baby polar bears on the cushion on which Buddy rests his head.

"Neither did I," I say. "Well, I didn't want you to see that face of mine; I just didn't want to scare you."

"I'm sure it wasn't that bad," he smiles. "Are you hungry?"

"Not really."

We watch the show together like husband and wife, except that we're not sitting next to each other hand-in-hand.

Seeing images like this in my head usually sickens me; they make my stomach turn. But to my surprise, Helen seems to like it. I find her throwing hungry looks at Hank, hoping he'll look back.

"Can I ask you something?"

"Of course," he says.

"So you studied history at Miami."

"Yeah."

"Was it hard for you to leave Miami behind?"

He strokes Buddy's head. It's a relief finding Buddy all comfortable and safe near Hank. I figure it's a kind of compassion that I can't give.

"When my father died, my mother wanted to sell the farm and move to New Haven. But I knew that my Dad wouldn't have wanted her to do that. So I came back from Florida to take care of the place, and I fell in love with Pamela once again. We used to date in high school before I left for college."

He lowers his head for a moment.

"The rest," he continues, "seemed to have fallen into place."

"Do you ever think about returning to Miami?"

"No."

The cook has spilled some olive oil on the stove.

"How about you?" he says. "Do you reckon you'll stay in New York for good?"

Who is he speaking to? I wonder who is going to reply – Helen or me.

"Is Buddy asleep?"

He glances at him and says yes.

"Put him over there, will you?"

Hank obeys and places Buddy and his polar bear pillow on the single sofa. Tom Colicchio's voice begins to fade into the background.

Next, I find myself on Hank's lap, kissing him hard on the lips and ears, while he grabs hold of my buttocks and occasionally runs his hands softly up and down my hips.

He smells clean – the hygiene test is a pass.

Then I consider knocking him out with that desk lamp next to us, so I can check his blood, but it might be a bad idea without a microscope.

"When did you last have sex?" I whisper, aware that my underwear is soaked.

"Not since…"

He hesitates, and I stick my tongue back into his mouth.

Next, I take off my top and then unbutton his pajamas. Pressing my body hard against him, he sucks at my breasts and neck.

Next, Helen brings out his erect penis, rubs it a little more before putting it inside us. She is more interested in his penis than his heart. His heart rate is increasing, but it doesn't mean anything to me.

I wake up in Hank's bed covered in sweat, trying to remember what happened.

"I didn't come," I whisper to myself.

I turn around and see Hank asleep. I reflect on the images of our intercourse and remember each step – from kissing, sucking to penetration. I used to be so out of touch with myself during sex, but it's different now. I am aware of it, and I am focused; I just don't feel anything for Hank.

Looking across the bed, I notice that he has taken down his wedding photograph. I sneak out of bed and go back to my room to play with the toys in the treasure chest.

In the morning, Hank wakes me up. I must've fallen asleep on the floor with a stuffed kitten in my arms.

"Are you OK?"

He lays himself beside me on the rug, and we kiss.

"I should have gotten rid of this box years ago," he says.

"This room makes me sad."

"I'm sorry, you should've said. I mean, nobody ever stayed in here before. I thought you would like it."

I stay quiet, unsure whose sentiments I'm expressing.

From my position on the floor, I can see a child's suitcase underneath the bed. I turn back to Hank. Before I have the chance to ask him something, he says, "I don't remember the last time I was as happy as I am now," and kisses me.

My eyes remain open during the kiss. I examine the sad wrinkles on his forehead, the frailty of his eyelids, and his thinning hair. I'm numb and empty, but it seems to be the happiest moment in Helen's life.

"Are you OK, Helen? You seem miles away." He looks worried.

"Hank, I'm..."

Buddy walks into the room and pees against the leg of the bed. Hank jumps up to grab him.

"I forgot to let him out. He has been doing quite well, actually, hasn't he?"

Hank turns this journey into a vacation well spent. I feel invigorated at his place, although the idea of settling down in Connecticut makes me want to die.

It's only been two days, and I have met some of Hank's close friends already. I know they've been encouraging him to make me stay longer. They are good people and happily married, even his brother.

But Hank should know how city people tick, and that's why he knows he is powerless over my will. And so is Helen.

I switch my mobile phone on for the first time since Friday, and I see several missed calls from Stuart. There are two voicemails, one from yesterday and another from six hours ago. In the first one, Stuart says, "Parker, turn on your phone, or open the door, please!"

In the second one, he says, "All right, Parks, I spoke to your landlady. So you really *have* gone away. The good news is she won't call the cops on me for the disturbance. The bad news is..."

Long pause – I hear the rustling wind in the background.

"Mr. Whitley's in a critical condition again. Listen, I need you. Your vacation is over. Get the hell back here."

He sounds drunk.

My throat is dry, cold sweat running down my back as I crawl into Hank's bed, but I can't sleep. For the first time, this entire journey seems wrong and ludicrous, as if I've followed footsteps into the unknown just to find some more puzzles. Or perhaps I'm looking to find a new purpose. Whether or not it suits me is another question. Is this the nature of being human? The inability to appreciate what you have because you believe there is something more significant to aim for?

Connecticut is beautiful and will always be my home.

But what am I doing here? Who is Helen?

Stuart needs my help.

I sneak out of bed again to take a walk outside. There's less light pollution here, but I don't need *tapetum lucidum* to see in the dark. Buddy follows me out. His eyeshine reflects the moonlight. It is only now that I notice how much he has grown since last week. Hank feeds him better than I do. If it hadn't been for Hank, Buddy would have died on me.

The cold air invigorates my senses, and I feel good.

I enter the barn to check on the animals. A couple of days ago, I would have dreaded this smelly place, but I've grown accustomed to it now. I would like to ride across the field on a beautiful horse like Dexter, but he doesn't seem to like me.

Some animals begin to stir when I turn on the barn light.

Buddy makes himself comfortable on a bunch of hay and falls asleep almost instantly. The goats and cattle are sleeping, but I hear heavy grunts coming from the back.

The two pigs are mating. I watch the male fall over as if embarrassed that I've caught them in the act. Then I realize that he is ejaculating continuously, but the sow, still standing on all fours, pokes at her mate with her snout, waiting for the male to continue, but he is still ejaculating.

I shake my head at him and watch the sow turn away and lie down.

I find a pair of rubber gloves for gardening, which Hank wears to clean the equipment in the barn. I put them on in the way I would put on my surgical gloves in the operating theater. The rubber gently snaps against my wrist.

The sow looks dissatisfied, kicking at her mate with her lower legs. I can imagine what that tingle feels like.

I kneel down to find her vagina. It takes a while until my fingers have located it. Then she starts to twitch and grunt at the same time.

I do this for about three minutes until finally, she comes.

"Helen?" I hear a voice behind me. "What the hell are you doing?"

Helen does not exist.

And if only he knew that Helen would never do such a thing. If I were Helen, I would never forgive myself.

Not that I care. I have done several bad things in my life. I have lost count of them.

Helen does not exist.

I'm in my car, thinking that I should've never left New York. A sense of dissatisfaction engulfs me because I'm leaving Hank without unfolding his secrets and learning about his blood type.

I'm not worthy of knowing anyway. I'm too selfish. Whatever was in that child's suitcase – a part of me is now buried in there.

On the morning of my departure, we have nothing to talk about. Apparently, he separates the pig and the sow from each other at night, but I didn't tell him that they could somehow unlatch their gates because I did not release them. Whether I have disappointed him or infuriated him, I'm not entirely sure.

"Trust me, Buddy is in good hands," he says, holding the little puppy in his arms like a kid cuddling his first pet. Only that pet doesn't realize that it won't ever see me again. It doesn't even understand farewell.

"I'm sure."

I don't believe that all dogs have a sense of time passing, especially if they get a good healthy routine like Buddy will. Soon I'll just be a shadow in his memory.

We part without saying goodbye. Hank turns away before I even turn on the engine.

CHAPTER SIXTEEN

The moment I hear honking cars and swearing people, I know I am home. Despite the sense of loss or what people would refer to as a missed opportunity, I am convinced that it was for the best.

My landlady, who lives across from me, steps out when she hears me open the door to my apartment.

"Oh, Miss Parker! You're back! "

"Hello, Mrs. Meyer. Yes, I am."

Mrs. Meyer is a widow in her seventies with perfect hearing. She looks down the staircase to check whether someone is coming.

"Listen, hon. That doctor of yours…"

"My supervisor?"

"Yes! He was a nuisance."

"I'm sorry. Don't worry; it won't happen again."

She looks disapproving. "The sound of that motorbike, oh Lord!"

I catch Helen laughing at me on the inside.

"But he seemed very worried about you. So I forgive him," she says. "I was worried, too. It's good to have you home."

She pats my shoulder gently and goes back into her apartment. I linger outside for a moment, savoring the feeling that there is nowhere else I'd rather be. The silent cold dark corridor brings a sense of peace to my mind.

I'm home.

It's Wednesday – I'm on my way to work. The smell of disinfectant tickles my nostrils pleasantly; my lab coat's fabric provides my body with perfect warmth and smoothness.

I don't even want to slip into Prada or Ralph Lauren clothing anymore. My colleagues' eyes brighten up as they see me. They all assume that I was in the Bahamas, and I do not deny it.

I see Sarah walking my way with the happiest and most genuine smile. As she puts her arms around me, I don't know whether I'm supposed to return the hug in the same manner.

"Ellen! You're back! You look tanned. So, you did go to the Bahamas!"

"Yeah, something like that."

She proudly shows me her ring finger on which she's wearing Jay's engagement ring. I don't know what to say, so I just smile.

"Congratulations."

I carry on walking towards Stuart's office, where I sense a heartbeat already – not his, but Mr. Whitley's. Is he there?

I knock on his door, but no one answers. It's locked. It's only twelve in the afternoon, and he doesn't eat lunch until three, or not at all.

"Dr. Parker!"

I turn around and see Julia.

"You don't look that tanned," she says. "Did you really go to the Bahamas?"

"Well, no."

This is like a dream. I'm unsure about the reality of my first day back; it has this surreal element to it that I can't fathom.

"We missed you! It's been hell without you here! Poor Stuart has hardly had any rest. There have been so many surgeries."

"Well, I'm back and not going anywhere," I say.

"That's nice to hear. But listen..." She looks around and then lowers her voice. "Ellen. This is just between you and me, OK?"

She hardly ever calls me by my first name.

"Is something wrong?"

She's looking for the right words, or she's hesitant to share a secret with me.

"It's about Stuart. He used to be such a hard shell to crack, long before you came."

"What do you mean?" I say.

"Come on, I'm not blind, and neither are you."

"Seriously, what do you mean?"

"You really don't know?" She sounds almost desperate, even sad. I can't help staring at the side of her nose, looking for answers. I only identify some blackheads.

"He's in love with you!"

Apparently, Stuart is on the roof, playing mini-golf with a friend. Taking the elevator up, I wonder who his friend is.

When I reach the rooftop and step outside, a sudden cold breeze brushes against my face. The air in New York smells homely, whereas everything in Connecticut was simply wishful thinking and illusory.

Like Helen.

At least here, you can be the same height as the sky.

Stuart is sitting alone in a beach chair with a golf club under his arm, his back facing me. He tilts his head slightly when he hears my steps.

"I've been told you're playing golf with your pal. So, where is he?" I say.

He exhales and lowers his head. The golf ball hasn't been touched, and the exquisite golf course is undiscovered territory. It's hard to believe that some colleagues decided to install this little course for relaxation purposes.

"Nah, he just leaped off the roof. If only you had come two minutes earlier."

It doesn't sound like a joke.

"Should we save him?" he says.

"What's going on, Stuart?"

I hurry to the railing and look down, but I see nobody. Is he referring to Mr. Whitley? The hospital is approximately two or three hundred feet high, and if someone were lying dead at the bottom, there'd be a crowd forming.

Stuart stands beside me and reaches the golf club over the railing, as if trying to save someone who might be holding on.

"Help me, Parker. He's heavy."

I can't describe the look on his face. A sudden collage of images is shooting before my eyes: I see the two of us in the OT performing another valve replacement, at

Aureole discussing metaphors for female genitalia, and then...

His face turns red; I see the veins in his temple. He is pulling hard.

"Come on!" he says.

I grab hold of the golf club, my hands touching his, and we both start to pull as hard as we can. Eventually, we both fall backward.

"What was that?" I say.

The huge Stuart McCormick grin has returned from the dead.

"Welcome back, Parker!" He stands up and walks to the door, whistling.

"Where is Mr. Whitley?"

"At home with his missus. What did you think?"

Sarah and I are sitting at a bar downtown. It's different being with her now. Before she was like a little stepsister. A month ago, I never would have agreed to go out with her again.

This evening, I would rather go through my new patients' documents, but I guess I owe her that one glass of wine. I'm guilty of going to Connecticut. I had to lie to Dad that I was too busy to come home.

"Have I told you that Jay is super cute, Ellen?"

"Um, no."

I reckon that she must be seeking assurance from me with these girl talks. I don't know what to say. She circles her finger around the edge of her wine glass, practicing in her head what to say next.

"I asked Jay about you," she swallows, "and him."

"I told you there's nothing. What were you trying to find out?"

She shakes her head in shame. Her hair moves with her.

"No, no, it's not that," she says. "We were talking about something else."

The bartender shoots a flirty smile at the two of us, but we ignore him. A few lonely creatures are whiling away the hours in dark corners, nursing their glasses of numbing substances. How old do you have to be to realize that sorrow can swim?

"I wanted to make sure that you really didn't have any feelings for him."

"I told you."

"I know, I know. I'm sorry! I should've spoken to you from the start," she says.

The silence reveals a tense pressure in the air; it makes me realize what friendship really involves. Is she asking for forgiveness, advice, or trust?

"Well, Jay was useless."

"What did he say?" I say.

"I was puzzled about something." Her voice is firmer now, condemning, which reminds me of Mother when Dad has done something wrong. A woman tends to exploit a man's misdemeanors because she believes that it emphasizes her spotless innocence. But if *she* commits something wrong, the man will defend his pride by dispelling all available access, and you'll never know what's on his mind. Then the woman will figure that he is for real.

But can you blame him?

I ask no further.

"He said," she begins, "there was someone in your life."

"I don't remember saying this to him."

"Well, you must have said something."

"I don't know. So, what if I did?"

"Ellen!"

Now she sounds upset. And I don't know why. Why is she condemning me for rejecting Jay?

She downs her wine and asks for a refill. The bartender hurries to fulfill her request. Judging by his handiwork and boyish lips, he would do anything for a girl he likes. What kind of woman would want that? On the other hand, what kind of man would want a woman to be clingy and needy? I have put a lot of value on independence in my life, and I have benefited from self-reliance. Whenever you ask someone for help, you always have to return the favor. I'm too busy for that.

"I'm your friend, Ellen," she says. There is sadness in her voice. "While you were away, you didn't reply to any of my text messages."

I roll my eyes.

"I don't know where you went, who you were with, let alone who you're seeing!"

I finish my glass of wine, but I decline a refill. The wine is taking effect on me. My cheeks feel warm.

"I'm not seeing anyone."

"You're such a..." She shakes her head, tailing off, but instead, I hear Norman finishing for her.

Liar.

He is probably pushing the little girl on her swing. I still haven't got a clue what links that little girl to demon Norman.

"According to Jay, I said something after the accident, but I don't recall," I say.

"Was it *Georgie*?"

I look at her and wonder whether Jay ever fantasizes about impaling her during sex.

"My little sister," I say.

"Don't lie to me!"

When people are overly confident about knowing the facts of your life, you shouldn't take them seriously. In fact, you're lucky, because no one will ever understand you the way you do. If you have feelings, fine, because I'm sure no one will ever feel the same as you do. Calling me a liar doesn't make me feel anything.

"How special is Georgie?"

The bartender isn't that bad after all. If I asked him to brush my Prada pumps, he probably would.

"Ellen, don't shut me out, please."

I bet his name is Mark, recently graduated and now worrying about the uncertainties of life. Unsure of what to do with himself, he contemplates finding a girl to marry; at least that would keep him from being alone in the big city.

Can you blame him?

"Right, I will get to the point then," Sarah says, exhaling heavily.

I look at her again. She is too young to get married.

"Stuart was a completely different person when you were gone," she says.

"How?"

Mark is throwing me an I-should-ask-her-out look. Unfortunately, he makes me think of Zach. A woman shouldn't go out with a younger man. It does her ego no good. Besides, she's living her dream while he's still searching for his purpose, which means he won't stick around for long.

"We've never seen him so absent-minded. Did you have a fight?"

Sarah's mouth is wrinkled at the corner. Maybe she is old enough to get married after all. Focusing on my mirror reflection in the wine bottle, I see only a disfigured version of my head. If I move further to the right, it looks a little heart-shaped like Mr. Whitley's. I wonder whether he has officially swapped the Yes word with those augmented buttocks.

"Stuart is going back to gynecology," Sarah says.

"*What?*"

"We thought it was a joke, too, but he has already signed up for that department. Isn't that crazy? You'll be assigned a temporary supervisor, and I'm sure you'll soon be head of cardiac surgery."

Staring at my deformed head gives me nausea.

"Ellen? Don't tell me you didn't know."

"We'll see about that!"

The suitcase is throbbing under my bed. As soon as Mother has left the house, I open it again to let the frog out. It hops onto my head and disappears in my hair. And then he bounces towards the window. I make a grab for him, but he jumps onto the chair and hops out of the window.

I can't get him. Climbing onto the windowsill from my desk, I see a pile of steep running concrete roof tiles on which he is resting.

"Don't go!"

I reach down for him, but he bounces off again. My arms are too short, so I grab my mini golf club and carefully climb back up again. This time I step out onto the roof, lying on my belly, holding my golf club in my right hand.

Unfortunately, I hit the frog a little too hard.

"Ellen?" I see George shouting at me from his backyard.

I let go of the club, which first hits the porch roof below and then the ground. The dead creature is about to roll down the tiles as well. I take a small step further onto the roof and watch George jump over the fence to our yard.

"What are you doing?" He looks alarmed.

"I killed something."

"OK, don't move!" he says and starts looking around for something. There is a ladder in the shed, but I'm not telling him.

"Will you catch me if I fall?"

"I'm not sure about that, little girl."

"Why?"

"The roof tiles seem loose. They'll probably hit me first before I can catch you."

I touch the tiles below me, and he is right. Now the frog rolls down the roof and falls right in front of George's feet.

"Is this what happens when you play with animals?"

I smile, and suddenly my arm slips, and I slide further forward.

"OK, listen to me, Ellen, don't move!"

He climbs over the fence, goes into our shed, finds the ladder, and leans it against the porch roof. As he climbs up the ladder, he checks the condition of the roof tiles. He carefully steps on it and walks towards me. My heart is beating fast, and my cheeks are blushing.

"I'm glad you guys have a low pitch roof."

With my belly on the tiles and my body leaned forward, I find it rather steep. As it gets a little steeper on the way up, he bends his knees.

"OK, Ellen, I want you to slowly lift both your hands like this."

He holds up both his palms, and I do as I'm told. I feel some kind of spark when our warm palms touch. He is looking at me as he pushes me back through my bedroom window.

Sometimes I find myself waking up on Buddy's cushion on the floor. After a while, you do get lonely in a king-size bed. I never sprawl; each night, I choose a particular side of the bed, and when I wake up, I often find my knees pressed against my chest. I wonder why every time I open my eyes, I am out of breath.

Dad has been chasing me about my planned visit, which I had to postpone. Speaking of which, this morning, I received a letter from Connecticut. Dad never writes letters or postcards – he calls – and Mother wouldn't have the guts to send me anything.

The letter is written in Dr. Dick's handwriting:

Ellen, dear Ellen,

Now I wonder; why on earth am I worthy of knowing about the skeletons in your closet? Did I say skeletons? I'm sorry, there is just one – however, a bad one, and it has almost blocked off all available access that people have to you. You must find him and face him.

We both know that he is a demonic fellow, but it's not me he wants to talk to. So how about, my dear Ellen, you trap him? He knows something about you, and I'm sure you are dying to find out, but you lack the courage.

Why is that?

I'm sorry I lied; there are actually two skeletons. However, you have to invite both in. I have no idea how much space you have in your apartment, but the three of you have some serious things to discuss. Trust me, you are strong enough to win this argument. You women are always stronger and shrewder to whip us men with words. I have resented you for inviting me into this demonic district of yours, but on the other hand, I am grateful for your trust throughout the years. I was happy to be your mentor; I still am.

Ellen, I personally take no advantage of having my eyes open all the time but be clear about other people's good intentions; you will see they mean no harm.

Please, don't hurt them. They don't deserve it. They care about you.

The skeleton with horns will destroy you if you don't open your eyes to him. And the other skeleton with wings has his arms wide open for you, and you refuse to see it.

It may sound like an exciting threesome, but it's not. I understand if you are afraid. I won't deny it; I've lived in fear, too. But I'm no savior. I don't even want to save myself, not even in my most vulnerable hour.

Dear Ellen, don't lose your grip; it's not the time. You have to hang in there. The pain will be over once you have accepted it. You are not alone.

With all my love,
Phil

I can't breathe – cold sweat and tears are blurring my vision, but I make no sound as if I'm in a cyborg's body with a system failure. An ice-cold shiver has eaten its way through my limbs – there is nothing but numbness. Perhaps I should gasp for air like an asthma patient. That's what people do when they cry.

My entire past is an accumulation of dirt and has just overflowed into my present. My inner morass is no longer keeping the dark faculties at the bottom. My body is fighting hard against this heat that I'm generating underneath my comforter. The heat is coming off me in waves; there is a bitter flavor in my mouth.

It's getting damper. The air is thin.

What have I done to these innocent men? And how come they don't resent me? I will no longer inflict anguish on anyone. But like a cloud, I was made—a cluster of little particles aiming to evolve. It's nothing but chemistry. And like each creation, you believe in good and evil, but there is no definition for them. It's the same as there being no God unless you believe. God exists in the heads of those who believe strongly that He is good. It's the kind of autosuggestion to help make you feel better—believing that a higher power watches over you just so you are not alone.

But the truth is, we're all alone.

Ultimately people have created something in their heads. They are the producers of their own good. Is humanity even real? It's human nature to doubt oneself, so instead of trusting what is inside, man creates a God. How is a Christian any different from someone with an authoritative voice in his head?

The voice I hear has temporarily stopped asking for blood; that voice that has been feeding the purpose of my existence every day is now silent. And I am lost without it.

Since the transfusion, my needs are no longer excessive, as though Scott has cleansed my body. But my inner self hasn't altered; if anything, I've become more aware of it. I've begun to view it with less fear. My cells are feeding my blood flow with courage.

If you have a sharp eye for detail, you can see blood cells' peculiar movements under the microscope. Some cells may look deformed; they may be loners or clingy bastards. Even if you have the same blood type as someone else, no two slides can be identical, except for Scott's and mine.

All cells, although unaware of good and evil, have a job to do. All my life, I have related myself to them. I dedicate my life to a job that defines me.

The only thing that distracts a cell is a bacterium or a virus. The cell's instinct will incite destruction mode. If a cell kills, it will be for a good reason, which is to save you.

In the end, no matter if good or evil, there is always a creator—a creator that might not care about his creation. And this is where the problem begins.

CHAPTER SEVENTEEN

Dr. Dick is gone.

My father woke me in the middle of the night during his late-night shift. It's like pulling me out of a nightmare only to tell me that the nightmare is real. When your eyes are open, things aren't usually as vivid as behind closed lids.

After hearing about Dr. Dick's death, I realized something. It's the first time that a sense of loss triggers the fear of another loss.

If only I had known that leaving Connecticut for a new job in New York would have been the last time I saw him or if only I had listened to Dad and come home sooner.

Even though we lose people in the OT, I have never experienced anything like this before. Those losses only count as failures, your failure to prove your ability and capacity to preserve life. Events and tragedy in the OT are ways of measuring your proficiency.

It's different when you actually believe that you have lost someone who was a part of you, someone that has made you who you are. Dr. Dick is now a big chunk of me crumbling away. When people die, you sometimes wonder whether they have ever existed at all or whether they were only part of your imagination, like the God you created in your head.

In my compendium of philosophical wisdom, Nietzsche announces that God is dead. Isn't this the moment we feel fear, abandonment, and loss? If so, one should see it as the best lesson to teach oneself self-reliance and courage.

I can't go back to sleep. Staring at my plain face in the bathroom mirror, my green eyes appear to be sharper and more menacing under the halogen light. My curls have lost volume. Now they resemble a middle-aged woman's wavy hair, a woman who has reached the peak of her life just in time. What if she never intended to get there?

I get dressed immediately.

Ringing Stuart's door at 1 a.m. is probably the most daring thing I've ever done. I should be in bed, dreaming about fine incisions, the luscious sound of cuts through flesh.

He answers the door without his glasses. It makes him look vulnerable: the hollowness in his eyes is the same as mine.

I didn't wake him.

"Parker."

I enter his house, not waiting to be invited. He steps aside to provide me some space, almost stumbling over his houseplants.

"You're a heart surgeon," I say.

Digging my fingers into his hair, I kiss Stuart hard on the mouth. As he places his hand gently behind my head, I feel his fragile posture. I taste the bitter grief on his lips.

"You're a heart surgeon," I repeat, and somehow this saddens him.

We reach the same heart rate again – the exact same as last time. Even on a dark night like this, we have created a bright enough shield to fend off the dark – make it disappear, at least for a while.

While we kiss, his body over mine, I bring forward a lancet that I've been hiding in my right palm and cut the left side of his naked chest.

He groans.

Then I cut myself above my right breast. Stuart sits up anxiously and takes the lancet away as though fearing the worst.

"What is this?"

I press my fingers against his lips and raise my body. Stuart leans back as I swing my thighs over his to facilitate penetration.

Blood is oozing out of our chests and running in several lines down our bodies. He pulls me closer, and both our wounds meet. The spark traveling through my cells reaches my cerebral field of perception, and there is this tingle in my spine, which I've missed ever since our first time together.

"We're the same," I say in one breath.

The blood smears all over our chests like crimson on canvas. I place my tainted fingers between our mouths while our bodies move to the rhythmical dance. A sweet-tasting stream runs down my tongue and again sets the center of my brain on fire.

The dim light in the room somehow fills the hollowness on our faces. There is something after all, something that can diminish the feeling of loss. And that is a heartbeat that backs you up when you need it the most. I'm looking at Stuart McCormick, aware of his presence and mine, aware of the sensations in my body.

The blood has dried on our bodies. We are wiping each other's mouth clean like two cannibals – two humans who have only just come to their senses. Stuart is no cannibal, but I could make him one if I don't watch what I do.

Even without my makeup, he looks at me in the same way, like I'm all that matters right now. Having shared our blood, we've risked sharing our diseases, our hopes, and losses. If life were to end this very moment, I would eagerly follow the footsteps into the unknown with him.

But that would be too easy. My inner faculties have taken over so intensely that I've almost forgotten that I came here for a reason.

"You're inscrutable," he says.

Now the dim light has brought back reality. This is when your brain tosses you out of the trance. And the least you want to do now is talk.

I kiss Stuart while my hand glides longingly towards his genitals again.

But he hesitates. "Parker…"

Reality always ruins the moment with hesitation or a guilty conscience. I don't know how to comfort him.

He turns away from me onto his side; I stare at his back. I touch my wound with dirty fingers and feel a slight burn.

"He was my godfather," Stuart says with pain in his voice.

Father would sound more convenient, and I would've believed him, too.

"You know what he said to me?" he says.

Dry blood gets really uncomfortable on the body after a while. You want to scrape it off like a scab.

"He said that I was a heart surgeon. But I didn't believe him, and then you echoed his words."

I wonder whether he would let me touch him now.

"Maybe you're right," he says as he turns back to me.

"What?"

Stuart looks at me differently: a strange spark has ignited in his irises as if he were under some kind of spell.

"You're right."

He moves closer, his eyes ready to devour me. I pull my head back a little. My eyes blink uncontrollably to his smile and rush of emotions.

"There was a feeling," he says.

"A what?"

"For God's sake, Parker. In the last eighteen months I've known you, I witnessed no emotion whatsoever."

There is a hunger tantalizing me, but this hunger knows very well that it will not be fed again tonight. I don't feel like I can open up to him right now. My wound is burning, and I don't know what he wants me to say. Throughout my life, I was certain that my heart had been stolen and that this pumping organ in my chest was merely a prototype for my android self—an android that longs to be human. To get there, I've succumbed to the abyss, dwelt in the past, and let nociception bring me pain to remind me that I am a human being.

"Phil saw something in you that I didn't. Until now."

"What?"

"He saw a heartbroken woman," he says. "He sent her to me and said, *show her how to heal hearts.*"

I feel a lump in my throat.

"Parker, it doesn't always have to end in pain."

Watching Stuart asleep evokes a sense of solitude in me, which is more intense, more drastic than being alone in an empty room. When someone is sleeping next to you, you become aware of how vulnerable they are. It may sound illogical, but it can fill your head with strange ideas. You could watch them for hours, paint them, inject them, operate on them, or kill them, and they won't even know. Stuart is asleep, not on anesthetic or unconscious, just naturally asleep.

Never have I really fallen asleep before anyone. Once the other person is sleeping, I can't overhear their breathing, which makes the process of falling asleep even harder. And they always wonder why I never stay the night. I enter Stuart's bathroom to cleanse and disinfect my wound. It's deeper than I had intended it to be. Looking at the neat scar on my waist, I wonder what the scar on my chest will look like once the scab has fallen off. At least both of them will hold beautiful memories.

Back in his room, I find him still asleep. I get dressed, and before I leave, I slip my journal into his bedside drawer.

"You never cared about Dad and me!"

"Don't you talk to me like that!" she yells.

Dad is sitting at the table with both palms pressed against his head. He is not looking at either of us. How much I need his support in this argument, his silence just seems to fuel my anger. He just came back from work and smells of disinfectant. He is wearing a navy-blue polo shirt and a white pair of jeans, whereas Mother is wearing a wide airy chiffon dress, which neither of us has seen before. It's unusual to see her wear something that doesn't emphasize her slim waist. She doesn't seem to like the dress, judging by how she grips it at the waist like she wants to tear it off.

"You thought you could leave Dad just like that, didn't you?"

She sobs. Dad raises his head and looks at us. Mother seems to lose her tenuous balance against the side of the fridge and slowly sinks to the floor.

"The truth is you are nothing without Dad."

"Ellen! Enough."

He is yelling at me. Have I said something wrong? He doesn't look happy with me. I watch him rise from the chair and move towards Mother. He carefully places his hand on her hair, petting her like she was an anxious dog.

"I don't understand, Dad! She was going to leave you!"

"But she isn't," *he says without looking at me.*

I run through the back door into the garden, where I bang my head several times against the wooden fence. I wish I could fall unconscious and wake up at Yale University already.

"Stop it."

It's our neighbor George leaning over the wooden fence. My heart is pounding hard. His green eyes glow at me. He is so beautiful, but the look on his face signals seriousness, perhaps a little concern too. We look at each other for a long time.

"Madness doesn't go away. OK?"

Then, he moves away from the fence. I don't remember the last time he spoke to me. He and his wife Maureen have been keeping to themselves most of the time. He doesn't hang out in the garden much anymore. In fact, the only time I see him is at night when he drives off in his truck. I wonder if he is working a night shift somewhere.

I squat down to observe my little peeping hole. I don't actually remember the last time I peeked through it.

"I remember when you drilled that hole."

I look up at Dad, who is casting a shadow over me.

"You were ten and couldn't keep away from my toolbox."

I rest my gaze on a daisy, and then I see Dad's hand reaching down to me. Instead of responding, I brush my fingers across the daisy.

"Please, Ellen."

I look up at my father again – this beautiful man reminds me so much of myself, except that I still have a long way to go to become this perfect entity.

At last, I reach out to him.

He embraces me.

"You are the best thing that's ever happened to me, princess. Please remember that."

***

My parents' new home is in West Haven, about fifteen minutes outside New Haven. They now live in a two-bedroom apartment near the former Bayer Cooperation building. Dad frequently communicates with pharmaceutical researchers at the university and has also been giving seminars lately. In fact, I don't see him retiring any time soon.

Coming back to New Haven's outskirts makes me feel fifteen years younger and guilty for how little I have visited.

At least Dad is happy to see me treat Mother kindly. Since she has started treating Dad with the kindness he deserves, I have decided to respect her. She cries during our embrace.

"I'm so happy to see you, Ellen. It's been so long," she says.

I wonder how one can fathom the richness of happiness and how to take a bite of it.

We are awkward with each other at the dinner table. It was often the trigger for arguments in the past, giving one another the silent treatment. This was why the food never digested well.

"Ellen, do you ever cook at home?" Mother says.

"I haven't got the time, Mom."

She has cooked my favorite childhood dish – pasta bake with mushrooms. The smell summons a pleasant childhood memory. The last time she cooked it for me was many years ago, shortly before she broke for good with her lover. It tasted terrible back then, but it tastes OK now.

"We're glad you can find the time to eat at all," Dad says.

I feel as if I'm seventeen again, envisioning my life at college with the scholarship in my pocket. From seventeen onwards, my life went uphill. I was working towards my future while my parents were putting the pieces of their marriage back together. Perhaps everything does happen for a reason. I just don't like the idea of being powerless over my actions or intentions. I suddenly feel so small.

I eat the pasta slowly, undecided whether I'm actually hungry.

"Is everything all right, Ellen?" Dad says.

"Sure."

He smiles as he continues eating. Mother is smiling too. Together they appear older, grayer. It has been a while since I've seen them together at the dinner table.

"Didn't I tell you, hon?" He addresses my mother. "She's made it further than me!"

"We both knew that right?" she says.

Dad asks me to do the dishes with Mother since the new dishwasher hasn't arrived yet. It's going to be just this once, and I won't object. Back in the old days, I used to help her, but we never exchanged a word, and I hope it won't be any different this time.

"Ellen?"

"Yes?"

Also, doing the dishes reminds me of the time when I was a teenager. I often had someplace to go after dinner, such as meeting a boyfriend, but I had to help her scrub the pots.

"Have you ever considered marrying?"

If only I understood why, of all people, she has to bring up this infuriating topic. Never have I considered marriage, and never will I consider it.

"No. I haven't."

"How come?"

"I'm focusing on my career, Mom."

She smiles. "There must be some nice men at your work, right? At your job, it shouldn't be difficult to meet someone of the same type."

"Same type of what?"

She looks slightly stumped. Why do older folks urge younger people to get married and squeeze out some grandchildren? Don't they understand the joy of solitary activities? Or setting goals and eventually reach them with hard work without having other responsibilities that might hold you back?

"You know, find someone who is like your father?"

"I heard that!" Dad shouts from the living room.

Mother giggles. "It was a compliment," she shouts back.

She is rubbing her left arm, which makes me think that the stroke must've affected her right brain.

The white plates are almost twenty years old. I remember that each of us used to have a personalized plate, and mine was the one with the knife scratches in the center. I never realized that she served me food on my own plate.

The kitchen atmosphere has quietened slightly, and I have no small talk material to break the silence.

"I'm glad that you're here," she says.

"Yeah, me too."

In fact, I'm happy they've moved. The more modern architecture gives the apartment a more comfortable ambiance compared to our old place in Cheshire Village.

She rinses off the washing up liquid and dries her hands with a towel.

"Listen, Ellen. I'm sorry I've not been a good mother to you."

"Let's leave it in the past."

There is a little uncomfortable pause.

"I...found love letters in your old room."

The plate nearly slips from my hand. Her voice resonates in my ears, and the image of me writing letters at the age of eleven flashes before my eyes.

"They sound poetic, but very sad," she says.

I put the plate down.

"You were young, and I wish I had been more aware of what you were going through."

My hands are trembling like they did after Mrs. Hughes' death when I sterilized the surgical instruments.

"I was just imitating books that I'd read as a kid," I say.

"Which ones?"

"I don't know, the Brontës? Why did you read those letters?"

When I moved to New York, I remembered to bring all my forty-six journals with me, so how could I leave those letters behind?

"I'm sorry, Ellen," she says. "I was trying to reach out for you somehow. I feel like I've never really known my own daughter."

The world stands still for a second, and my mind begins to dig into the past. Why am I really here?

"It's OK, Mom..."

"That day I found you bleeding in the garden..."

"Mom! My hymen broke. No big deal." I try to keep my voice down, but Dad walks into the kitchen to check on us. "Everything OK?".

"Everything's good!" Mother says and smiles at the two of us. "I'm going to make some tea in a second."

She walks into the living room.

Dad is smiling.

"Dad?"

"Yes?"

"Have you sold the old house yet?"

"There have been a couple of interested viewers, but we haven't got a potential buyer yet. Why?"

"I was just wondering."

He smiles as he puts the kettle on for Mom, and then he kisses my forehead before returning to the living room.

*

New Haven is the second-largest city in Connecticut. I can't help but grin from ear to ear as I park my car at Yale hospital. This place awakens my former self, a highly motivated student who wanted to become a successful surgeon.

Before I get out of the car, I double-check the message that Julia has forwarded me via email. It's marked as urgent. I'm starting to become a little bit nervous. Apparently, one of the surgeons here named Dr. D. has some confidential documents for me.

I feel my bowels stir when I enter the hospital. It's awkward watching these students, who appear so much more confident and efficient than those at Mount Sinai.

Back in the days when I was a student, studies of anatomy were all I lived for. I enjoyed every minute of it. Never would I have thought that I would come back one day to relive my past. But of course, it's no longer the same, especially when I know that my mentor will never enter this place again.

I make towards reception, where for a second, I mistake the head nurse for Julia.

"Hi there. Ellen Parker. You have something for me."

I show her a copy of the email stating that I've received a special delivery, which is not deliverable to the house.

"Oh," the nurse says, turning slightly pale. "You're Ellen Parker?"

"Yes."

She lifts her finger in a friendly manner, signaling for me to wait. Then, she walks away from me swiftly.

About five minutes later, she returns with a tall doctor, who is a consultant judging by his white hair and exhaustive face. The number of new faces here brings home to me just how unfamiliar the place really is. It's probably a good thing.

"Good afternoon," he says, grabbing my hand and shaking it firmly.

"Hi."

"So, you're Dr. Parker! It's a pleasure to meet you. You're no fairy tale after all!"

Instead of picking up my delivery, I find myself sipping a coffee with Dr. Desmond. He is a human anatomist teaching medical students at the University. He is another Harvard graduate with a similar story to Dr. Dick. He transferred himself to New Haven because his wife was born in Connecticut and intended to settle down here. Why would women who come from Connecticut opt for Connecticut when they could be in New York? I'll never understand it. Do they ever ask the men what *they* want?

"He often mentioned how this student of his had redefined precision."

"What else did he tell you?"

"Dear old Phil adored you. God bless him."

"I assume you were good friends?"

"Oh yes. We played golf together," he says.

I used to play mini golf as a kid, but only because I never played with dolls. And because Dad didn't like me playing doctor, I said I wanted to learn golf, except that I ended up using the golf club for other purposes.

"Please tell me he didn't suffer," I say.

He is the last person to deserve that.

"Phil refused to take painkillers. Besides, he was too distracted to feel any pain. He was delirious in his remaining days, lost in his own thoughts."

I imagine him wandering through the chambers of his own heart, where the walls are throbbing.

"How is his godson? Stuart?"

"He's good."

"He's an excellent heart surgeon. You're definitely in good hands."

Dr. Desmond is a friendly man. I picture him dissecting a corpse's chest and wonder what he sees in people's dead flesh and what he perceives through the smell. But I don't know how to maneuver him into this subject. All of a sudden, I remember something.

"Dr. Desmond," I begin. "Just to let you know, I do not intend to take my gift home."

He nods understandingly.

"But...can I have a look?" I say.

After providing me with a spare lab coat, he leads me into the anatomy room. where a few students are busy dissecting. I remember being all alone in this big hall once, surrounded by cadavers – previously known as people, who choked to death in pain or bid farewell to the world in their dreams. Dying in your dreams, apparently, is the less painful shortcut to the other side. If my dreams were less terrifying than dying, I'm sure I would think this too.

I've almost forgotten the fierce, foul smell. I associate it with the cadavers' unfinished business in life. Now the unfinished business is rotting and decomposing along with them.

Dr. Desmond and I walk into the cool room, where they keep specific body parts for further examinations. I used to call this room the mortuary of incompletion. There are over twenty large metal drawers in the cool room, divided into five rows.

"I'm sure you remember this room from when you were at university," he says.

"I do."

He uses keys to open the second drawer from the top left. But before he pulls the drawer open, he asks, "Are you OK?"

"Yes."

"Are you sure?"

"Please, could you go outside for a while?"

He nods.

Amazingly, my hands are still warm as I approach the drawer. I have never had the chance to open any of these drawers. Whenever I used to enter this room, I never even thought about it.

I carefully place my hand on the handle and begin to pull.

In front of me is Dr. Dick's beautiful naked chest; his body, finely cut into pieces by professional anatomists, has already been parceled out. At least through the fine cuts, you can tell that whoever did this had dignity and respect. The flesh, muscles, and bones sticking out of his shoulder girdle were neatly trimmed, the same with the neck area. I see his sternohyoid muscle, which depresses the U-shaped hyoid bone known to support the tongue. On his left are bits of the coracoclavicular ligament, which connects to the clavicle. And judging by the fine smooth surface of the trapezius muscle, his head had been cut off neatly. From his ribs' appearance, it seems that he must have lost his appetite shortly after the stroke. I remember him being slim but not undernourished.

Who knows what I would do if I had my instruments on me now?

I lay my palm on his heart as if to transmit some energy, some warmth that may revive his heart, awaken some memories. And maybe I will get something in return.

I press my ear against his chest, but I hear nothing. While his heart was still beating, I never had the chance to touch it and knew that I never would.

With this cold air spreading through my eyeballs, I feel my eyes tearing up, but it's only a reaction. I feel unsteady and fall on my knees. I can't feel my legs. I see my breath in the air; they are forming images. It's as if I'm in a deep hole looking up at a tiny light. It has never dawned on me how much beauty there is in disrepair – a beauty that needs to be protected, like these heart-shaped photographs of Dad and me, me in the OT, me at my graduation.

On the outside, my life is without clutter. But I have spent so many years rummaging around in the OT, unable to let go of the past. Perhaps all those photographs aren't meant for me after all.

All the other pieces of my mentor have been scattered on different campuses, except for one piece. He wanted me to keep his best part. Do I even deserve it?

Looking up again, I see Sarah and Jay having dinner at Aureole. I see green tomatoes and a vaginal speculum in between bed sheets.

I picture myself in Stuart's house. I walk into the living room and find him wiping the leaves of his houseplants with a damp towel. It feels like I have entered an indoor forest or something. He greets me, and we kiss.

I open my eyes. What am I doing here?

The hair on my arms rises. I hear a voice calling my name, but I don't know where it is coming from. My knees go weak as soon as I recognize the voice.

I'm standing inside my old house. Someone is knocking on the door.

"Little Ellen? It's me. Can I come in?"

I remember. I remember now. This is the day my heart dies.

CHAPTER EIGHTEEN

It's dark outside when I watch Georgie leave his house. Under the porch light, I see his clean-shaven face for a second. He gets in his truck and turns on the ignition. The tires squeak as he rolls down the street.

I connect my phone to the audio recorder that I have installed in his truck. I start my car and begin to follow.

I hear him crank his car window shut, despite the pleasant evening air. However, the sound is better without the rustling wind.

We are now driving through Brass City, where he makes a few spontaneous turns. I know that Cheshire Village is not a place where you can dive under. Waterbury, aka Brass City, is not much different; it's a city of neighborhoods. I wonder if he has a mistress here.

It's quiet in his car, as though it were driving itself.

I can't help but believe that he wants to be somewhere new, where he is a welcomed stranger. In New York, every corner has a stranger. George wouldn't have a problem there. He wouldn't have a problem anywhere as long as he has his black Grand Cherokee.

New Haven County is a decent county, so are many places in Connecticut with dozens of desirable places to live in. Many people who choose to live on the East Coast opt for a homely state like Connecticut.

But every town has a shadow that hides the light, and Georgie knows all the dark corners. I hear him exhale through my phone, and for a second, I feel something brushing against my ear. I know that breathing – deep and moist against my ear.

It's late in the evening. It's the time of the day where he fears the sound of silence. Only the sound of his truck's engine preserves his sanity. Many years ago, I would watch him pull from his driveway at 11 p.m. and leave his wife at home all alone. But it never occurred to me that I should get to know him better – until now.

I stop the car a few times when the roads look empty and start the engine as soon as I see some cars lightening up the roads. I follow a residential vehicle down the street where George is. Before I spot his car, I hear him turn off the engine. As the car in front of me drives further down the street, it throws some light on George's Grand Cherokee. He is a couple of houses upfront. I immediately park on the side and turn off my engine. In fact, he is not parked in front of a house but on a construction site. Residential streets are not as well lit as the main roads, but we have a full moon tonight. There is no sound in the truck, and I wonder whether he has spotted me.

"I'm here. Come on out," he says, and my heart beats faster. There is silence again, but I do not dare to move.

Suddenly there is light in one of the houses ahead of him. A tall teenage girl sneaks out and makes sure to close the door behind her quietly. She walks down the empty street towards George's truck. She looks no older than fifteen and is wearing tight shorts and lipstick, judging by her dark lips. Before I can make more observations, she has already stepped into the vehicle.

"You want to watch yourself at night, sweetie, going around dressed like that!"

"Don't make fun of me," she says.

"Fancy a ride?"

"Where are we going?"

"Wherever you want."

He starts the engine, and I watch them go up the street. I wait a little longer before I follow.

"Did you get me some vodka?" she says.

George laughs, and I hear the rustling sound of a paper bag followed by the girl's jewelry hitting against the vodka bottle.

"Oh yeah, Smirnoff! Party time," she says.

"So how did you like your first week?" he says.

"Well, for an internship, it's not too bad. But honestly, stockbrokers are assholes. My dad is anyway."

"Why did you agree to hang out with me, then?"

While she sips at her vodka, George takes the interstate towards New Haven. Before I hit the interstate, I make sure my phone is charging as this application is eating a lot of battery. The sound quality is too overwhelming, especially when the girl's rings and bracelets clash against the bottle.

"You are different," she says. "I don't have the impression that you care about money as much as they do. My dad loves money more than me."

George doesn't respond, and while she continues to unload her teenage dramas, I try to imagine George's face. I haven't really seen him properly since the day I left for college. I only ever used to read despair, lust, or provocation in his face – through the peeping hole and through the window.

"I think you're really nice," I hear her say.

I imagine how she runs her fingers through her long soft hair, hoping for some attention. I was more advanced at that age and wouldn't say things like that. I would show it.

We are somewhere in North Haven or Hamden. The roads aren't busy. We are close to William D Bertini

Park, where Dad used to take me hiking. I did go there again before I headed to college.

"Don't you think it's a little too dark for a hike?" she says.

"It's a beautiful night," he replies.

He cuts off West Dayton Hill Road to access the car park, but I keep on going, again, hoping that he hasn't spotted me. I make a halt at the pond nearby and continue to listen.

"Can I tell you something?" she says.

"What's up?"

"I was having a few drinks in my room before you came."

"You knew that I was getting you vodka, right?"

"Yes, but…I was nervous."

George has stopped the car, probably in the parking lot. I grab my phone and get. I walk through the woods and make sure I am walking parallel to the road. The moon lights only a part of my pathway. For a moment, I recall my most recent dreams in which I was running through the woods, looking for shelter, unknowing if I was being chased or not. Unlike in my dreams, I know where I'm going. And yet, it's still so precognitive. I hold the phone against my ear and hear moist kisses. Memories are flashing before my eyes – my first cunnilingus. I hear them move around inside the truck, and a sudden female moan fills my ear.

As I reach the parking lot, I see the Grand Cherokee. Through the back window, I see a head appearing in the backseat – it's Georgie. Judging by his heavy breathing and sucking sounds, I believe she is blowing him.

"You feel so good," he says.

I imagine him grabbing her by the hair, pressing her head harder against his body. The choking sounds become more intense.

"Turn around," he says.

She is breathing heavily, and it doesn't sound like she's still enjoying it. I approach the car by walking around it. I see her head for a moment as she rolls onto her stomach, probably raising her behind.

"You're so sweet," he says through his breath.

She lets out a cry as he enters her. I suddenly recall the pain from when I was young. There was lots of blood: period blood, broken hymen, and a wounded cervix. I was bleeding for weeks. My heart was aching too, and I felt like dying. After all these years, does he still think about me?

When hearing the girl's painful moans, I notice that I am on my knees – my phone lying in front of me. It's like watching myself lose my virginity once again. Georgie is not aware of what he is doing. I tilt my head to the right and see Dad's bamboo stick sword in the living room. Its sight has always made me stronger.

Why George of all men? Boys her age must have doubted her abilities and her beauty. What can possibly make her think that George is different? She doesn't need him; she doesn't need him like I do.

There is blood on my hand. I must've opened up the pocketknife in my jacket and kept on playing. Strangely enough, I don't feel anything. It doesn't feel like it's me that's bleeding.

"It can't be! You lied to me," he says through my phone.

The teenage girl sobs.

You have seen this before. The blood will always remind you of what you've done. Do you remember when you removed your hand from my mouth? I did not sob. I did not make a single noise. I know you admire my maturity and modesty; you always have.

I'm still in my car by the pond when he drives her back to Waterbury. They remain quiet for most of the drive. Upon arrival, they are still not talking, and no one is stepping out of the car.

"Despite the gray in your hair, George – you look like one of the boys from my school's soccer teams."

I hear him exhale.

"I'm sorry about your wife."

*

"Why are you taking me out? I ask him.

George hasn't told me where he is driving. I don't know why I stepped into his car in the first place. Perhaps because it's a nice day and there's still too much tension at home, where no one is talking to each other. I can't imagine what my dad is going through. It must be tough for him, knowing that I'll be moving to New Haven next week. I've never lived away from home. It's going to be tough for me too! I can see that Dad is trying to alleviate my mother's guilt trip by looking after her. But I don't think I heard them talk to each other in the last few days.

"Pardon?"

"Why are you taking me out?" I repeat.

"Well, your old man told me that you were off to college. I didn't just want to say good luck and goodbye."

"Maybe you should," I say.

"Listen, I'm just trying to be nice," he says.

I sip at the Corona that he got me. When he goes off Interstate 91 into Woodhouse Avenue, I realize that we're in Wallingford on our way to William D Bertini Park. I used to come here with Dad when I was younger. He has been asking me to go hiking with him, but I didn't want to. I've been too busy drawing my own blood and analyzing it under the microscope. I still need to practice the insertion more as I still tend to bruise myself with the needle. I've been wearing

long sleeve tops to cover up my arm when I'm around
people, but today I am wearing a tank top and shorts.

"I'm sorry about your cheating mom."

"What do you know about it?"

"I'm not blind, sweetie. Which mother needs four hours to
do grocery shopping? And that every day?"

She would leave the house at lunchtime and come back at
around four o'clock or later.

"Can we talk about something else, please?"

"Sure thing. Who's that fella that you're seeing?"

I look at him, irritated. He pulls into the parking lot and
parks at the bottom of the Bertini trails.

"You're an asshole," I say and get out of the car. I make
my way to the trail.

"Ellen! Wait up."

He catches up with me, and our arms touch. I hear a
heartbeat for a second, but it is not mine, and then he grabs
my arm.

"Why are we here?" I shout as I push his chest. "Why are
you doing this? Why are you talking to me all of a sudden?"

All he does is sink his head.

People view him as a decent man, but since his wife's
death there have been a lot of rumors and speculations
concerning his private life. When Dad told me that
there had been a murder in the neighborhood, he

didn't say that it had happened right next door. There was no clear evidence of suicide, so some suggested George might have been involved. But I know he is not at fault. Cutting someone's wrists in the bathtub is not his style.

Poor Georgie.

He could easily leave Connecticut and start anew. However, that would make no difference. Wherever he goes, the nimbus above him will follow him to the end, just as mine will. Unlike me, Georgie has no particular passion to pursue.

When I arrive at his company in New Haven, dressed as a businesswoman, I'm determined to approach him. Prada is keeping me warm and confident. It's a medium-sized corporation with five departments – nothing compared to what you'd find in New York. How I miss it there. I think about Stuart and wonder if he's operating at this moment.

The reception area of George's workplace doesn't look formal. The female receptionist is chewing gum while swiping away on her phone.

"Hi, I'd like to sign up as a visitor, please," I say.

Without looking at me, she says, "Who are you visiting?"

"Your hard-working brokers on floor three. My niece is an intern."

"Oh yes, Holly! What a sweetheart she is," she says and passes me the sign-up sheet and a visitor's sticker. By the time I make it to the elevator, I tear off the sticker.

I step out of the elevator into a busy office environment where every second person I see is on the phone doing their sales pitch with that arrogant tone.

I spot George right away in the right-hand corner at a desk, which is facing the elevator. He's not on the phone but looking at his reflection in the office window, and I must say he is in good shape despite his age. He still has full dark blond hair with some gray, and there's only a slight receding line visible on his forehead when he brushes his hair back. I still see his sharp green eyes close to mine. I wonder how he feels in comparison to when he was thirty. I feel like we're both inside a bubble, and every person in this room has vanished.

He stretches his arms and rubs his lower back. The way he rubs it, I presume it's a compressed spinal disk causing him pain. My hands shake as I slowly walk towards him. And then he looks up with the receiver in his hand. Our eyes meet. The receiver is about to fall. I see how all his memories are flashing before his eyes. It must be like seeing a ghost. But all I see is George – nothing but George. With me being the product of his memories, I'm sure that the past unravels itself to the fullest in the young girl's eyes. He is looking for reminders that will eventually lead him back to me. Back to that one particular girl: a quiet girl full of erotic fantasies and desires. Something happened to him that day; that girl implanted an insatiable hunger into his brain.

He gets up from his chair, and I stand still. My lips tremble while painful scenes of the past begin to display in front of me. When he steps away from his desk, I turn around and walk straight into the open elevator.

It is a chilly evening. Winter is near. I spot his Grand Cherokee in the lower ground parking lot. I know he has a bad habit of not locking his car.

I get ready to face him when he walks towards his truck. The neon lights flicker the moment he opens the door and sits down. I jump forward from the backseat and administer a dose of etorphine to his neck via a hypodermic needle.

***

I bet in his dreams he sees numerous young girls. He hears them giggle, whisper. But they are not special compared to the little girl with the blonde curls, the girl who wrote him love letters expressing infinite love.

"Here we are, reunited. No more hurting," I say.

He stirs on my bed, still half asleep.

"I never hurt you," he mumbles.

He isn't supposed to wake so soon. After the etorphine dose, I shot him some spinal anesthetic and some cyclobenzaprine, a directly acting muscle relaxant. That will paralyze his body for a few hours. Will has taught me the procedure well.

He slowly opens his eyes.

If only there was a mirror on top of my bedroom ceiling, he would see a reflection of his naked body, his erection, and the entrance to his half-open thorax exposing the pumping heart. Since he doesn't look pretty with a rib spreader, I have removed two ribs from the cage to facilitate a better view, a better view of his heart. How can one not view the heart of their loved one?

"Where am I?" he says, "What's that noise?"

I smile.

He is glancing at the pink walls and me.

"A shame I could never invite you up to my room."

"I can't move."

My fingertips gently glide along his stomach and right breast. I don't think he has quite registered his surroundings. I haven't revisited my old home since I left years ago. I'm surprised that all these years, my parents have kept it the way it is. Obviously, this makes a beautiful child's bedroom.

"Georgie."

"I can't move," he repeats.

I taste blood on my lip. His nose is bleeding.

The smell in this room awakens a past sentiment, even when intermingled with the antibacterial liquid scent. The past is pulling me further to what I used to call emotions. I think I am very close to becoming the old me again. A familiar sort of warmth engulfs my heart, the exact same warmth my childhood self used to feel.

I wipe the blood away from his nose. Then I approach his ear with my mouth.

"Do you remember our memorable moment? Downstairs?"

He responds by breathing heavily; his body is still motionless. I see fear in his eyes like I was a nightmare from which he can't wake.

"I missed you, Georgie."

"Why are you doing this, Ellen?"

I clench my fists.

I move towards my drawers and begin to rummage around. Finding some packs of expired tampons, I pull out a thick one for heavy days.

As he watches me remove the plastic wrap in front of him, his breathing accelerates, and his heart rate goes up.

"One hundred and twenty," I say, counting.

"What? What are you doing to me?"

"You're supposed to say *I missed you too*," I say.

"What do you want?"

"Nothing. I just..." I lick the tip of the tampon.

A spark has just flashed in his eyes.

"I just want you to see how much blood I've spilled for you."

"Please, please, I'm sorry!"

I spread his legs slightly apart, and with some effort, I bend his right leg and then stick the tampon up his anus.

"NO!"

"Come on, Georgie, you never used to wail like that."

"Oh my God," he groans.

The anesthetic must be wearing off.

"Maureen couldn't give you what you want, so she killed herself, didn't she?"

I unbutton my lab coat.

He is now looking at the beautiful naked body of a child – her undeveloped breasts, the absence of pubic hair, the softest skin he has ever seen and touched. He closes his eyes, tears of remembrance running down his face.

I'm climbing onto him. The next thing he feels is his penis inside me.

"One hundred and thirty-eight," I say, making love to him on my childhood bed.

"Look at me, Georgie. Don't you like the way I turned out?"

Astride him, he sees a little girl, the same girl from almost twenty-one years ago. She has not changed one little bit. And yes, she is beautiful.

As the two of us come simultaneously, I sigh somewhat painfully while he groans again. Rubbing my cheek against his stubbly face to seek a kiss, my lips encounter salty tears. My fingers are running delicately through his hair, down his neck, and around his chest. I make sure my breast doesn't get in contact with his open thorax. I taste disinfectant on my tongue – my bedroom smells like the OT at work.

"I can feel your heartbeat," I say. "I can hear it, but..."

Georgie continues groaning and sobbing in pain.

"I've loved you all these years," I say. "Don't you feel the same?"

"You seduced me," he says.

My hands turn cold.

"You tricked me."

I freeze on top of him. Next, I find myself climbing down from my bed. His sobs make his torso vibrate.

"You didn't tell me that you were a virgin, Ellen."

"What difference is there? So it never occurred to you that I was in love with you after that one time? Does that mean nothing to you?"

He moves his head to the other side, where my Walt Disney treasure chest is located, showing the face of Briar Rose on the front.

I rest my behind on my desk, still naked. Each beat of his heart freezes a different spot on my body.

"This is it, but virgin or not, what does it matter? You forced me down."

"No!" he shouts. "*You*! It was *you* who told me how to touch you. You made me…"

I loosen both of my shoulders. No matter how hard I try to imitate Briar Rose's smile, I see that of the witch's.

"Don't you remember at all?" he says. "You lured me into your house with your love letters, telling me about all the sexual things you'd done."

I see us on the floor, the way I grabbed his hair and told him to fuck me harder. I dismiss this image immediately.

Georgie's groans continue, and this time, they touch the spot of satisfaction in me.

"You did something to me. You passed something on to me! I wasn't me! I loved Maureen!"

A sudden image of Maureen's childless face appears in my mind – how I used to shoot her nasty looks without her ever knowing it. She wanted a child, but she couldn't have one.

"Maureen found those letters. That's why she killed herself." Georgie is out of breath, his chest rising and sinking. The sight of his heart reflects that of any other man that loves his wife. He continues, "I should've burned them all."

What I thought was special over the years has never been there, to begin with. In his heart, there is only one woman – it is not me and never has been.

"You passed something bad on to me. Something evil. If I could undo the past, I would!"

I should have realized a long time ago that I was never meant to play Briar Rose. It was Alicia all along, and she had deserved that role – deserved Dad's kiss on her lips and his hand on her chest while trying to revive her on stage.

I try my best to replace Georgie's heartbeat with the sound of Mr. Whitley's just to remind myself that I have done something right in this life. I lie next to Georgie's body and carefully place his hand on my chest. His fingertips are cold, transmitting nothing but cold. Then I press my lips against his dry lips, which are almost as cold as those of a dead body. Only the tremble of reluctance proves that he is not dead.

Ten minutes have passed. I feel the shiver of his hand on my chest. My nipples have gone hard from the cold, and I realize that it is not getting any warmer.

"I feel cold. What are you going to do to me?" he says and swallows hard.

While holding the two pieces of his broken ribs, I draw lines with them on his body. For some reason, the sound of his heartbeat has dissolved in my ears.

I walk towards my bag and return to Georgie, holding a pair of surgical scissors.

He screams, but the sound emerges as a painful cough. "Oh my God, oh my God!"

His eyes are glued to the instrument that I'm holding. I wonder how objects trigger fear and horror in someone. Does he picture the object inside his body? You are supposed to fear the hand; it's the hand that practices the act of horror.

"I'm sorry, Georgie. I'm trying to put things right. Don't you understand?"

He is not listening. He shuts his eyes and shakes his head pathetically. I watch how his limbs are gradually regaining their senses.

"Please, please, don't. I'm in so much pain already!"

He does not understand that pain defines us, unites us, and fulfills us. It stimulates our survival instinct and encourages us to make life worthwhile.

"Georgie," I say softly, "I'm taking it back."

"Taking what back?" he sobs.

I hold up the pair of scissors. The higher I hold them, the more terrified he becomes. I grab the lab-on-a-chip and hold it in front of his eyes.

"You see that? I gave you my youth. You're healthy and as fit as a horse."

His lips have turned blue. I cover his body gently with an antibacterial blanket, but I give his heart one last look before that.

"Please let me go," he begs.

The literary notion of letting go usually has a revealing effect on the person who lets go, as it means giving up on what makes one's life worthwhile. He doesn't understand that he has made my life meaningful all this time by giving me a reason to become who I am—a heart surgeon. If I let him go, what will be left of me?

I hop onto my desk and crouch in front of Georgie like an animal. He looks at me, estranged and dazed. As I place my finger on the tip of the surgical scissors, I begin to press down. The sight of blood has never terrified me in any way, except this time. I have to think about Scott, who would not tolerate what I'm doing. I think about Stuart, who did his best to sew my wound shut. All these people care about me for no explicable reason, yet I have nothing to give, nothing but an apology.

The color of my blood is interestingly bright, and it feels cold.

I rest my behind; press my legs against my chest to expose my vagina to Georgie. Instead of looking at it, he's looking me in the eyes. The only thing I see is Norman's doppelganger, sad and fragile. And I see me.

The bleeding finger is drawing several lines down my legs. I lick the blood off my knee, hoping to remembering Scott's smile.

Slowly I spread my legs open and place the cold instrument on my naked thigh.

"What are you doing?"

"A shame we never talked about it, Georgie. We could have fixed it."

He twitches. I notice movements underneath the blanket, but each movement triggers pain in the open gate.

"I'm sorry I dragged you into this mess. I will make it right, I promise. Now I need you to watch, Georgie."

While pressing two fingers against my labia, my clitoris exposes itself – this weird looking mouth of arousal resembling the snout of a newborn hamster or hedgehog. Sexuality is right there with you, right after birth. From that moment onwards, your body develops sexual desires, and you fall for the first person you see. For me, it was Dad. You also masturbate at an early age while fantasizing about that person. A lot of people may not remember it. However, I do, and I chose to express it. But who knew that the concept of love would reveal itself in the form of an obsession? Norman knew. He knew that the way I saw love was through a tube. I didn't see the big picture. Even Bruce had seen more than I ever will. In the operating theater, Dr. Dick had tried to aid me through this journey by helping me believe in the power of my own hands, the way they could conjure miracles into reality.

In the end, sex is a guilty pleasure if you have lost your feelings in it, oblivious to the blindness that has overshadowed your sense of reason. What are feelings still good for, without reason?

I move the instrument closer to my vagina.

George begins to move underneath the blanket.

"No, don't do it! I forgive you!"

I smile at him. "I am not a good forgiver."

You should never come to realize the lie that you've been living, even though it's you that buried it in your mind. But most of all, the cells don't know it. They just move on. They will always move on except you because to you, life is absurd.

Stuart slams the door open and doesn't even need to register the scene to know what I'm about to perform. He only has eyes for me. Rushing towards me, he grabs my wrist tightly until I let go of the scissors. My perception of sound and touch has ebbed away. I'm no longer there; I got sucked into the black hole of my inner faculties, like a star that collapsed inward. I have swallowed myself entirely. I see a ribcage and find myself walking on this beautiful piece of art. However, I'm moving quickly along with my new friends. We're traveling through a tunnel towards the chambers of life. I can hear them welcoming me.

There are things in real life from which you can't escape, only delay. Life is all about delaying things by creating reasons to live and by watching over the friends inside you. The more meaningful your reasons, the longer you want to delay it. However, when you realize that your motivations were based on a lie – the entire world shatters. You can't restore equilibrium when you're falling down a hole.

And this beautiful man has veiled my body underneath his coat. I think he is telling me to look at him. It's a familiar voice, but so quiet, as if he's speaking to me through a wall of glass. I'm listening. I'm looking at him.

STUART

Fall is coming to an end. At least that was how her journal ended. She also wrote that a walk in Central Park would have been nice, but she didn't have the time. If she had told me, I would have taken her there. I didn't know how fascinated she was by the Hangman's Elm and how the scent of sticky Elm leaves on the ground made her feel alive.

The journal told me the story of a girl that never recovered from the spindle incident. This person that we all knew was just a camouflage for who she really was. My godfather knew.

Before the police pulled her away from me, she'd told me to burn it. I did as I was told without ever rereading it. Mr. Heyman and I were the only witnesses of her attempted self-mutilation, but of course, the police had a different theory. She was charged with physical assault and rape. When they dragged her away from me, one of the officers told me to watch Mr. Heyman before the ambulance came. He was crying in pain, throwing nonsensical apologies at me. I didn't have to look underneath the blanket to see her excellent handiwork. Though, a sudden reality came upon me. Is this what we do as surgeons?

Due to the danger of catching infections, an immediate surgery took place in the bedroom, and they needed my help. His heart was no different from any other heart that I've seen on my operating table, yet her obsession was built upon it.

I sewed his chest shut for good in that room, and he is recovering well. He didn't press charges against Parker; she didn't want a lawyer, either. At least she didn't respond to anything they asked her.

After she attempted to gauge her vagina with a fork, they assigned her to a psychiatric center where they kept her in a straitjacket. A passage in her journal described a funny feeling in her vagina – a guilty tingle that she wished she could remove. She wrote that she was no longer feeling any pain, as she'd already gone beyond natural pain, human pain and that no pain was too foreign to endure. She was convinced that love's knife was exceedingly sharper and intelligent as it would cut the heart first. Only if we let it. It's the sight of blood that stirs our perception and delivers a signal of pain to our nervous system. Feeling each other's pain is how we empathize with one another. If pain still exists, that is. Her final wish was to become a blood cell because those cells are the only good things in the world.

The many plants that I keep in my living room remind me of her. The color green makes me think of our first date. Green's association with new life often gives people the impression of hope, but hope does not come with color. Hope emerges from nothing; it's a human sentiment, a belief in preserving human life – something I thought I knew well. But when her mind degenerated, that sentiment had no more meaning left for me.

I recall her outstanding skills in the OT. Her android-like performances always impressed me. Everything was fine back then.

Last week I spoke to her through the glass, but she said nothing. She merely pressed her hand against the glass with an empty smile that was no longer hers. Her short blonde curls had turned greasy and frizzy. She had an eczema flare-up on her face, all around her neck, spreading across her body. The startling green in her eyes had faded to grimy gray, as if her spirit had escaped her body. What I saw was the remnants of the woman that I once knew. The disrepair was always there. She camouflaged herself, rejecting who she really was. My godfather gave her a purpose to bolster her inadequacies because he believed that good would come out of it. And it did.

I told her that I'd get her out and everything would be the same again. For a second, there was hope, but it was crumbling away at our feet. The doctor told me that they couldn't get her to speak.

During bath time she had a panic attack at which she broke a mirror and attempted to cut herself with the broken pieces. I remember reading about how much she hated the sound of breaking glass.

Her father was most devastated when he learned about her condition. If there's one thing about parents, they know their children the best, and the least well of anybody. The Parkers told me that she had a mild dissociative identity disorder when she was younger. She would tell her parents that her name was Helen. Helen wanted the same things as Ellen, except that Helen was more optimistic and conventional. But that identity had soon merged with Ellen. That explains the episode in Redding where she'd tried to weigh out her options and adapted to possible married life on a farm. But she couldn't handle the love. She was too unaware of its meaning; however, Helen was aware. Ellen was a perfectionist who wanted the best she could get, whereas Helen was glad about what she already had. She would return the love that she received while Ellen would reject it. She didn't believe that she deserved it, and yet she was aiming for it. Though, it seemed that Helen had no power over Ellen.

I miss sharing Parker's skills in the OT. We'd cut open a lot of chests together; our hands had washed in blood together, and our hearts had raced together.

Now all that is lost.

She was allowed nowhere alone, not even the bathroom. They installed a video camera in the isolation room. In her journal, she also wrote about the necessity of loneliness; it brings one closer to oneself, it urges one to think. Loneliness is an inborn sensation, which the artist uses to create meaning.

The doctors applied cognitive behavioral therapy with no success since she gave no response.

The nurse bathed her in a tub only yesterday evening despite the orders to only wash the patients on a chair in their rooms. Like many nurses, she felt sympathy and took pity on Parker, letting her hold the showerhead without knowing that Parker would knock her out with it.

Still naked and soaked, Parker escaped to the nearest laboratory, where she locked herself in. Nobody knew about her disappearance until an hour later when the security guard found the nurse lying in the bathroom, unconscious. He was following wet footprints that led him to the lab floor. There he noticed a blinking red light signaling that a lab was in use and entered it. A trail of blood led towards a dark corner underneath the examination table. There he found her lifeless body with blood all over her legs and a red pool forming between her thighs.

They found a pair of scissors with bits of her labia attached to the blades. According to the autopsy, she had cut off her clitoris as well. The piece, however, was never found. Additionally, she'd slashed her cervix, which triggered the excessive bleeding. Her entire vagina was ripped and torn, as though mangled by a wolf.

She was wearing a lab coat.

Before the incident, she'd intended to cut her chest open, judging by one deep cut down her sternum. They didn't know why, but I believe that she might have wanted to view her own heart and then decided that there was no need. She must have realized that she was real – that all her work was real. She saved lives.

In her journal, she wrote, "Everybody dies alone."

Retrieving my earliest memories of medicine, I remember fixing up my dad on a hike where he stepped on a loose rock and fell down a ravine. He hit his head and needed immediate stitches. That was the first time, at the age of fifteen, where I held a needle and some thread. Instead of following his footsteps into science, I chose a slightly different route. I've always admired my godfather and pursued the path of a surgeon.

Parker died of guilt. Mr. Heyman, for this part, had already forgiven her, but forgiveness is never complete if you can't forgive yourself. With her death, she made people believe that her femininity was the trigger of all her troubles. Women criticized her for being weak and giving them a bad name. Perhaps she had tried to save the men from her, I don't know. She used the idea of love as an excuse to become who she was—a cardiologist. We all rely on excuses to become who we are. It's up to us to create meaning. We are people, after all, and we have a choice. Parker made her own.

When I think of her, I see a woman that didn't give herself a chance. When I touch the scab on my chest, I feel that she is still alive.

Since her death, I've had a recurring dream in which I see the image of a blooming daisy; someone walks past and brushes a drop of blood on its petal. It's my little girl Helen.

"I have to ask you for a favor," he says.

"Why did we have to come all the way out here?"

I grab hold of both my arms, shaking. I don't remember the last time I felt so lost and disoriented. He looks at me with guilty eyes and then squints at the sun.

"Talk to me!" I say.

"Ellen," he says, as he comes closer. "Look at me!"

I look him in the eyes, and I feel how my knees are going weak. His breath is brushing against my face, and my lips begin to tremble.

"You need to stop writing me those letters," he says.

I don't really have friends, so there are not many people to say goodbye to. There is no farewell party, either. I'm alone on the swing. I remember when my legs were too short, and my feet weren't touching the ground. If anything, you have to learn to keep your feet on the ground at all times. It took me some years. I stare at the fence but hear no voice or movement on the other side. Most of the daisies in the garden are still in bloom – some of their petals tinted purple. Some rues are seeping through from under the porch, growing with the flowering weeds. I've spent lots of time out *here despite my allergies. I also dissected a dead cat, rabbit, frog, and hedgehog here. Animals just don't seem to get much of a life in this garden, and yet they proved to have been my only friends. I even talked to them.*

If I want to have a fresh new start, I will need to change. I will need to be more in control, more reserved, and study hard. The only thing I can do now is making my dad proud and get out of this godforsaken place. I need to give my life a purpose, as otherwise, something drastic will happen.

Dad steps out and approaches me with a smile.

"How did I know that you were out here?" he says.

I jump off the swing and run straight into his arms like a little girl.

"I miss you already, princess."

ACKNOWLEDGMENTS

I want to thank Elizabeth Wells and Sam Whittam for editing this book. Your help made the publishing process possible. I would also like to say thank you to Egemen Oezyay for your patience and the awesome cover design. A big shoutout to all my dear friends and loved ones for believing in me and supporting me all these years to make this book happen.

PAULA C. DECKARD was born in Hamburg in 1984. She completed her (MA) Creative and Life Writing degree at Goldsmiths University of London. *Heart Like A Hole* is her first book of fiction. Paula lives in Canada.

Learn more about her or subscribe to her writer's page for news, blogs and more:

https://paulacdeckard.com